To XueLong

The Burden of my Red Lips

in Tehran

By Shaghayegh Farsijani

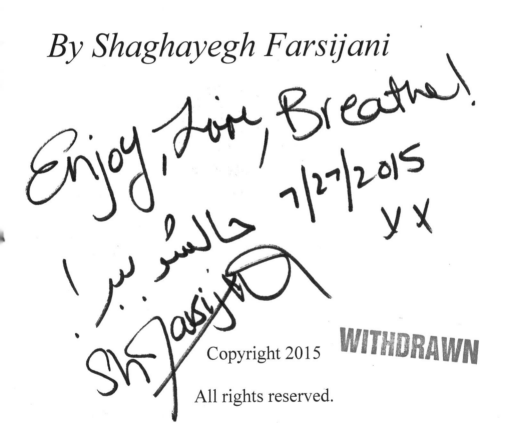

Enjoy, Live, Breathe!
7/27/2015
X X

Copyright 2015

Note from the Author

When I returned to Iran with my parents in my late teens, I embarked on an exciting and life-altering journey. This story is based on my true life experiences of moving to a culture rich in history but torn by religious controversy. I was firmly grounded in the Western culture of my formative years, which began in Brooklyn, NY. I plunged through transformational challenges in Iran and guarded my Western identity. Within a short amount of time, I grew confused and frustrated. Without solid, true life skills, at the time the best choice was to run away.

This novel is my story of how an adolescent girl—equipped only with fearlessness—sets goals and begins a journey with insurmountable odds. I was an American Iranian teenage girl singlehandedly struggling to navigate through one of the world's oldest and most tabooed countries in the world—Iran!

When I took flight over two decades ago, I couldn't possibly have anticipated what I was about to experience—the journey of a lifetime. I have and always will be thankful to my parents and to all the Persian people who contributed to my very existence and, ultimately, to the person I am today.

Dedicated to the pillars of unconditional love,

Mahboubeh & Farshid.

CONTENTS

Chapter 1: Goodbye, Brooklyn

This was bad. Very bad. And despite many days of trying to figure it out—and *much* labored thought—I still couldn't understand why my parents had decided to move back to Iran. Yes, I knew it was my home country, and I'd been born there, but we'd moved to America when I was three years old, leaving Iran a dim, dusty memory in my mind. Now, at seventeen, I didn't have any connection with it. I hadn't heard anything fun about growing up there, so why would I want to return now, when I had friends, hangouts, and a guy I kind of liked—although that didn't end up going far—here in Brooklyn? Brooklyn, where a perfect summer day meant some punch ball in the playground, followed by an iced gelato. My crush sometimes took his shirt off, allowing me to admire his soon-to-be six-pack, but that was as far as our dates went. Robert was his name, and I had the hots for him.

And now I'd have to say good-bye. For reasons that I absolutely couldn't understand.

I racked my brain again, looking for anything I hadn't thought of yet. What reasons could my parents possibly have for returning to their homeland? My cousins all longed to come to the US, and yet here we were packing up our bags, headed back to the country of burkas. My mother's side of the family lived there still, but I hardly ever spoke with them. I hardly spoke to anyone in Iran, truth be told. They didn't have what I wanted there—freedom, and my friends here in Brooklyn. Krista and Bianca, my Italian buddies … what was life going to be without them? What were the Iranian girls going to be like? Would they be fun and exciting, and go out on bike rides with me? Wait … would they even know *how* to ride a bike, when they always wore those long burkas or coats over their clothes? How did you ride a bike with a foot-long garment wrapped around your hips, anyhow? This was going to be … interesting.

Then my mind flew to the next question: Why me? Why did *I* have to go to Iran?

Who could blame me? Even the slowest, most bee-buzzing days in the neighborhood offered many charms: dog-walkers (each, like their pets, bearing unique quirks) lawn-tenders and their weekly rituals, and guys fixing and washing cars with scientific intensity. Sometimes with their shirts off. A sight to see while eating a gelato!

In Iran, I knew for a fact, I'd find none of that, and I'd been struggling with dull nausea over the very idea of leaving my home for weeks. The truth was, I had no idea what to expect in Iran, and my mom and dad had no right to take me there. Away from my neighborhood, my life, my friends, my way of living ... The many unanswered questions about Iran frustrated me, and they were topped with horror stories, told in whispered voices, by people who said that *they* would never want to return to Iran. I still didn't know the real reason for going. Just that my dad had—somewhat marvelously—reached the conclusion that he wanted me to become acquainted with my Iranian roots and language.

9

I already suspected that his real reasoning was to have better control over me. My mischievous ways were leaking out slowly, and it must have frightened him enough to finally decide to pack up. But shouldn't I have had a say in it? I didn't. And anytime I'd asked, I was hit with, "Because this is the best route for you," followed by a sentence I learned to hate: "You will love Iran!"

Why would *I* love Iran when so many kids and their parents were migrating across the ocean in the *opposite* direction—toward the land of the free?

I already knew that I wouldn't be allowed to do what I wanted there. I'd be restricted, simply because I was a girl, and I hated that. I knew I wasn't going to be able to ride my bike like I did here, anytime I wanted, or go on a date with a guy. And forget about prom. I didn't even think they had that there. My cousins had told me that the schools were separate—one school for boys and one for girls—like some Catholic schools in the US. Asking them about something like a prom had them LOL-ing, and forget about reaching legal drinking age, since alcohol was banned for all ages.

I wasn't religious, but I did believe I had a right to choose. I would respect Islam and the beliefs that followed, but wasn't keen on someone else telling me what to worship, or what I could and couldn't do. How was a girl to have fun?

And if my parents loved Iran so much, then why did they leave for the US in the first place? When I was a child, I would eavesdrop on my mother's conversation with her friends, and hear things like, "*Va,* it was the best decision to come here... Tehran is not made to live in anymore. Inflation kills!" Then, at other times: "There is no opportunity *there* for children to grow, so I want her to grow up *here*, speak English fluently, and get a good education and job." This was all said with a deep Farsi accent, and the obligatory *va,* which was uttered in the slanted attitude kind of way that all Iranian moms used in conversation. It basically meant, to my way of thinking, *whatcha talkin' about.*

Those conversations meant, though, that they'd brought me to the US so I could have a good education and future. But I knew how that had gone: Suddenly, when I got older, they saw the devil sneaking out of me, and thought, "Crap! Forget good job and education, let's split and head back to the mother ship!" They called it a parental decision.

And the deal was sealed. So I decided to spend what little time remained living it up in the neighborhood that had given me so many memories. I chose to live in the moment, and where could I have done that better than Brooklyn? Usually, I wasn't allowed outside after sunset, but the night before we left, I asked my mom for permission to take one final bike ride. She must have known how unhappy I was about moving, because she granted this request.

With greater-than-normal anxiousness, I pulled on my favorite sneakers, clumped none-too-slowly down the stairs, and climbed onto my bike—another thing I was going to have to leave behind. This bike had always been my ride to Coney Island, to the playground where we played punch ball, and my ticket to watching a shirtless Robert while he was hanging out with his buddies. It had even been my savior once, providing me with a quick getaway when those very boys started walking towards my hide out spot. Now I was going to have to leave it behind, along with all my other friends.

"Well, here I go. One last bike ride…" I whispered to myself.

Pedaling along the sidewalk, I caught isolated whiffs of grass clippings, flowers, and phantoms of someone's backyard barbecue— a greasy smear of hamburger. Then suddenly I slid to a stop. "Hi! *Hey!*"

Here on the twilit sidewalk were Annie and Larry, out for an evening stroll with one of their four dogs. "Delkash!" called Annie. "Don't run us over, girl!"

We all laughed, but my joy quickly turned to sorrow, and I nearly wept over my love for them—our two-doors-down neighbors. Tall, debonair Larry was as handsome as they made men. Annie, a true Italian beauty, had fashion sense and a uniqueness that often had her sporting a new pair of funky earrings and toe rings, simply to walk the dog. Although I was perhaps too young to know such things, I'd always thought their lovemaking had to be the tops. They showed lots of PDA, but it was the way they talked to one another— so flirtatious, smoldering, and intense—that made me think it had to get hotter under the covers. I sometimes talked to Annie about having the hots for Robert, since I couldn't talk to my mom about it. One word about a boy and she'd become fearful that I was having sex with him, pack up her bags, and leave yesterday. Iranian parents—another issue that bothered me! But with Annie, I could have fun talks—talks that ended with, "Remember, pumpkin, you are the cream of the crop, so make those six packs run for *you*!"

Oh Annie, Larry ... I'll miss you.

I swallowed hard before I came to tears, and pedaled past them, then past my favorite deli—with the best pastramis—where friendly faces were eating and talking and laughing. Not much further and I was at Ming's Golden Wok, exhaling its garlic and stir-fried pork scents beneath the buzz of crimson neon. Ming's pork was my favorite, but my parents never ate it, and now I was heading to Iran, where I could probably forget about all things pork. That fell in the religious country category, along with no prom nights; it was a category that would soon be in overload mode.

I coasted, resting my legs, as I wheeled past the pizzeria—another symphony of aromas. The cozy heat, swirling with molten mozzarella, spicy sausage, oregano, and the holy promise of olive oil, surrounded me.

"Delkash!" someone shouted through the bright doorway. I knew it was Mario from the pizzeria, by his deep Sicilian accent. Over the years, he had treated me to one too many slices on the house, and on slow days had even taught me how to make pizza dough the Italian way. This included understanding the physics of tossing the dough up in the air, allowing it to form a disc, and then grabbing it at the right moment, while it still had momentum. I'd thought it was too complicated for something as simple as making dough, but he'd made it fun by teasing me for not getting it right. I waved sadly at him and pedaled away, dreading tears but taking comfort in the realization that nearly everyone who visited these happy establishments knew my dad and me. If nothing else, they'd remember me when I was gone.

Next, I passed P.S. 200—Benson School—and the park where I'd punch ball, my consciousness swarming with smells of freshly made Italian tomato sauce and sights and sounds of all kinds ... all marking my sweet childhood. This place had been everything to me, and I pedaled on, leaving behind the village that represented what little I knew, and grasped, of the world.

15

As I pedaled up 21st Street, the occasional stranger favored me with a smile, and I recalled the ice cream truck that had first acquainted me with its sugary cargo. I didn't really enjoy it, but loved asking my mom for money, simply to have a treat with the other kids on the block. Of course over the years, I'd started to gain weight from that particular habit.

My parents had always warned me to watch myself when it came to sweets. "A tummy isn't good for a girl your age," my mom constantly said. Ignoring them (as I sometimes had to do), I carried on with whatever suited me. Anyway, it didn't matter now; I was going to have to cover up my body and trash my jean shorts. So who cared if I had a tummy?

Krista and Bianca had always joined me at the ice cream truck. They were *my girls*, and together we made the Two Italian 'n a Persian Musketeer trio. We'd been inseparable in school and when the clock hit 3, we were already outside playing punch ball. Bianca had a crush on Robert's brother, Jason, and her parents were just as strict as mine, so we spent a lot of our time going out on imaginary double dates. Krista was the listener and a self-proclaimed nerd, but always brought in good food during lunchtime. My lunch, on the other hand, was either a simple bologna sandwich or something from the Iranian end of the culture spectrum, called *kookoo*—an herb soufflé with a strong herb smell that prompted whomever was sitting next to me to ask, "*What* is *that*?" The answer, depending on how nice I felt like being, would either come with or without translation. If I didn't translate, the only thing the person got was the word '*kookoo*' with a *mind your own beeswax* tone and my finger twirling in circular motion gesture.

My parents had introduced me to the more contemporary Iranian dishes and food products while we were having dinner at home, or when I opened the fridge and dug in between the shelves, but these were just a handful of the possibilities. Same with the Farsi lingo – I knew some Farsi words here and there and my ears were acquainted with simple, informal Farsi from my parents speaking with one another in the house. But my own personal Farsi was a mess! Sometimes we had Persian guests and sometimes American, but I never hung out with any of them. I didn't really know, at that time, whether I was Americanized or Iranianized, because I didn't want to hang with anyone other than my own friends – who were not Iranian.

The girls, though … we'd all been friends for the longest time, and now, right before prom year, right before the year we turned the big eighteen, my parents were separating me from them. Krista, my best friend, the one I would run to if anything ever went wrong, had said that our bond would never break and was "stretch worthy"—which was true—but I would miss our days and evenings together. Forget about writing—the post office in Iran would probably throw out letters with an American address.

Okay, so I was exaggerating, but the time it took to exchange letters between two countries in two different continents could be a month! And my parents weren't up for a hefty phone bill, either. I was scared I wouldn't find friends I liked in Iran, especially since my Farsi sucked. If I couldn't communicate, then how the hell was I going to establish relationships? Especially with guys? How was I going to *find* the guys? Was there some sort of underground *Sexiest Man Alive in Iran* magazine out there?

And what about dancing? I loved dancing, especially ballet, jazz, and hip-hop. I'd even dreamt of being Michael Jackson's choreographer—or, okay just *a* choreographer—after college. My hips and feet couldn't stand still when the beat hit me ... but I knew for a fact that there were no dance classes in Iran. You had to cover yourself up, and move the curves of your body in ways appropriate to Islam. The girls had told me not to worry about it, but they weren't the ones in the hot seat.

Personally, I knew I was headed toward big-time trouble.

But did my parents care? *No.* Dad was an entrepreneur, and had already closed his jewelry business in Brooklyn to start a curtain business in Tehran. Mom was a hair stylist, and would probably join my aunt in her female-only salon. Easy breezy. And then came me, who would, according to my parents, adapt. "She is so talented and flexible ... she will adapt within days," my school counselor had told my mom. *Oh Ple-ease!*

One thing I knew was that this Delkash was not the giving-up type. I would find a way to hold onto myself, cherish my own inner child—that sweet, playful, and vivacious person I'd grown to be. I was determined not to let Iran change me, no matter what.

*

After pedaling through block after block of memories, I finally made it home to start packing. I labeled some boxes "not trash worthy—EXTREMELY valuable" so my mom didn't 'accidentally' throw them out. I'd been told that I could have a certain number of 'important' boxes, and that was it. The boxes that weren't labeled as important … well. I'd just have to make sure that the things I really cared about were in the boxes that *were*. I believed that my parents would try to take care of my things, but I had no way of knowing for sure.

They'd always been strict, though I'd done my best to get around that. I called my mother 'Ziba, H^2O,' and my father 'Kaveh, The Emperor.' It was flattery, plain and simple—one was the essence of life and the other a powerful king. They might have thought it was disrespectful, but they'd also given me whatever I wanted when I used the nicknames. A little info regarding the two: They were total opposites, and I didn't know how or why the powers of the universe brought them together. My mom was full of love and life, and very fun to be around—and, even though I was her daughter, I had to admit— very sexy, with a good business head on her shoulders. She hadn't allowed me to talk about sex or boys, but that never eliminated her own powerful attraction. My dad was serious, had a dry sense of humor—though he occasionally grinned—and was only enthusiastic about basketball, baseball, and the occasional hike. He was a great listener and an awesome poker and backgammon player. But I was certain that this wasn't what brought them together. Their resumes and my grandfather's firm and angry eyebrows had been the cause of this marriage. I don't think they even went out for one date with each other.

They'd been told to marry, and that was that.

I was their only child, and I knew they adored me and my love for life, dance, food, *Looney Tunes*, *MacGyver*, *Saved by the Bell*, *Melrose Place*, and a good Scooby Doo mystery. But they were taking me away from my home, and I was scared to the bone. I didn't *want* to grow and understand life and my culture in Iran ...

Chapter 2: Hello, Tehran

The pilot announced that Iran Air would be landing shortly, and my mother turned to me, her gaze serious.

"Put on your scarf before you get off the jet. You'll have to get used to this style of dressing from now on."

I didn't really mind donning my scarf, which I'd decided to think of as a new addition to my wardrobe, and nothing more. But her eyes made me rethink that, shouting as they were that I was about to make my way into deep culture shock, or maybe even a coma. The good part was that I *knew* I was headed into a coma. It wasn't going to take me by surprise.

Though I wasn't sure how much comfort I could garner from that.

Still, it wasn't like I could do anything about it. Jump off the plane, try to take my own life? No. The flight attendants would catch me before I even got to the door. *Bad plan.* With no money and no one I could trust, the backup plan was to suck it up. I'd been telling myself that I was a warrior from Brooklyn, and that I could handle this, for the entire flight. Whatever it was, I'd get through it.

At least until I knew how to get back out again.

And so we landed, and the passengers started cascading out of the plane. There was no line or order … just everyone on top of one another, trying to get away from the plane. A bus took them all to the airport customs area, while my parents and I waited until everyone got off. We were the last to exit, for fear of being run over.

My first impression was that everyone was complaining to everyone else, speaking Farsi at lightning speed, and pushing at everyone else. I couldn't understand what half of them were saying, they were speaking so fast. All the women wore *burkas*—making them even harder to understand—and the men wore long beards. The clothing was a shock to me, and I ran back through what I knew: The *burka* was a combination of a wimple and depressingly long cape

24

that went all around the body. Only very religious women wore them. Those of us who were more … casual, I supposed, could get away with just a scarf or wimple.

Everyone looked either terrified or mean. So I kept my mouth shut and let my mother do the talking.

My dad was pretty good at saying the right words with the right tone, so we got our Iranian passports stamped without any problem, and passed through the security line. That's when it really started to hit me. This was *it*, and there was no going back. The journey had begun! Now it was bag pick-up time and then meeting Mom's mystery family, who were either going to be like the Adams family or the Brady Bunch.

The baggage check was fun. They basically dug through your bags to see if you had porn magazines, sex toys, Madonna CDs, or anything illegal. They could have been searching for guns, but no; this was much more than a security search. This was a *religious* search. I had to remember that I had stepped into the religious hot tub and had to be a zombie from here on out. At least in public. No more *People* magazine or *TV Guide* to check out the latest steamy encounters on *Days of Our Lives*, and definitely no more *Star* magazines.

I watched nervously as they went through my bags, and then we were moving forward again. We went into the greeting section, where all I could see were big flower bouquets, people jumping into each other's laps, men throwing themselves at their 'brothers,' and people weeping as if someone had pushed their cry buttons. There was a sea of scarves and black *burkas* and … the best part of all—men with so much facial hair that it looked like the country was short on razors and shaving cream.

I didn't remember what my mom's side of the family looked like but they knew exactly what *I* looked like, thanks to the pictures from my parents. They ran right up to us, and I saw, to my surprise that they weren't religious looking at all—nothing like the scenes I saw on TV. Instead, they were groovy and hip. Scarves and coats were mandatory, but these women had made them into a fashion statement! Their make-up was impeccable, and everyone smelled of perfumes and colognes. Some even had their blonde, brunette, or highlighted hair hanging out of their headdresses. My guy cousins were studs, and they were kissing and hugging me! I'd thought that was illegal, but now I found myself ambushed by kisses and hugs from all directions. I had no idea who was who, or whether I was even related to these people, and my parents were too busy to notice. It occurred to me briefly that at that moment, *anyone* could have gotten away with a kiss.

The family's love hit me like a warm wave, and I returned every drop. It had been a while since I'd been the center of so much laughter and so many smiles. It was as if everyone was high on ecstasy—they had loads of energy despite the pre-dawn hour, and seemed to be oblivious to whatever duties lay waiting after sunrise.

My mother was in seventh heaven, obviously enjoying the presence of adored nieces, nephews, sisters, cousins, and of course her own mother, *Aziz Joon*. She wore a *burka*, and was the only one of the bunch that *did* look religious. When she came toward me, I wanted to run away. I just knew that she was going to pull me under her *burka*—my first experience with that particular piece of clothing—so that she could kiss me. In the end, of course, I had to give in. She was my grandmother, after all. And her eyes told me that she might be an important ally, in the end.

Personally, I couldn't stop grinning, and had to constantly be aware of my scarf slipping off my head. I'd already started hating the damn thing for its inconvenience. Still, the joy of the family was contagious, and I couldn't stay angry at the headdress for long.

After the mushy stuff, the men started fighting about who was going to carry the suitcases for us. That was all right with me; I don't know if they wanted to spare us back pain or if this was Iranian hospitality, but giving my bags to someone and only having to wait for the car was like a frequent flyer valet service. Even my dad, considered powerful and muscular by most, was pushed away from the luggage. Outside, though, we started to experience Iran in truth. And it was terrible. The smoke was so bad that I thought for a moment the airport had been built right next to factories. There was a short scuffle about who would sit with whom in the car, and then we made our way to the parking lot. Dad went with another crew of distant relatives toward a different car, saying that he wanted to go straight to my grandmother's house to rest, and leaving us on our own.

The cars around us were atrocious, and looked like nothing so much as turtles, with the name 'Peykan' engraved in the back. They looked like cheap frogs made with steel and four wheels, and the insides were absolutely archaic. Out of this mess, though, a new Mercedes suddenly popped into view. It must have been dropped down by God himself, I thought—a miracle from Vogue car magazine. Even more surprising—that was the very car for which we were heading.

Then, since we were the guest arrivals, we got the best seats in the house, in the Mercedes SUV. Everyone else was driving these ugly Peykans, which I later found out were actually foreign luxury cars. And then we were off to Aziz Joon's house, captive to my mother's family.

A cousin sat next to me and started pouring out Farsi in line after line of conversation. I sat there smiling, nodding, and agreeing with everything she said, and when appropriate, my mom dropped in a line or two to save me. She knew I couldn't understand half of what the girl said. And even if I'd understood it, I wasn't sure I trusted it. Now that we were held prisoner—to my mind—in their car, I'd started questioning all the joy and affection. Was it even real? Or was this some sort of grand welcome that would end up being fake?

These people were my family. But could I trust them?

My mother, seeing my blank stare, quickly introduced everyone in the car—Kamran, Bahareh, Ghazaleh—the cousins—my aunt Elahe (their mom), Aziz Joon (my grandmother), and H^2O, and I. The passengers in the other car with my Dad were too many and too hard for me to remember.

We started moving, then, and instead of trying to understand the conversations around me, I zoned out to focus on the city. Tehran's weather in the summertime could get as hot as the Sahara desert, but it was still early morning, so I put the window down to breathe in the cool air. I saw a billboard of a guy with a turban and white beard, and laughed to myself. Certainly not the Sexiest Man Alive. I didn't know much of Iran's history—I'd learned American history at home, after all—but I knew that this was the Islamic leader, whose name I could never remember. The ugly Peykans filled the streets around us, both as cabs and commuter vehicles. Man, did they make the flowers lose their shine. Cabs were also parked in front of a busy square, which looked impressive—like it was from a war period—with the drivers' legs hanging out of the cars, indicating that they were having morning naps.

The square in question was roughly the shape of a sumo wrestler spreading his legs and trying to accomplish a split. Despite that, a strange intuitive feeling told me that it was the equivalent of our Statue of Liberty, given the size, and its central location.

My cousin looked at me, and must have read my mind. "Delkash Joon, this is Azadi Square, or as you call it, Freedom Square. It's a big deal, and people gather here for protests. Especially during the revolution." She said this partly in Farsi and partly in English, knowing my Farsi was on special crutches. Then again her English—with the accent—was also on crutches.

But my mind was caught on the world 'revolution.' The only revolutions I knew were the American and French revolutions, and at the risk of sounding dumb, I asked, with the crappiest verb and noun placement in Farsi, "Freedom from whom and why?"

My mother looked at me as if I had to know the answer to that question, and was asking this rhetorically. "Delkash, *Jan*, you know about the revolution *azizam*. You know about the Shah leaving and the Ayatollah coming and … the regime change. That is why everyone has to wear the *hijab*. This is the famous square where they had all the protests. It's a true symbol of your country," she said firmly, as if the revolution was still rotating around her, coloring her words and attitude.

Jan and *azizam*—both terms of endearment in Farsi—should never have been used in one sentence, as far as I was concerned. Too much foreign language in one place for me, and it made me feel dumb. Not that I cared what anyone thought. I knew my mom was only trying to pull the famous Iranian *aberoo dari*—covering up my lack of knowledge of my *own* country before I could embarrass her.

"Oh…" I said, sounding surprised even to myself. I loved the US—it had given me Brooklyn, good pizza, the Backstreet Boys, and awesome memories—but here I was next to the Freedom Tower, where many years ago, the thread of communication between the country where I was born and the country where I grew up were permanently disconnected. Sounded like a bad relationship that had come to an end. Even divorced parents communicated to keep the kids happy, but here, the relationship had been completely severed.

Were the kids happy in Iran? I wondered suddenly. I guessed not, because many—including my parents—left during the revolution to pursue better lives. And now here we were, back at square one. Pursuing a better life for the family evidently meant controlling me and helping me get in touch with my roots. I thought I could have accomplished that in Brooklyn and continued going to the Iranian school on Saturday mornings in Queens, New York—the one that had taught me the little Farsi I knew.

But no, it had to be on a grander scale than that for my folks!

Around me, Tehran's streets were dirty, with lots of construction going on, and gutters on either side of the road with little streams flowing through them. I saw some professional graffiti on the walls as we drove up the street, then, and gasped. It was like Picasso had stepped out of his grave and drawn the Statue of Liberty herself in a skeleton outfit. Right below her was an illuminating and gleeful picture of the Islamic leader. Whose name I still couldn't think of. But whoever he was, he wasn't the president of the country.

That was someone *else*.

Who was who? I didn't have a clue what they did, or why two people were leading the country. I had learned, though, while the emperor watched the news, that Iran had a leader like Khomenei— although I thought he was dead now—and the president. I wondered who picked who. What if they didn't like each other? Why did one have to wear a turban, and the other a beard?

I put that thought away and glanced once again at the graffiti. A two-sentence description of it could have been: 'America is dead to Iran, and Iran is in rock 'n roll shape.' Shivering, I turned back to the street. As far as I was concerned, America was my home, and I wasn't sure how I felt about anyone saying—or illustrating— anything against her.

As we got further away from the airport, the streets began looking more contemporary and clean, the people wearing tight pants, more make-up, and high-heeled shoes. The women began wearing their headscarves far back on their heads, just covering their

ponytails or enormous fake buns. Instead of the Peykans, the cars

were Maseratis, BMWs, and lots of Mercedes Benz's. The guys were

hot, and the girls beat any Vogue or Versace model, hands down! I

guessed that this was northern Tehran, where the rich lived, and

wondered if this meant I could also dress like the women here, rather

than trying to keep this piece of fabric from falling off my head. My

hair was already getting tangled from constantly pulling the fabric to

cover the front portion of my hair, and I was over it. If I had a

chance to dress differently, I'd jump at it.

The buildings, too, were different here. I'd thought the city

would have more Arabesque architecture, with gold and turquoise

popping out everywhere. But this looked almost modern. Some

buildings were tall; not as tall as the Empire State Building, but two

to four stories. We passed a huge, burnt building that had the logo of

a hotel, and I saw that it had been a Hyatt. Probably from the Shah's

time, when they still did business with the US. Now the building was

unused. The water gutters on each side of the street had expanded in

width, and some even had flowers growing in them. Trees lined the streets on both sides, but grass was a rarity. The sidewalk designs changed frequently, as if the task had been given to every house or property owner: "Please design your own sidewalk."

Drowned in these thoughts, I was surprised when my cousin Kamran, sitting behind the driver's seat, posed the golden question. "Do you guys want to get some *Halim* or *Kaleh Pacheh* for breakfast?"

My mom—and, for that matter, everyone else in the car— favored *Kaleh Pacheh* over *Halim*, which was similar to oatmeal, but had chunks of turkey meat and cinnamon in it. *Kaleh Pacheh*, or anything associated with sheep's heads and hooves, disgusted me. I preferred a serving of good ol' wheat toast and feta cheese, accompanied by a glass of orange juice. In fact, the very *smell* of *Kaleh Pacheh* made me sick to my stomach. I didn't understand why or, better, *how* my cousins could even be excited about it.

I voiced objection to the breakfast suggestion. "Why *Kaleh Pacheh*? Gross!" I said with a moan, trotting out my mistake-laden Farsi.

My cousins grinned, and Kamran said, "It's the best, Delkash! This place has the best and freshest—with my stamp of approval!"

Your stamp of approval ... what does that even mean? I wondered. Who was he, and how should I know what his stamp was accountable for? How could eating the brain, tongue, and hooves of a sheep be delightful in any way?

Still, it didn't look like I was going to have any choice in the matter. The morning was getting busier, and now buses, people going to school with their backpacks, and office workers with their suitcases were popping out in the streets. And we were in the middle of them, heading toward the restaurant.

"This is the north of Tehran, called Fereshteh, Delkash Joon. We live right in this street," my female cousin, Ghazaleh, said. She pointed as we parked in front of the sheep's brains and hooves place.

I was disgusted about the food, but looked up the street, impressed. Wow! North of Tehran meant *fancy*. And this was where they lived? My estimation of the family went up several notches. Then it plummeted again, as they directed me toward the eatery. The brains and hooves restaurant was covered in marble tiles and designed with elegant calligraphy and metal workings. The art scene was very unique, but I couldn't understand why anyone would have decorated a restaurant like this in such a beautiful way. Inside, it was purely functional, with a big pot sitting in the corner. It looked like the one our Italian neighbors used to make tomato sauce.

But that wasn't tomato sauce bubbling away, with the chef guarding its side and slowly stroking it.

The chef himself was a piece of work: A burly man with a thick gold necklace over his hairy chest. Nothing like you would find on the Food Channel. The sous chef next to him was busy filling baskets with special bread baked in a stove oven. Pots of tea were perpetually boiling.

There was no table service, so we just sat down at the table Ghazaleh had found until the guy who was walking around the restaurant approached us.

"Do you want anything specific, Del?" Kamran asked, dropping the latter half of my name to be friendly.

I couldn't answer because I thought I was going to barf at what I saw: The chef holding the sheep's head in the air with a long fork.

"It has exactly the same ingredients as a human head. We just don't eat the skull," he explained loudly, chuckling to himself.

My urge to throw up got even stronger.

"Relax, Del Joon, it's really tasty. Put some lemon and cinnamon over it and it'll be a delicious start to any morning. It's just too high in cholesterol, so having it every day may kill you," he continued calmly.

Customers started to come in then, their taxi drivers parking their cabs outside to wait. "One brain soup, please," a man carrying a suitcase said.

"Can I have hooves and tongue this morning, *Hassan Jan*?" another guy asked.

The next order reminded me of the movie *Return of the Living Dead*: "Can I have an eye sandwich?"

I gagged. What the hell did *that* mean? Now we were extracting eyes out of animals and making hearty sandwiches? If

Krista or Bianca were here, they would get a kick out of it. And then they'd run for the nearest pizza parlor.

Having sprinkled the remains of the sheep's eye with salt and drops of lemon juice, Hassan—evidently both owner and chef—stuck it between two pieces of bread and offered it to the customer. The eye was crushed, the lemon and salt adding to the oily texture.

Kamran ordered a couple of eyes, some tongues, three brains, and some hooves, while everyone started gossiping and talking at the table again. By the time the order came to the table, I was longing for a simple everything bagel with cream cheese. My mom saw the fearful and disgusted look on my face and shook her head.

"You'll like it. It might seem gross at the beginning, but you're a good sport. Give it a shot! It's full of calories. Very meaningful and refined in our country."

I felt my mouth sealing itself shut. How could she be okay with this when she'd spent the last decade and a half eating normal *American* food? How could she expect *me* to be okay with it? The only piece I was willing to even think about trying was the tongue. It looked like roast beef, and I could at least eat it with my eyes open.

I fought to open my mouth. It wasn't working.

"*Kaleh Pache* has been passed on for centuries, Del. Like old letters or songs passed down for generations," continued Bahareh, my other cousin—Ghazaleh and Kamran's older sister.

I knew they were all staring at me, and my mom was right—I had a personality that could try anything once. But I needed a wingman. I needed someone to point me in the right direction, or at least understand that I didn't *want* to be here. I'd been forced into it.

Suddenly my aunt Elahe stepped up to the plate. "So this is the gist of this place. The hairy dude, Hassan, runs the place with his four brothers, all named after the prophets. They prepare one hundred sheep heads every morning, when one brother—Saeed—brings them all to the restaurant to cook. He's a real treat—usually stays in the room downstairs, but sometimes he makes his appearance." She looked over my shoulder and her face lit up. "There he is now."

Overwhelmed with curiosity, I spun around to see a guy with his long hair tied in a ponytail, John Lennon shades covering his face. His entire upper arm—the one I could see—was covered in a tattoo of a cross.

A Brooklyn heat wave came over me and I felt at home for the first time. Now that was someone I could understand. Someone who was just himself, rather than doing everything he could to fit the mold of Iran.

"People think these guys are rich," she continued, "but the elder brother is the only one who owns a house." I still had my gaze on the bad-boy tattoo guy, and my aunt laughed. "If you want to marry a *kalehpachei* guy, I will forbid it!"

I turned away, blushing at that. So I was attracted to him, who was going to tell me no? He was hot, and the tattoo on his arm was sexy.

Instead of answering, I pried my mouth open and shoved a small bit of the tongue in, chewing as quickly as I could before I had a chance to rethink it. Then I paused. It had a powdery texture, but … was surprisingly good. "I want another," I told my mom.

Instead she put a pile of brain on my plate. "Taste this, and you'll be hooked!" she said.

Slowly and carefully, I put lemon juice on the brain and slipped it onto my tongue. I closed my eyes and told myself, *This is not a brain.*

To my surprise, the piece of meat melted like a Hershey's bar on my tongue. It was … delicious. For the rest of the meal, I stuck with the tongue and brain, and passed on the eye and hooves. Could I be hooked on sheep's eyes? No way! I would have to have it with *lots* of lemon juice! Then again, who would have thought I'd get used to eating brains?

Not that I was allowing myself to think about it much.

We finished breakfast and got some to go for the relatives that were already at my grandmother's place. I figured the meal for the whole table would probably cost $100, plus a good tip. It came out to $10, and *forget* the tip! No one paid tips in Iran, evidently.

When the first rush of customers left, Hassan stepped from behind the giant pot and lit a small bunch of herbs. He blew the sweet-smelling smoke to disperse it throughout the restaurant. "Against the evil eye," he explained, referring to an Iranian custom to prevent misfortune. "We might be complaining about the things that've happened, but many people are jealous of us. They might curse us for what we have. Though I don't know why, when it was God who gave us this food. *Shokr!*"

The last word meant *thanks*, I knew. The prayer was akin to what the pilgrims would say at the Thanksgiving table. The Mayflower was nowhere to be seen or found, though. We were land locked in Iran. And so far, it was better than I'd expected.

My family stayed for his ceremony, then left the restaurant and piled back into the car. Hopefully, with no more stops, we would soon be at my grandmother's place. My folks planned to stay at her house until we bought a place of our own. In the Iranian culture, it was considered rude to go and get a room in a hotel when your family was there to help. Hotels were mainly for tourists.

As we drove, I continued taking my catalog of the streets of Tehran. My grandmother's street had flowers lined up on every side, and the homes were made of brick and three to four stories tall. When we got to my grandmother's house, we found a big black garage door, which opened automatically when my cousin pushed the special numbers in.

Inside, the parking lot looked like a car showroom, with everything from BMWs to the German Opel cars to a black Lexus. Whoever had said that Iranians were poor was wrong, I thought, smiling. There was also a BMW motorbike, so I suspected a hot guy lived in one of the condos. To the right of the parking lot, there were stairs leading to my grandmother's backyard. I jumped out of the car and followed my cousins up the stairs to the backyard, where we found a garden planted with herbs and every kind of fruit you could find in the fruit market: figs, persimmons, mulberries, peaches, and even a walnut tree. Who said Persians couldn't plant? A big barbecue lay to the left with a fire pit smack in the middle of the yard. I could only imagine how cool it would be at night to go out there and read my favorite book under the stars. I never saw anything like that in Brooklyn!

"Delkash, come on!" my mother shouted. "You're holding us up!"

I ran back toward the parking garage, where everyone was waiting at the head of the stairs to get on the elevator.

"Don't worry, cuz," Ghazaleh said. "Later in the evening, when the sun is setting, we'll go eat our hearts out in the yard. That's the time to go!"

"Ok," I replied enthusiastically, smiling. Food in Iran was becoming the number one hit with me, and if we got to eat in a place like that, it would be even better.

*

My grandma had a nice pad to herself on the first floor. The house was huge: four gigantic bedrooms, three bathrooms, a large kitchen, a living room, a dining room, an indoor garden … and the list kept going. There was enough room for two more families to live there with us.

I'd thought that once we got to her place, we'd deliver the food my dad had requested to eat after he woke up from his beauty sleep—now that we'd caught up to him again—and all lay down for a nap. But everyone around me—except for the emperor—seemed to be able to function without sleep. The sun was fully out now, and even though they'd risen in the dark to come get us, everyone was wide-awake and happy. Could it be that the *Kaleh Pache* was fortifying their blood?

As for me, though I was dead tired physically, we'd changed time zones, and my body said that it wasn't time to sleep. Instead, my mind was running with questions: Didn't these people have to go to work? Wouldn't they miss the train or bus? Were they all taking vacation or sick days because of us?

"Are you going to the bazaar?" my aunt Elahe—the same one who had forbidden me from dating a *Kaleh Pache* restaurant owner—asked Kamran.

"Yeah, but later on. I want to chill with Aunt Ziba for a bit," Kamran said as he tossed his car keys on the table by the door.

My grandmother, who had been silent throughout the car ride and restaurant stop, quickly went into the kitchen. "Welcome, welcome. My house is your house. All these rooms are yours, too. You can even use my room. Whatever you want," she told my mom eagerly.

The first course of action after the welcome was turning on the teakettle. I thought this odd, but then remembered the boiling teapot at the restaurant. Evidently tea was *the* drink. Kamran, Ghazaleh, Aunt Elahe, my grandmother, my other cousin Bahareh, my mom, and I all sat in the living room to have another chat. I couldn't imagine what they wanted to talk about now, but told myself to sit and look nice. *Just keep your mouth shut if you don't have anything to say,* I lectured myself.

"Are these guys still hanging out? Don't they have lives?" I asked my mother out of the corner of my mouth.

"Of course they do! But we have just arrived, and this is part of being hospitable. They are all going to head out for work soon, though. Stop complaining."

Though we were full of breakfast, my grandmother had put out some pastries, and everyone took one. They were Danishes, and far better than any peanut butter or chocolate chip cookie I had ever eaten. Everyone else told jokes, while my mom told them everything under the sun about my life (the impressive stuff, thank goodness, and not the embarrassing or bad stuff). Then the clock hit 11 and Kamran trooped out to go to work.

Who goes to work at 11? I wondered.

"Well, see you tonight, Aunt Ziba. I love you!" he said as he kissed her.

Gay flag. Surely he was gay. The whole way in which he said it and kissed her was totally gay. Dudes just said "Later," shut the door, and got out. I scowled.

Then he kissed me and said, "Can't wait to hang out!"

The tone was—again—gay. I could have bet the whole cash pot in *Ocean's Eleven* and *Twelve* that he was, but word had it that you couldn't come out of the closet with that sort of thing in Iran. Some kind of embarrassment issue. And it didn't work well with the Islamic rules, either.

Everyone else cleared out or went to a bedroom to take a nap, and I finally had some privacy. I laid down on the couch and found the TV control, then sat in a dreamy haze, watching a riot of brightly colored censored cartoons. The channels were:

1- News

2- More News

3- Sport News

4- A cartoon with Japanese-looking logos on the upper right hand side, probably piped in from Japan or China or one of those countries

5- Cooking with female *wimple*-wearing chefs

6- International News

Anything above channel 6 didn't get a signal. Then suddenly I hit gold: MTV videos! My eyes weren't playing tricks on me, because the next channel was a soap opera. *The Bold and the Beautiful!* Where were the *mullahs* and *burkas* in these? Suddenly I craved watching some good drama, like *Melrose Place* or even *Dynasty*, but the other channels were in Turkish. I even hit a Bollywood movie where the main actor and his lover were running around in a garden and swinging on a branch, with the dude grabbing the girl. But nothing else. Where were HBO or Showtime when you needed them?

I settled on the one (and only) cartoon channel on the Islamic channels … some non- *Scooby Doo* or *Thunder Cats* cartoon. These cartoons, the imports, had no action scenes, no funny parts like with *Scooby* or *Shaggy* or *Lionel*, but were more inspirational and

50

heartwarming and—at this hour, in my jetlagged state—kind of surreal. I later learned that these cartoons didn't fascinate my Iran-born cousins as much as they did me, but regardless, I genuinely enjoyed them. One of my basic joys in Brooklyn, whether early in the morning or at 3 in the afternoon when I came home from school, was my cartoons. I just hoped they weren't all going to be as inspirational as these, because after a while that could transform to *boring*!

Suddenly a thought rose in my mind as I watched the Asian characters on Iranian TV ... *How will my life change here?*

This thought eclipsed even the blaring TV, and it possessed a certain gravity, like some huge beckoning challenge ...

Whatever it might be, I told myself, I'd be meeting it soon.

*

I got the second to biggest room at Aziz Joon's, and learned that we called her that as a nickname, meaning "the dearest." The room was isolated, so I had privacy, and had a full-blown king-size bed, armoire, and a huge closet that could fit however many guys I chose to bring home. If only I could actually speak the language!

My windows were huge and received plenty of sunlight, but the curtains were absolutely gorgeous—something straight out of the Shah's castle. They were designed with such elegance, and made with lace and satin in champagne-colored fabric. I didn't dare open the window because I was frightened I might ruin the design. Half of the room was wallpapered, and the other half was green paint.

"You like your room?" I heard Aziz Joon say behind me.

"It's awesome! Was it anybody's room before, or it is just the guest room?"

"It was your mom's room before she got married. The armoire, she picked out and bought with her own allowance," she said, grinning.

"Must have been some allowance! This French design, classic grey, and gold lines running vertically on the sides..." I replied as I looked more closely. It was absolutely beautiful.

"She has good taste, and now it's all yours!" Her energy surprised me, and suddenly I felt as if I was with Krista and Bianca ... as if there was a young girl living inside her—an old friend that I could tell my darkest secrets to, without worrying about word spreading around town. She wore the *burka*, and was religious, but her heart was soulful. Why, though, did she take the *burka* off now that she was in the house, when my dad and other men were still walking around?

"Aziz Joon, can I ask you something? Why do you cover your face? And now … why do you take your *burka* off?" I asked, hoping I didn't step too far.

"Weird, eh? I have my beliefs about God, but in Islam you can take your *burka* off in front of your son-in-law and grandsons…"

"What about in front of me?" I asked, baffled.

"You are not a man! This is only in front of men that are strangers, who you have no close family ties to … you know, including that Mr. Tattoo you were gazing at in the *Kaleh Pacheh* place!"

Ha! She had noticed that. Old, clever, and wears a *burka*! Accepted in my book!

"Wasn't he cute?" I gasped, dying to talk about him.

"No! And you'd better be careful. Your dad is a strict one!" she said, smiling and walking toward the back room. "Unpack, now. I made *kebabs* for lunch and we'll have tea afterwards."

"Another round of tea? With the amount of tea you consume, you should have a hose attached to your privates and just forget about bathroom trips!" I said, giggling.

"We will ... soon! *Yallah!*" she said.

Yallah meant *hurry up*. I grinned and turned to my unpacking, thinking that I'd already found a friend here.

I started to love staying at Aziz Joon's. We soon became buddies; sometimes we were like the characters in the *The Three Stooges* and sometimes we were like *The Three Musketeers*. Staying at her house was like staying at a bed-and-breakfast place on the Upper East Side; she was gracious and welcoming, and cooked and served up huge meals. The house was old, but fully renovated and charming. It also had great views of Tehran at night, because it was on a slightly elevated hill. Before long, it had become home.

*

Soon the time came for me to actually register for school, though I dreaded it. Perhaps this fear came from knowing that the academic level in Iranian schools in Tehran was different from that in America. Or maybe it was my own perception of how school would go. I was starting my senior year, turning eighteen, and here I was a foreigner. I didn't know the language well, had no friends, and had to wear this wicked *wimple—mandatory—*in school!

Initially, my dad and I went to the regular Iranian schools to register—you know, the public ones filled with regular students— and *boy* did I feel lost. I stayed for the morning and sat in on a class. Not too much time had passed before I decided to check out. It started in the morning when they were singing their national anthem. I was a turtle trying to interpret the non-groovy, opera-like song, which seemed too depressing for me. I could sing the *Star-Spangled Banner* in my sleep, but then again, it had a complete different feel to it. Or maybe it was because I'd been singing it since my childhood. The Iranian anthem was strange and unfamiliar to me.

While listening to it, I suddenly felt disloyal to the *Star-Spangled Banner*. After the feeling sank, I realized I just missed it … Missed it so much I could moonwalk through it if I sang it!

Thank God the anthem wrapped up at that point. I stood up and got in line to follow the other girls upstairs. My dad wasn't really allowed inside, so he stood in the yard to smoke a cigarette while I walked around and tried the school out.

From what I could gather, this was the way it was at a *P.S.* Iranian School:

The *wimple* and the coat had to be worn at all times with the front root portion of the hair completely covered. Question: If we were all girls, what was up with wearing this uniform at *all* times. I thought the purpose was to cover up in front of dudes (especially horny ones)?

To elaborate, the *wimple* was like wrapping one big scarf around your head, covering north, south, east, and west of the head. The only opening was for breathing purposes, and to see what was in front of you.

It didn't come with any medical insurance coverage if you happened to fall or slip on something.

A dudette, since everyone was a girl, would get up first, followed by all the other girls, once the teacher walked in. Getting on your feet was some sign of respect, like in the army when a higher-ranking officer walked in and everyone stood to attention. On your feet, soldier! I totally ignored that, though, and kept cozy on my chair, with a nice smile glued to my face. Then a green *burka*-wearing teacher came in with her purse and a book in her hand, and commanded everyone to please take their seat.

"Have you studied the chapters from the last session? Because it's question and answer time," she would say.

She lined up ten girls in front of the class, like they were in a police line-up, and zipped a question at each student. They would get a positive or negative sign, depending on how complete and right or wrong their answer was. Some girls cared and some just answered, "I haven't studied!"

I wanted to clap my hands for signs of bravery and courage the *non* kiss-asses displayed.

Then suddenly, I noticed a girl in front of me had a football (the Iranian-Persian version of soccer) player picture on her desk. She was totally checking the guy out.

"Oh, he is so hot!" she said to her friend.

"I would kiss him up and down until my lips dr-" said the other.

"*Khak bar saret!*" said the girl with the picture. "He is mine … only mine!" They both giggled at that, and I smiled to myself.

Khak bar saret literally meant *soil on your head*, but metaphorically meant *go die in a hole or gutter,* or *bury yourself alive*. I knew enough to know that she was actually telling the other girl to get lost, because he was hers for the taking.

Wowzers, I thought. Iranian public school girls were *human*! Sweet!

Unfortunately, the rest of the day didn't go so well, and my dad told me immediately that we had to find an alternative means of education. Even the girl with the magazine had been shy about having it; she'd hidden it as soon as the teacher looked her way. I'd never be able to fit into an environment like that. Not with my personality, and not with the way I'd been raised.

Beyond that, I was behind in both Farsi—their everyday language—and my education. The biology text had been far too advanced for me, and even informal conversation confused me.

So, though I'd found the girls there to be at least human, and people I thought I could befriend, my father and I continued our search for my new school.

*

After calling around to every friend or neighbor they could reach out to, my parents finally found a place for me to get my diploma. It was better than going around uneducated, I suppose. God forbid I not live up to the country's standards; my father would rather be hanged!

They decided to send me to Tatbighi, the international school for children of families unfamiliar with Farsi or Iranian culture. Maybe it was a cushion for culture shock—or maybe it intensified it—I didn't care; I was just relieved that I wouldn't have to go to that public school, where I was sure I'd end up embarrassing myself.

Besides, the place I was going was perfectly respectable; students from all around the world were registered here. The catch was the school fee, which was through the roof. Luckily, almost every other currency was worth more than the Iranian *toman*. So families moving to Iran could afford the hefty fees, especially if they came from the US.

Tatbighi was different than the public schools in Iran. There was freedom; although I was required to wear a *wimple*, I could take it off in class and dump it in my bag to wrinkle up. The teachers weren't so strict, either. Sometimes they even seemed scared of the students. The school also had all kinds of girls from all over the world. One girl from Sweden was very open-minded, and constantly talked about sex in class, even showing me the condoms she had brought from Sweden to use. I wondered if condoms were available in the pharmacy in Iran, like they were in the US, then realized that even if they were, they wouldn't be given to a seventeen-year-old girl. There was also a girl from Germany, who was a tomboy and talked about car races, sports, the Bundesliga, and her crush on

Michael Ballack. He was what Pele was to Brazil, but the German version. I had to admit she did have good taste. Yum.

Then we had the UK crowd, made up of four to five girls who frequently changed channels to Brit English to talk to one another. Some girls were from Canada, and the rest were from the US. Ah! Now this was soothing; these girls looked normal to me, and we hung out frequently. Sometimes when we were in the yard, there were so many ethnicities that I felt as if the FIFA games were underway, but with Tatbighi rules. Team US versus Team UK versus the remainder of the European countries. Everyone had a slightly different cultural attitude thanks to those homes from which we'd come. Those of us from the US were, for the most part, laid back and relaxed, while the Europeans were more traditional. The girls from the UK just needed to speak slowly so that we could understand them.

Since many of the girls were from my side of the Atlantic, we connected quickly. It was like going to school with Krista and Bianca. Turn the Italian to Persian and replace the meatball sandwiches with *Joojeh kebabs* (chicken *kebabs*), and there you had it.

I missed my girls back home in Brooklyn, but these *mammas* had lots to offer, and there was a certain cultural familiarity between us—strangers in a strange land—that made our connection even stronger. It was as if they knew my secret and I knew theirs; we had all been to the other side and seen what the world had to offer. I personally felt I was really different coming from NYC—I'd seen drug busts and mafia dons, and the other girls hadn't—but I enjoyed hearing about the other states, too. One girl was from California, Sunshine State, and—I didn't understand how these two ended up where they did—one was from Oklahoma, and one from Idaho.

The classes were more like my classes in Brooklyn. They were trying to help us comprehend a lot of the material in very little time, but progress was slow for most of us. At least they cut us some slack. I could speak some Farsi, thanks to my classes in Queens, but everything was different here, and I was struggling. It was like trying to learn everything from scratch again. And it was frustrating.

We had six to seven different classes: Farsi (language and literature); Arabic, which was replacing Spanish as my second language; and the Koran class, which we were required to take, even when we didn't understand a word of what we were reading. Then we had religious education, history, geography, math, and the arts.

The art class was the tops. We had to knit, sew, and even learn to wash stains off fabric. There I learned that washing blood off silk was the most difficult thing, and best done under cold water. They were turning us into good ol' Iranian housewives, I realized, but I wasn't too worried about that. Something told me that I wouldn't be there for long. And at least the company was nice.

Whether you liked the school subjects, were slow in the subjects, or didn't understand the subjects was irrelevant. You had to memorize all paragraphs word-for-word and get a good grade, which led to a good reputation. This kept the ego fuel going, and had me studying even when I normally wouldn't have.

The most annoying subject was religious education. It was too complicated for me, and was something I didn't believe in. Nor would I ever, ever practice it in my life. But I had to memorize everything in the book to take the exam and pass the stupid test.

"Why do I have to study this nonsense? It's not like I'll be *applying* any of it!" I complained to my mom.

"You won't lose anything by becoming familiar with it. It's your religion anyway," she answered.

"My religion? I haven't picked one yet!" I fired back.

"We are Muslim, though we don't practice it," she said firmly.

I narrowed my eyes in fury. This was exactly what I'd been afraid of—someone telling me what I should and shouldn't believe. I would make up my own damn mind, thank you very much! "Leave the determining what I am to me, Mom. I may choose to be a Jew or become a Buddhist," I said chuckling.

"A Buddhist?"

"Just sayin' ... you push me and I fly to extremes!" I answered back, turning my head to indicate the conversation was over.

"Del, relax. No one is pushing you. In your own words, 'take a chill pill,'" she said, no doubt thinking that if we got into a fight about this, I'd go into attack mode.

I decided to take her advice for the moment. But I knew that this fight wasn't over. Not by a long shot. I could pretend to respect the society and wear a *wimple* outside. I could also pretend to study and waste my time over crap I would never use, just to get an A grade. But I couldn't force a religion down my soul and pretend to care about it. I would have preferred to read the Koran and not understand one word of it than pretend I cared.

The school's general direction was to turn you into a nationalist—to make you understand Iran's position in the region and the Islamic world, understand how its democracy came about and how it worked, and respect everything about *Jihad* and martyrdom. But *Jihad* was the fight a Muslim put up to defend their beliefs! Shouldn't I be allowed to do the same? Besides, learning about religion wasn't going to make me a better scholar.

So my studies were heavy, but my friends were the best. We had lots of fun, which took away some of the pain of being from another world. I looked forward to seeing them every day and exchanging gossip. Everyone behaved like a leader, or representative, of the culture they'd flown out of!

And I was determined to learn, so I sat at the front of every class and became a straight-A student. It was a real mission, but I banged out the books with lots of overnight study sessions and coffee. Competitiveness ran in my blood and I was hungry to learn. I just wanted to do it for my own reasons. I never did manage to admire my teachers, who I envisioned as females stuck in a world where they'd lost the key to freedom. In my opinion, they were zombies who had forever surrendered to their circumstance, which was to say: They led very boring lives. Ambitions crushed, goals not achieved, hobbies ignored. Some due to traditional families, some culture, some the country.

My math teacher had an edge, which I liked. Talking with her was the tops, because she was open minded and we were comfortable with her. She didn't like living in Iran and wanted a way out, so she was in the process of applying for an education visa. She was also smart, and I could easily think of her as the next Nobel

Peace Prize Winner if she did manage to make it to the US. Smarts topped with edge was a *great* formula for a girl ... at least in my opinion. But in this country it was grounds for destruction. Girls should obey and follow. No entrepreneurship for a woman ... or she would be above a man. At least that was my impression.

I felt some women had lost the ambition to even want to *feel* the rush of that ambition and freedom or—worse—didn't even want that particular key. They'd become followers with an unclear destination. I couldn't summon the will to interact with all of them, and geared that energy instead toward girls in class. Ones who were less anal about stuff, and shared my wish for more out of life.

As we got closer, we got more daring. We paid less attention in class, spoke more freely, and talked about our dreams. Then one day, we decided to ditch school entirely. Neda, the girl from Idaho, had found a short wall leading to a forest behind the school. This, we decided, was the easy path to getting out of there.

We jumped the wall to just wander around a green, leafy area without rules, and without people forcing us to do this and that. We returned three hours later, resulting in the principal escorting us straight into detention. It turned out that our absence hadn't gone undetected, and I wondered what they'd looked like when they found us gone. Had they been surprised? Dismayed? They shouldn't have been; they should have seen it coming. Learning, pretending, and disobeying school authorities were becoming my daily routines. I wanted my space, and I was going to do whatever I had to in order to get it.

As time passed and the pressure for studying and being a certain way mounted, I started feeling an even more rebellious side rising up. I wasn't angry with my parents, but really disappointed that they'd taken me to this place. I didn't like being told what to do by my own parents, and now I had to obey the restrictions the religious government put upon me. Before long, I started thinking about running away. But I had no idea how, or where I'd go if I left. How would I get out of the country? I missed Brooklyn, Annie, and Larry. I missed Krista. I missed admiring Robert's six-pack on the playground.

But how was I going to get back there?

The one positive aspect of the detentions—which became more common—was that I got to know Neda better. She was going through everything I was going through, and sympathized with my suffocation. Only her parents were planning to leave the country by the time she was nineteen. Her father loved the US, and had only returned to Iran because his mom was dying of cancer. I didn't know if this meant he was waiting for his mom to die, or if he was trying to get rid of her himself. But he'd decided that it would happen before Neda turned nineteen, and had already set his plan for going home again. I was more jealous of her than I could say.

I also became close to another girl—Saloomeh—who was from California. Her dad was going bankrupt, and had run to Iran with the family for fear of getting arrested. That sounded like a longer-term stay to me, and I immediately asked about it.

"So, you guys aren't returning anytime soon?" I asked curiously.

"Well, my dad isn't, for sure. He also has this school loan that he hasn't paid back yet!" she said, without thinking that I might go report her dad's whereabouts.

"Do you like it here?"

"It sucks, girl. I can't wait to turn eighteen and get the hell out!" she said.

That meant, I assumed, that she was planning to leave without her parents. Which seemed sad. If I were going to get out, I would have preferred to do so with my folks. But it looked like her family was a broken one anyway, so maybe it was different for her. Her parents were divorced, and her dad had dragged her back with him, insisting that she be under his supervision. Her brother, from what she said, was a pothead and refused to come to Iran with them. She was trying to keep it together.

"Sometimes I just want to give in!" she said.

"Give in to what?" I asked, completely confused.

"Disasterville! These books are a horror story. I can't find a place to dance and have fun, and I miss wearing my ripped jean shorts. And I *hate* being told to be Islamic! I hate, *hate* my life and my dad doesn't help, either!" she said, shouting toward the end.

"You're not thinking suicide, are you??" I asked, a bit fearful for her mental issues.

"No. Well … sometimes. But *no*, not really…" she said in beats.

"So which one is it? Either kill or save yourself?" I asked, a bit scared to hear what the answer might be. "Let's save your life for now. I may need a friend to talk to!" I added sarcastically, not wanting to give her time to answer.

"Deal!"

"That's a girl!" I said, giving her a hi-five.

Then I took a breath. That was pretty deep, and this girl seemed on the verge of collapse. Maybe all the girls were thinking these thoughts in this country, though. I felt as if I was walking in and out of twilight zones, and although she sounded angry and suicidal, I understood where she was coming from. We were all the same: a bunch of girls being told to convert to a certain way of living, but resisting the path. Being teenagers just added to the idea of resistance. We didn't want to do what *anyone* told us.

Our main bond was jumping back and forth between Farsi and English. Everybody knew how to speak Farsi at a different level. Thanks to the Emperor and H^2O speaking Farsi at home and on the telephone, I was able to pick up a lot, though I was nowhere near proficient. Others had it a bit more difficult, with one parent American and the other Iranian; they didn't have as much exposure at home, so they were slower to pick it up.

So we spoke a mixture of English and Farsi to each other. Five words in English, one word in Farsi, or five and a half words in English and a preposition in Farsi. To those fluent only in Farsi, we must have come across as nonsensical. Occasionally—when in a bind—we used hand gestures to convey what we meant, along with our awkward and bi-lingual communication. At times when the all the techniques failed, I just gave up on the conversation.

We were only a year away from graduation, and considered to be adults by the country around us, but our theme was *girls just wanna have fun*! So when the teachers hadn't come into the office yet or we had a break, one of the girls would shut the door so we could start dancing around. Someone would bring out a radio and we'd shake it to Vanilla Ice's "Ice Ice Baby" and M.C. Hammer's "Hammer Time," just to show that we could.

"Shake that ass, girl!" shouted Neda to one of the UK girls.

"Shakin' every little part I can," she replied with her Elton John accent. She wore the same glasses Sir John always wore, and could have passed for his Iranian cousin.

Then suddenly, the teacher would come in and see a music video in production, frown, and demand that we take our seats. But what could she do? Punish us? We were in school and there were no men to be sexually aroused by our dance moves. The whole lesbian thing wasn't even a concern, as Islam strictly prohibited homosexuality, so she couldn't accuse us of tempting anyone.

Once in a while, the teacher would raise her voice and softly yell, "*Khanoom*, take your seat fast! Stop these moves and steps!"

Khanoom meant *missy* or *young lady*, but with an imaginary pointed finger, and we never took it that seriously.

Instead, we'd just shrug it off. We always sat down. But that didn't mean we wouldn't try to dance again. It was exciting to be doing something that wasn't allowed, and it was even more exciting to be doing it with other girls who were in the same boat.

For me, though, Arabic and Farsi grammar killed even the good times.

"Study these," advised my mom. "Memorize them. I'll help."

"I don't *want* to memorize them. I just want to understand the language."

This conversation was replayed often, and often expanded to other classes, including science, social studies, and religious studies. What was the point of memorizing? I wondered. Then I came to notice that it all came with a label. All the parents tried to impress each other with what their child was doing in school. I wanted to think that my parents were still the same parents I'd had in America, and that they'd only moved me here to broaden my mind and expand my horizons. But the more they tried to make me adhere to Iranian society, the less I believed it.

I started to feel isolated and lonely, cut off from the people who were supposed to love me the most. I was on an island, all by myself. And I wanted to escape.

My parents must have realized that I was getting restless, because before I could move into graduation, they started shopping for a new school. Evidently the foreign school was only meant to be a temporary resting point. Once your child acclimated and started

74

making progress, you had to put them into a regular school. I had to leave mid-school year and was to be transferred to an outside, public, school. Which meant goodbye Tatbighi. And goodbye to all my new friends.

I didn't think I could do it. I wasn't ready to be thrown into the culture outside, and I certainly wasn't ready to leave the safe haven of my friends and teachers. But no, my parents were convinced that I would be flexible and adapt. I wasn't so sure. The other side included speaking completely in Farsi, understanding where to say what, and knowing how the culture operated. The *absolute Iranian side*—no more joking around and no more *wimple* freebies! No more Hammer Time. No more New Kids on the Block crush talks.

No more of my small, hard-won freedoms.

I was scared to the bone, but I had come this far, and I wondered if it could actually get any worse than what I'd already seen and heard of. Outside, I knew, there would be one restriction after another: the society's religious rules; my father's rules, which revolved around how he wanted me to behave in Iran; my reputation, which included what I studied, how I dressed, how intelligent I was portrayed… And forget about looking forward to sex. I didn't even want to bring that up.

I'm a warrior, I told myself … but was I? I would soon find out.

Chapter 3: Strange New World

Months passed, and we moved into a condo on the top floor of my grandmother's building. My father bought the place so my mom could be near her mom, which—I thought—was one of the reasons for our return to Iran. I liked it, though, because whenever I wanted to do something private or needed space, I would just go to the first floor, to my grandmother's. The problem was all my cousins also had the keys to her place, and would do the same! If they wanted to bring a chick home, call a boyfriend, or get with a fling, where did you go? *Grandma's!*

Not that there was anything wrong with our house. It was a nice condo, and my mom had decorated it and emptied my father's wallet in doing so. Everything was custom made, with the latest in fridges, stylish cabinets, furniture, artwork, and antiques. My bedroom was twice the size of my bedroom in Brooklyn, and I decided to paint it purple on one side and cream on the other. I told my mom specifically to stay away from decorating my room. Her opinion didn't fly with me, and she wanted to make it look like a museum more than a room in a home.

My furniture was white, and I had posters of New Kids on the Block, Christina Aguilera, Madonna, and Guns 'n Roses on the walls. I found an old armoire from one of my grandmother's rooms that I decided to paint grey and make my own. Had my own stereo, TV, and VHS player, which blasted Ace of Base and La Bouche whenever I felt like it. And I could always go watch my American movies in my room if I needed the feeling of being back home again. That room was the place I called home and connected with. Best of all, I could walk around in my underwear if I wanted to, without any *wimple*, *burka*, scarf, or *manto*.

Coming home from school was not the happiest time of my day, though, because aside from the TV, there wasn't much to do. No bike rides or walking down to the pier with friends, and definitely no pizzeria or parks. No punch ball. It was terribly boring, and I wondered—often—how people managed to live there at all. Girls couldn't ride bikes in the streets because it wasn't normal. But I had heard from my cousin that there was a certain park called *Cheetgar* for girls to bike! A park with a certain section just for girls! I was determined to go, though I didn't know how I'd manage to ride a bike with a manto or burka on. Could I just wear a scarf? Or would that be showing too much skin? But if we were in a section set up just for girls …

The difficulty with Tehran was we had to think about things like that. There were no hangout spots specifically for girls; instead, you had lots and lots of family time. The food was amazing, except for the eye sandwich. Everyone was very nice, but extremely nosy, and school was like a girls-only sauna. If I was going to go outside, I needed to dress up in a burka or nicely ironed scarf. Plus my father had turned into a true despot. He wouldn't allow me to go to the parks or green space without supervision, and supervision meant that I couldn't do anything that I wanted to. This off-limits policy came from his awareness that soldiers (*sarbaz*, in Farsi terms), went to the parks when they were released from their designated stations on break, and my parents didn't want me interacting with them.

Who are these soldiers? I wondered. Could they provide some entertainment? Perhaps some … romance?

"Can I just take a walk, Dad?" I would sometimes ask.

"No, walking alone in the park is not suitable for a girl," he would answer back.

"Dad! It's just a walk! You don't trust me?" I asked, furious and annoyed. He'd allowed me to go all over the place alone at home, and now—suddenly—I couldn't be trusted?

"Of course I trust you, Delkash Jan, it's them I don't trust!" he would always say, as if he was on the US Supreme Court, attempting to defend his client.

What was that supposed to mean? He never said that stuff to me when we were in Brooklyn! But then again, my mom had always made sure I was in the house before he got home at 8. So maybe he'd never realized how much I was out on my own. He'd certainly never complained about it.

Of course she was no help once we were in Iran. "Your father knows best. Listen to him, beautiful," she would say.

I almost asked her—numerous times—how *she* would feel if she wasn't allowed to go out with her sisters and mother. How would she feel if she was stuck in the house all the time? Women had to follow specific rules, yes, but those rules were even *stricter* for girls my age! And it was completely unfair, from my point of view.

But I bit my tongue, because I knew I would regret saying it.

Later, I found out from Ghazaleh, that those so-called soldiers were actually teenage boys trying to hit on every girl visiting the park. It was their way of dating and hooking up. They placed prank calls from the heavily trafficked yellow telephone booths around the park or called their girlfriends to talk without anyone disturbing them. It was some awkward way of dating and communicating.

It was all we had. And I wanted to experience it for myself.

I got a more complete answer about how it worked from Kamran.

Iranian boys who were too lazy to study for the university exam, had to enter the military at eighteen. Some did full service, while others leaned on the ol' *party bazi* to get out of it. What was *party bazi*? It was the underground, essentially—a way to pay your way out of military service. These boys paid to be labeled 'disabled' so that they wouldn't have to serve. Clearly, not everyone wanted to be a soldier. My cousin said that being a soldier made a man out of you, but I had trouble seeing any of them as manly at all.

What was the point of all this nonsense anyway?

I couldn't understand their system. Could those guys just go to work, or get married? I knew things weren't that simple, though, especially considering Iran's economic woes, which were worsening every month. Some days, you could buy a piece of gum for 5 cents one hour, and the next hour you would buy it 1.5% more! Eventually, as it got more expensive, you just stopped chewing gum. I didn't understand what was going on, but I did know that it affected the poorer classes in Tehran, and made it difficult to feel any consistency in the city.

So they made their boys join the military if they didn't want to go to college. They had to join the group and learn how to handle the weapons … how to kill. How to do it and deal with it, and how to go to war, if it came to that.

This duty extended six months. More, maybe, for some.

What a waste of energy. Of life!

According to my cousin, some of the soldiers were normal boys, even handsome. Others were outcasts. Many of them climbed the walls to try to get away from their military service, though they rarely escaped. If they were caught, they earned another six months. The few times I saw them—always with a family member—I found them to be bad mannered and offensive. With that in mind, I couldn't really question my parents' wish to keep me away from them.

But what *was* a girl to do after school? Everything I was used to doing was not allowed there. How could someone live *and* have fun in Iran?

Studying and knitting became my after-school rituals. My parents were still diligently researching where they should place me for school, and I didn't interfere. I didn't *want* to know. The outside world was scary for me.

One day, I managed to endure roughly ten minutes of the knitting before I was interrupted by the benevolent presence of my grandmother, who—with utmost kindness—took the yarn and demonstrated the basic steps of my knitting project. I laughed at that, because she was actually showing me a way to cheat. This didn't surprise me; she was always showing me ways to get around things.

But I got bored watching her, too, and jumped up to put Madonna on the stereo.

"Get into the groove, Aziz Joon!" I cried, dancing around.

"This kind of music is not for me," she said.

"I don't think Madonna excluded you when she made this song," I answered, moving my butt.

"I don't think Madonna was thinking about me at all when she was producing," she laughed, gently turning one foot back and forth and starting to move around.

I was surprised and very pleased. The old lady had moves! Even though she wore a scarf and *burka* (that combo of a *wimple* and a long, long sheet of cloth covering your body) and was old, she had enough energy to have a pop concert!

And that was how it moved forward. To pass the knitting course I was taking, I smothered Aziz Joon with lots of love and kisses, and she, in return knitted a small baby sweater for me. I did eventually learn knitting, but the results little resembled an actual piece of clothing. Not that anyone else knew that. With my grandmother's help, I became the star student of the class.

Whether my teacher noticed this or not didn't matter; the combination of whatever I'd learned and Aziz Joon's time earned me a solid A+, and my fake reputation was golden. My parents were happy because it made them look good.

And that was how it went in Iran. Reputation was everything. Even if it was fake and forced.

The days passed, bit-by-bit, moment-to-moment. I slowly adapted to the new settings, although I still complained about having been moved to this boring, dark country. "This is your country," my mother would declare. "With so much love for you. Try to understand it, because you have Iranian blood. You are from a great country with so much history … with such a rich culture."

Ok so I was Iranian, a brunette, had exotic almond-shaped eyes, olive-colored skin, had two passports, and spoke Farsi like a five-year-old! What I had learned so far from my Iranian side was that I had to wear a mandatory *wimple*, have a good reputation, and be careful of who I talk with in the parks. What *else* was there to understand? The culture was vague for me, and they expected me to start learning it at seventeen, when I'd already grown up in a different country. They didn't understand I was more of a Brooklyn gal than an upper Tehran kind of girl. Many of the other girls did their hair and makeup under their scarves and burkas, and tried to be someone else.

Not me. I didn't care enough to do that. I didn't wear any makeup, and didn't do my hair at all. I hadn't even tried to adapt to the culture. All I could think of was what I'd lost.

Frankly, I felt as if no one understood me, except for maybe Neda and Saloomeh. But even my hobbies were different than theirs. The sun came up, the moon rose, and my days after school were filled either with studying (which was good as long as I wasn't knitting), watching taped music videos of favorite American artists (from the satellite dish my dad had put on the roof), or spending time downstairs at my grandma's, with my grandma or any family that randomly decided to drop in. Labeling these activities as bad or uncomfortable wasn't entirely fair or accurate, but I sensed that there was more out there for me. I just had to find it.

*

October loomed, and school transfer time was getting closer. My parents were eager to send me to some private school, called *geyre entefaii,* with regular students, teachers, a principal, and the requisite over-the-top religious clothing. All good things come to an end, and now Tatbighi was a dream I was letting go of. Why couldn't I just stay here? Maybe if I pretended I hadn't progressed in my Farsi or adapted—a teeny tiny bit—to my surroundings, they would keep me there. But I couldn't pretend. I was too smart. And I hated pretending to be something I wasn't.

And so the new school became a reality.

The class was all female, with around twenty girls. Twenty privileged girls who had the bucks to go there. It was better than a public school, but the girls seemed snobby, and most of them had actually been to England or France for vacation. Some knew English, while others spoke it in the way I'd spoken Farsi months earlier. They were smart girls, for sure. Neda and Saloomeh had been taken to other, regular schools, but mine was a class of its own. We were served *kebab* lunches and taught courses like French, which was not usually taught in the public schools. I still kept in touch with them once in a while over the phone, but I could no longer see them, and I missed our adventures. I missed feeling like there were people out there who understood me.

This school also had new rules for uniforms. My attire changed from a grey *manto* and black *wimple* (Tatbighi colors) to a green *manto* and black *wimple*. The green trench-type coat was made of cotton and polyester, and the heavy outfit was guaranteed to sweep up all dust and hair it encountered, thus reducing janitorial fees! Collectively, the class looked like a rain forest, and any girl who objected to wearing this attire would find themselves in the principal's office or out of the school. You didn't voice your opinion here.

I noticed that the place was furnished better than most public schools, with new desks and white boards instead of blackboards. They said chalk was bad for our lungs, but they forgot to look at the pollution in Tehran. It was even dirtier than Brooklyn.

All told, I didn't quite know what to make of this novel atmosphere at first. The girls were warm and well humored, which was a definite plus. Not exactly the type of dry Jewish and Italian humor I was used to, but pleasing nonetheless. I didn't know if it was a cultural connection, but I actually felt at home with them, and they didn't look at me like I was an alien from outer space. But simply coming from America was enough to draw heavy attention. Upon learning that I hailed from the USA, girls would besiege me with questions and comments.

"Could you please speak some English?"

"She has no accent ... that's so cool!"

It sounded like I had stepped out of a movie or I was a popular actor they were meeting live. Some took the easy way and just stared at me with intensity enough to be classified as creepy, remarking afterward that I was cute. Obviously I was foreign, but they didn't judge me harshly for that.

Best of all, they were educated and sophisticated. And they offered me something I hadn't thought to find again: a world of their own, underneath the restrictions and clothing.

Of course most of the clothing was only on when we went outside. While we were in class, the principal had given us permission to remove our *wimples*. In other regular public schools, this wasn't permitted. Sadly, a few would keep those bad boys on! I couldn't understand why they would do this, especially during hot days. I didn't know if they thought it would help them get the best grade, or if they were afraid that some man might be peering at them from a secret window, or maybe a male ghost was waiting to see their hair. The rest of the girls were laid back, and some actually had pretty nice hair when the *wimple* was removed.

My cousin Bahareh also went to that school. Her dad had died during the Iran/Iraq war—via a bomb that flew through his office window—and her mom (my aunt) was raising the siblings

(Bahareh, Ghazaleh, and Kamran) on her own, but their dad had been wealthy, and left plenty of money for the kids. They did just fine, and were certainly able to afford the school fees.

They were well-mannered, kind, and easy going, and usually went on summer trips to Turkey, France, or even Malaysia. So they had seen the other side as well. My aunt was strict with the girls, but also very good friends with them, and gave them freedom to be who they chose.

Our parents thought we would get closer, and become virtual sisters by going to school together. But I didn't trust her ... yet. What if I told her a secret, and she went right to her mother with it? It could ruin everything. Still, we did grow closer. In the beginning, my Farsi was weak, so Bahareh often came to the rescue and completed my sentences. She also began to teach me the slang of the area. I slowly, deliberately, picked up local slang and—from books and my cousin—proper usage of certain terms.

We had five courses and fifteen-minute breaks in between, with an hour-long lunch, and then prayer time. Which I refused to do. In the beginning I told them that I couldn't because I was on my period, which excused me from praying, but that only lasted for ten days. Then I started getting stomach aches (the fake kind), then headaches until they finally smelled it out. After that, I was told that I had to pray, and had no choice in the matter. So I started reciting Madonna lyrics to myself while I went through the movements.

Yet another lie. Something new that I had to fake, just because my parents had decided to move to Iran. And another piece of kindling on the fire of rebellion that was growing in my belly.

I liked the study-recess system, though. It allowed time to devour a Mortadella sandwich, or chicken *kebab*, which the school usually ordered for our lunch. If someone didn't like it they could head down to the cafe and grab a sandwich. No more pizza bagels or mac and cheese or ravioli with an apple for lunch. These were hardcore delicacies, delicious sandwiches, and sometimes *koobideh* (beef) kebab with grilled tomatoes. The kind of stuff that put you to sleep immediately after you ate. Best of all, it didn't matter if you were overweight; the *manto* concealed it.

During lunch the girls sat circled on the ground, discussing daily events, making jokes, or having water fights. We could do whatever we wanted in front of the principal, except—God forbid—get caught dancing, or wearing our *wimple* slanted or cut from the chin-piece to make it loose, or holding an unlawful item such as a CD or troll doll, or daring to pluck our eyebrows. This last was strictly forbidden. It made no sense to me; there were *your* brows! If your *parents* allowed this and you weren't doing it on school time, well, so what? But if you showed up with plucked brows, away you went into suspension!

So this new school was quite the maze, but it did give me a good laugh. After all, the girls were different but *sane* and—in a foreign way—*fun.* As I grew closer to them, they welcomed me into their circle by way of birthday parties, pizza parties, and even study parties. Thank God they were all female gatherings, or I would have been forbidden to go. The party had to be a female sauna; otherwise I was banned from going! *Emperor's rules!*

Four girls in particular became good friends to me: Bahareh, Mina, Azin, and Nooshin. The four of us hung out at break times, and I slowly came to think of them as my group. These girls and their families brought me a whole new world of education about

Iran. Mina's mom was a firm Shah defender and hated the current regime, and her dad was an American-educated electrical engineer who had gone to Stanford University. He didn't like the government either, but had his own company and made lots of money. They both lived in Iran because they wanted to be near their parents. Her mom still had hope that the Shah's son would gain power over Iran. Because they didn't really believe in the government, they followed their own set of rules under their roof. They threw parties, didn't require scarves, had plenty of alcohol, and allowed Mina to date as long as they knew the guy. The family was not religious at all, but still ranked in the upper Tehranian class. I'd had no idea that was possible.

Azin's mom and dad met at Northwestern University near Chicago, fell in love, and during the Shah's time came back to Iran to get married and establish a family. Then the regime went sour on them. She was a psychologist but preferred painting, and her paintings sold like crazy. She occasionally had a gallery show in Tehran, with art that resembled Van Gogh and put him to shame. Azin's dad had an MBA and was into real estate. His focus was building many of the high rises on the northern end of Tehran. Azin also had it easy. No scarves while at parties, and she could talk to guys without constantly being chaperoned. Her dad even drank and smoked.

Then we had Nooshin. Her dad had gone to Columbia in New York and was a bad boy turned good at forty. He had returned to Iran to find a wife and get married. This man adored Iran, and said that he'd never move back to the US. But he'd brought plenty of US to Iran with him, including tattoos all over his arms, only to be seen inside the house. He wouldn't expose them out in the streets. Tattoos weren't approved of in Iran, and if men had them they wouldn't be put in the highly educated or sophisticated category. In the US, he'd been the type to hop on his motorcycle at night, with his frat buddies, and drive near the tip of some mountain loop! Definitely not the type of guy normally found in an Islamic country.

"In my country, no one can tell me to leave!" he would sometimes say when I asked him why he decided to stay in Iran. My guess was that he must have had some traumatic experience with someone in the US who had told him to go back to his country. He was a confident and arrogant man, and I could see how that would have upset him.

He was a mechanical engineer, and her mom was an antique dealer. Too much money and sitting in the house had led to her traveling all around the world and buying old stuff. She was also an American citizen, and watching *The Addams Family* was her fondest memory of living in New York. Nooshin wasn't allowed to have any boyfriends because her dad was super protective like mine, and she too was only allowed to go to girl sauna parties.

Since Bahareh was also friends with them, and her family approval meant my family approval, my dad considered all of them legit and allowed me to go to their homes. But never to spend the night. He'd never allowed slumber parties with Krista or Bianca, either. I was Cinderella in both worlds and had to come home before a certain hour, or the pumpkin would be put in the garage for a long time!

When I did get to go to parties, I found them to be similar to the ones with the Tatbighi and Brooklyn girls, but warmer and friendlier. They were into guys, but not as much as we had been back home, and were only dating here and there. My Farsi had gotten better so that I could converse with them easier, and if I needed help, Bahareh always kicked in. Their families were very hospitable and I found a certain kind of cultural proximity and openness with them that I'd never had before. They had so much soul, love, and life, even though they were living in such closed boundaries.

One night that left a big impression on me that year was *Shabe Ahya* night. It was a completely religious night, and the first night of the holy month of *Rajab*. The month was considered one of the four sacred months in Islam, in which battles were prohibited. The nights of that month were the most fun for us in school, though the rest of Iran's population was supposed to feel sad, cry all night, and even faint! They were called the Nights of Awakening and were another way to attempt to revive the heart from all suffering while praying and reciting *Duas* (verses from the Quran). The nights were taken seriously, with all the gravity one might expect. *Duas* were considered weapons of the believer, affirming belief in the One God, and shunning all else.

The school's second floor was used as a cafe on those nights, and covered with expensive rugs and a type of tough fabric cushion that would lean on the walls. There were tablecloths spread out on the ground with all sorts of treats and tidbits of food and tea, which was served regularly. The room was filled corner to corner with all the religious—or those *pretending* to be religious—sitting on the rugs or leaning on the cushions in an attempt to listen to the *Duas*. Sometimes it would reach extremes: The girls or the school principal and her staff would start shouting prophets' names, striking themselves in ecstatic empathy with the sufferings of the diviners.

I would wonder then if they were crazy. I mean, come on! Shedding tears and showing compassionate understanding for the harsh deaths of the holy ones … well, I get it. But the rest … was it simply good acting, or what? Some of them looked like overheated fans passing out at Michael Jackson concert!

School authorities forced us to pray and recite the *Duas*, but afterward … well, we found other activities.

On one of the three *Ahya* nights, we gathered in an empty classroom on the second floor. I imagined I was at a slumber party, under the covers, in a tent in my bedroom in Brooklyn, with lots of my old favorites. My heart was forever with Oreos and Doritos, but the Iranian pastries were irresistible. Mina, Azin, and Nooshin would share their awe and slight fear of the rituals while I devoured some of the best pastries I'd ever tasted. This, and awareness of how the symbols and protocols connected them to religious mysteries, thrummed with magic. Occasionally, due to harsh restrictions imposed by the more traditional families of the other girls in class, these nights also meant a chance to go out on dates.

The process was simple—their boyfriends would arrange a pick-up at the school and, with their date's complicity, pose as a family member taking the girl home. Everyone knew and exploited the Nights as covers for meeting with dates. The school doorman was laid back, and usually snoring by the door, so he never objected.

Sometimes during these mandatory school prayer times, called *Namaze Jama-at,* meaning group prayers, I got caught singing Madonna's "Like a Virgin" while following the physical ritual. One time I was caught and pulled into the principal's office. By the way, thank God for satellite TV, otherwise I wouldn't have had any idea of who was new to the music world. News traveled to this country with baby turtle speed!

"Who do you think you are?" she growled, straightening her *burka* and wiping her mouth after she sipped the boiling cup of tea.

"Someone that doesn't like to pray," I said with hesitation, but with lots of determination.

"Start liking it, *azizam*. This is your religion, and if we don't teach you *when and how* to pray, when will you start?"

"How about we start learning what we are *saying* in the prayer!" I snapped. "It's bad enough I don't understand Farsi, but it's even worse praying and repeating Arabic words I don't get!"

"Don't you raise your voice on me, *Khanoom…*" she said again, keeping her cool. Maybe the tea was helping balance it out, because I could see the steam resting on the tip of her nose. "You will learn that too, but this allows you to feel it, especially in the *Jama-at* style."

Jama-at meant everyone praying together. They said it had a greater effect. This was the only part I understood.

"Well I'd rather pray solo. But I can't win in this conversation, can I?" I asked.

"We have rules that you need to respect, and you will respect them!" she said. This time I think the steam was coming out of her nostrils.

At that point, I started to get as angry as she must have been. "So I have to respect what you respect blindly, is that it?"

"No, not blindly. Not with the smarts that you have…"

Before I could respond to this lack of logic, the phone rang and she was summoned on a call. I blasted out of her office, but not soon enough. I was given a warning, and the next time the school cops caught me faking at prayer, I would be suspended. Since my honesty mattered more to me than suspension, I made a mental note to learn all the words to another Madonna song, or maybe do a remix. There was no way I was going to pray in such a group, using words I didn't understand. Who knew what I was saying? And why was I being forced to do this at all?

There came times—one in a million—when I felt content to recite from the Quran, *on my own,* even though my Arabic was still a mess. But all these prayers and rules brought me to a realization of my culture. Our rules were both religious and family oriented, and they put us into a box with their boundaries. It was almost like they were trying to make us all housewives who prayed after we cooked. I didn't understand the reason for it, though, and so I kept asking questions.

My dad never forced me to pray or do anything Islamic while in the house; I just had to be a 'good Iranian girl.' Somehow I made it work; I didn't have a choice. There was no way out—at that moment—so I decided that I had to be flexible, and at least *try*.

*

Of course trying didn't always mean that I succeeded. A new friend from school—who was also the daughter of the downstairs neighbor—had invited me to go mountain climbing, along with some others. I'd met Leila in the elevator, and we'd slowly bonded while sitting in the backyard a couple of evenings a week, having a barbecued *balal*, aka barbecued corn on the cob. So when she suggested going mountain climbing, I gleefully accepted, though I could hardly wait to hear my father's opinion on the matter. *If* he asked who those other people were, the best answer was: Leila's

cousins or someone related to her. That was the only way he'd allow

me to go. It was all about 'trust'. So if the guys were blood related

and Leila's parents knew about it, he would allow it. I thought.

"Horseback riding and mountain climbing," he said

suspiciously. "With 'friends' I know nothing about. *Out of the*

picture!"

"But why? You haven't even seen my friends! Anyway,

they're our neighbors!"

"Out of the picture. Completely." He sipped his cardamom

tea, its sharp aroma perfuming the room.

"You won't let me go outside and you make no effort even to

come with me. I want to go out! It wasn't like this in Brooklyn you

know ... Dad," I said.

"It's different here, *azizam*," he said softly.

"Um ... so what am I to do? Turn back time?"

"Del *Jan*..." he said with a smile. "Everything is so different

here, and it will take time for you to see this. But I guarantee you

will slowly love it here."

"Love what, may I ask? Honestly, other than the pastries and good food, there's nothing that I really, really, enjoy!" I said, irritated. Couldn't he see that he was shutting me into a box? Couldn't he see that it was slowly killing me?

"Okay, okay. Enough." He nodded, and sighed deeply as if he was defeated but strategizing. "We will go. Yes … Let's set something up with your aunt and cousins. We could make a day of activities out of it."

Of course he was referring to the *family* when I wanted to hang out with *friends*. My mom didn't mind going to the mountains, but all she and my aunt would do was gossip, and my dad would comment on how clear the air was. It was no fun for me.

I knew he was saying that so he could shrug off the conversation. But I also knew that it would never actually happen. He was just trying to restrict my movements even more. What was he so afraid of? Could it be that he got it from his family? Although my mom's side of the family lived in Iran, my dad's side was still back in New York City. They were into the homey stuff like playing pool and poker in the house, and always ordering take out. But they were 100 percent American. One hundred percent different from my mother's family. So why was he being so much stricter than my mom?

Chapter 4: The View from Darakeh

Later, when my dad finally managed to organize the family trip to the mountains, I decided that I'd rather stay home. Going out with my family wasn't going to do anything for the wanderlust growing in my heart.

I was determined to arrive at some solution for getting myself out of the house. Speaking and pleading with my dad hadn't worked, so that was out. And my mom, forget her! Despite exerting considerable influence on her husband, and maybe even having some affection toward me, I knew that talking to her about going out would lead to another dead end. After everything, she'd be on his team, not mine.

Finally, I played the "Why did you bring me here in the first place? There is *nothing* to do!" card. And it was a winning gambit!

Designed to evoke parental guilt, it worked without flaw. You turned

my whole world upside down by bringing me here, and now you're

opposed to me exploring because you fear the soldiers, or some dude

hitting on me? The list of their fears went on and on, and I showed

them how each point was actually keeping me from learning about

my new country. The place they'd brought me to supposedly expand

my horizons.

My dad was still hard to convince, though, so I had to bring

Leila over, introduce her, and let him talk to her. After extensive

talks and questions regarding what she did with her life (never mind

that she was seventeen years old), her goals and ambitions, what her

parents did for a living, and their ideologies, he surrendered and told

me to be back home in not more than three hours. Poor girl, Leila

left with a dry mouth. But we had won! He'd also met her parents,

and found them to be well-mannered and capable parents. And it had

all worked—I was free to go to the mountains!

As they say in the *land of the free*: Nothing succeeds like

success, and now I was excited to see Iran's mountains from up close

for the first time. Leila had told me *Darakeh* had beautiful vistas, access to hiking and climbing, a selection of awesome places to eat, and was hugely popular on Friday mornings to get away from Tehran's traffic, pollution, and smoke. From her standpoint, it was also very expensive, but nothing seemed cheap to her. She stacked a fairly good allowance from her folks but was stingy even when it came to spraying on her perfume or borrowing her purse!

I was pumped for a new journey. I thought we'd have a blast up there, joking with one another and—if we were lucky—tourists and everyone else who might cross our path!

But first and foremost on my mind was the *food.*

Leila had narrowed our choices down to one place for an excellent breakfast, where we could get fresh eggs taken directly from the farm. I could hardly believe it, and thought I had to see it for myself before I would give in.

Then the day was there. "Hey, you ready to go and have some fun?" Leila asked over the phone, impatient with my ponderous prep. "Shahriyar is going to be there, you know!"

Shahriyar was Leila's modelesque "friend," otherwise known as the heartthrob of Tehran. *The charmer.* She wanted to introduce him to me, which was all good, as long as the emperor didn't find out. If we liked each other and decided to date, it would be my first boyfriend. I didn't know how my father would feel about that.

The fact that he was coming was good news for me. Not permitted to date, I might be able to mingle with Shahriyar during the climb. No telling where it might lead. Perhaps the mountains would become the location of all future dates—*who knew*?

Vogueing before the mirror, I tried to decide which scarf to wear. Before long, Leila was coming upstairs to help me dress.

"That one," she said sarcastically. "Just pick one. You look good in all of them!" She had come upstairs to push me through the difficult task of the scarf and *manto* match-up. The *manto*, the long trench coat, was usually matched up with a nice scarf, just like you would if you were doing a blouse and pants or dress and stocking pairings. After you matched them, you also had to remember to match it to your pants and shoes and bag! At times, I thought of just putting on a *burka* and calling it a day because the black sheet covered you from head to toe. At least that way you wouldn't have to worry about matching.

Layers upon layers of religious clothing to live in this country! Who said everyone wanted this?

"Let me take two scarves just in case anyone in the family sees me, and I need to switch to change face ... my laser-sharp strategy!" I said, laughing.

Leila huffed and shook her head. *"Oh my God!* Just bring two, then hide somewhere, change, and walk down the mountain. Maybe on a different path.

I glared in the mirror. "Very not funny."

"Get over it, you know I've got your back," she said as she stood up to straighten her *manto* and retie her scarf.

I was glad to have her support. Before she came up, my dad had called me into his room for round two. "Who are you going with again?"

"Dad, you remember Leila who came over!" I said defensively.

"Who else is joining you, Del? You know exactly what my question is," he said firmly.

Suddenly my mom came into the room and asked the same question. *Crap ... two against one.*

"Del, answer your father," she said, as if he needed backup.

"You guys already know! Leila and her cousins," I said, biting my tongue. They could find out easily if they were Leila's cousins by going downstairs and asking Leila's parents, but they put their trust in my firm voice.

"Who are the cousins, Del *jan*?" asked my mom.

"Don't know, I've never met them, but the apple can't fall too far from the tree," I said, smiling.

"OK, have fun, but don't come back too late. Take my cell in case anything happens," said my dad. "Remember, I have to know everyone you go out with. I don't want you going out with this cousin and that cousin when I haven't met them. Leila is an exception ... I know her folks."

"Sure, Dad, *no problemo!*" I said, looking away and hoping he wouldn't ask any more questions. I was too honest to lie easily, and I wanted to get out of there without giving anything away.

The reality of the situation was that Leila, her boyfriend, one of his pals, and I were going to Darakeh on my first adventure. I imagined that this was a tight group, somewhat like the girls I had met in my new school. They were the contemporary version of cool, relaxed, and non-religious, and hanging out with them was going to mean that I could really be myself. In my view, they were free from all the mandatory Islamic stuff I was forced to abide by in school … at least much more so than anyone else I knew. They were far from mainstream, and I was excited to join them and see what they were all about.

But it was going to be tricky. Being with males—unless they were your husband, brother, or legal cousin—was not considered admirable on the streets of Tehran. Tehran was less restrictive than other cities in Iran, though, and with money—which Tehranians had a lot of—we could get away with breaking some regulations. Still, being seen with an unfamiliar guy was on par with being a bad girl according to society's standards, and not considered *halal*. It was a non-*halal* relationship, and it would be better to either get married or to have a *Sigheh*—a temporary marriage.

The consequences of my father or cousin seeing me with this Shahriyar dude was—first—that they would know he wasn't related to me, second, that the guy probably wanted me for sex, and third ... their first thought would be to start a fight with him. My father looked at girls and boys like cotton and fire—once the cotton was touched or lighted, there was no way to prevent the flame!

To eliminate myself from such rumors, I took two scarves so I could switch if I needed to, for disguise. The first and original scarf would be *me* and the second scarf would be *another girl you mistook for me* (of course not showing my face). The strategy was good for places with lots of traffic, where you could get yourself lost in the crowd.

I wondered how, if I took an alternate (sneaky) path, Leila would have my back. I didn't trust her fully, but let it go. I hoped I wouldn't get caught in front of Shahriyar! I was a teeny tiny bit horrified at the very notion of humiliation while he was around. I was seeing the guy for the first time. What, pray tell, impression would that leave?

Also, I had heard rumors that sometimes guys used girls with green cards to get married and make it to the other side. It was their lotto ticket out. So if he liked me, would it be for my green card? According to Leila, Shahriyar was young, a macho boxer, and super smart with lots of self-confidence. I assumed that meant he was looking toward his future, and would know full well what a green card would mean to him. With that in mind, I reminded myself to be careful. No matter how hot he was.

We stood up, ready to leave, and strolled into the kitchen with feigned casualness. There I plucked a tall glass from the cupboard without making eye contact with my parents; this was to avoid being assaulted with questions.

We both gulped water, and clunked the glass onto the counter. "We're headed out guys. Love you! I'll be back for lunch!"

"Be careful! This is Tehran!" my dad said loudly as I slammed the door. I felt two pairs of eyes beaming into my back.

Outside, I released a huge, anxious breath. We climbed downstairs, and I paused at a row of plants growing in artful clay pots and excavated my makeup kit from the soil. *Good thing no one watered these today!* Now it was time to prettify my face in the cab.

This was another obstacle: hailing a cab that didn't carry perverts in back, or—God forbid—in front. Leila was with me, and I assumed she had experience with this, so I let her do the job and just observed.

Contrary to some solid and secure regulations, the taxi driver was allowed two occupants in front and three in the back. *Four* were permitted in the back if one was a child, dwarf, or something that could otherwise fit in whatever space remained. So we would all be able to ride in the same cab. If we could find one.

A bunch of cabs passed right by Leila and me, as if we were invisible. Finally one stopped, bearing one woman in the back. We hopped in, hoping we'd be the first off. The cab drivers usually locked and broke one door handle, to make sure no one ran off without paying, so you had to get in and out of the other door. Which meant, of course, that we all ended up climbing over each other trying to get into the cab. The mountains were located on the far north of the city, so we'd probably have to climb out or move around if there was any dropping off or picking up. Good thing was I was wearing pants and sneakers, and it was neither raining nor snowing!

In the end, we got out having overpaid for the cab—thanks to the cab driver not carrying any change—and running late. Trotting toward the planned meeting place, I caught a sweet scent of black cherries and mulberry. A gathering crowd soon became visible, faces flushed beneath cool, crisp air. Some people still shuffled along in sleep-mode. Others (the real troupers) lugged kettles, rugs, portable barbecues, and *gelyoons* (*hookahs*) in their backpacks, and were heading up at Olympic gold-medal speed.

"Look at these people! How can they hike up the mountain carrying all the extra weight?"

"They don't. For them it's just a picnic Friday ... they are used to it. *They are troopers!*" she laughed.

After saying hello to her boyfriend, Ali, and Shahriyar, we started walking toward a path. Ali was a photographer in art school and wanted to some way, somehow dig a hole to France or England and become a professional photographer. He said that the career didn't pay much in Iran. Shahriyar was a boxer, and from the looks of it, had a six-pack under his shirt. He was also extremely handsome. I thought that I'd have to push my old crush, Robert, out of my mind soon, because I'd found a replacement.

Not knowing where we were headed, and trying to find a path that was less crowded and traveled, we continued moving on up with the guys leading the way. They were good company, and we laughed and mocked each minor mishap and absurdity. Leila was sweating bullets and turning red with the exercise. I was hot, but the *manto* was thin and unbuttoned, and my scarf was about to fall off (I had made an executive decision and unbuttoned the long mandatory trench coat), so I was staying cool. Leila kept telling me I better button up because the religious cops were always around, and I could be arrested for showing my body. I ignored her, of course. I was wearing plenty of clothes underneath, and wasn't showing any skin.

Leila was sweating profusely, though, and unfortunately this attracted bees and bursts of laughter from all of us. "Hey, Queen Bee!" I cried. "Look out! Remember the *Candyman* movie—don't get stung!" I continued giggling, knowing that there was a chance none of them had even heard of that movie.

Ironically, I didn't find Leila attractive or sweet, but the bees sure did. They were following her closely, and looking like they were going to sting, when a thick cloud of pungent *hookah* smoke scattered the buzzing menace, saving Leila (and everyone nearby) from pain and worse.

Aside from this near tragedy, we spent our time taking advantage of the fairly remote environment and laughing with each other, occasionally shoving one another, and telling silly stories. Being out of the so-called public eye was great. There was less traffic in the part of the mountain we'd found, *because it wasn't supposed to be hiked on!*

I started singing my favorite songs, as if I'd forgotten I stood in an Islamic country. Free to be whomever I desired—or behave like I had been allowed to in my hood—I went back to the person I'd been in the town I would always consider my home.

After a while, we stopped at an ideal spot: the riverbank, where burning feet could be soothed in icy rushing water. One of the guys found mint and Persian watercress growing among tangled weeds, and we all plucked enough to eat. I, delighted by the clean green tang, joined in. It was so unlike the commercial herbs, which were tainted with disinfectant. Back home, everything would be labeled, packed, and sealed with approval, but here we were eating from and with Mother Nature herself! It actually tasted better than the supermarket labels shouting "Organic."

Shahriyar stooped to wash his hands, and I tried pushing him into the river. "What are you doing?" he asked, joking and trying to keep his balance.

"Having fun ... what are *you* doing?" I flirted back.

Standing straight, blotting his hands on his pants, he said, "Staying dry—or at least trying to! I can't show up back home with sopping clothes, can I?"

"Okay, soooo, *take 'em off,*" I joked.

Shocked, then tickled by my dare, he smiled and hugged me, savoring my scent.

A thrill of fear and pleasure surged through me. *Oh wow, I can't believe this! What if the authorities see us?*

The authorities were the religious cops, also known as the famous bearded, gun-carrying, green-suited *Komitehs*. These guys were merciless and, in the name of *Allah*, would take you down to their headquarters, *pedeghan*, and imprison you for a couple of hours or interrogate you.

Sample interrogation question: Who is this man?

Sample interrogation answer (best choice): My fiancé.

Sample interrogation reply: Release them. They are *halal* (meaning Islamically okay to touch each other).

Other answers would risk imprisonment for a longer time period. You could actually bail yourself out, too, but the bail was set upon your status, and under-the-table cash. The fuller your pockets, the faster the process!

But Azin had told me about them, and warned me to be careful about being caught by them. If they were the wrong kind and wanted lots of money, they could sentence you to whippings or some other punishment they implemented during the Middle Ages for tortuous crimes.

Still, we were away from them, surely. The whole hiding in the mountains and hugging Shahriyar made me feel like I was in a 007 movie. *Am I supposed to be scared? Are the rumors really true, or should I just be cautious?* I preferred none of the above, and not giving a shit about what might happen. I wanted to be young and carefree, if only for an afternoon.

My stomach was beginning to growl, though, and we were all getting hungry, so we decided to head to the breakfast place.

Shahriyar put his arms around my neck, and for a few minutes we walked, until he stopped short.

"What's the matter?" I said, hearing his sharp intake of breath.

"It's the *Komiteh*. Let's put some space in between us ... as if we aren't together. Quickly, button the *manto* and knot the scarf tightly around your neck," he whispered softly.

In an "as soon as yesterday" mode, I redid my attire and looked in the direction opposite of Shahriyar. Trouble was coming right at us. All I had to do was act like I'd never seen him before, and we'd be all right.

Abruptly, Shahriyar turned and began gesturing, asking directions as if he were some lost tourist. The charade had to play until the green-coats wandered off to browbeat other innocent hikers.

Looking around me, I could see that Leila and the other guy were spread out too. Everyone was walking in a different direction and making their way back down the mountain's rugged face. But where had the cops come from in the first place? How had they found us? I thought this place was hidden?

Without giving it a second thought, we hustled down the mountain—separately—before the police could give us any trouble.

And that was our short morning. We had no way to contact one another (I had forgotten to give Leila the cell phone I had in case I died or was arrested), so the next stop was going back home. *Komiteh* had smelled us out, no matter how good our acting was. One of them looked me in the eyes as I walked by, and his silence meant get the hell out of here or pay up. I just continued walking and thanked God for the warning.

My only goodbye was to Leila, who returned a dry response, as if she was totally disinterested. The green-coats loitered, casting

122

what looked like sinister glances at departing hikers and picnickers alike. I was a little bit scared, but I was also excited; this had been truly dangerous, and required some good acting. Still, we hadn't really been able to do much, and I wondered if going out was always this hard and fruitless. I'd been well on my way to making out with a boy, but now we were caught and being sent home.

Chapter 5: SATs on Steroids

Like all potential college students, I dreaded taking the

Konkoor, Iran's version of the American SATs. There were referred

to—with no trace of humor or irony—as "SATs on steroids."

How could I survive that? It had been a total of eight months

in Iran, and now I had to get ready for college. I wanted to study

dance, choreography, and have a career in the arts. I despised the

thought of becoming a doctor, lawyer, or engineer—the three jobs

most respected in Iranian culture. If you were a doctor, you would be

highly respected and definitely the number-one pick on anyone's list

of "people considered suitable for marriage." The last two were both

rated as number two, but if you told anyone "my son or daughter is a

doctor," you automatically sat in the VIP listings and needn't explain

more.

There wasn't a dance major, but even if there had been, my dad would have strongly opposed it. He said *shaking my ass* was not a career, to which my answer was: "Dad, people make a living out of this back home! Besides, when I dance everywhere shakes, and it's just not that one place!"

I was good at it, and was convinced that it should be my life. I just had to figure out how to do that.

I taped videos from the illegal satellite TV and, after school, would push all the living room furniture to one side and make the space for my own private dance studio (this was the same satellite TV that was viewed by 70 percent of the population, who secretly imagined there existed no surveillance helicopters or well-greased bribes). Once the videos starting playing, I acted like I was a paid dancer, and learned all the choreography by heart. My parents would pass by the living room, shake their heads, and say, "May god help her...! She has to get this out of her system!"

But it wasn't some type of steam or sweat I could extract from my body. It was in my DNA. That, of course, never registered with them. They thought it was a teenager thing that would pass. The "teenager thing," though, had made a solid home within me, and every day it was my routine to dance it out, no matter who saw me. I even thought about selling tickets once or twice, given the way the entire family stopped to stare at me.

Dance was a dead-end in this country, and in fact, any discipline involving extreme physical movement—especially by a female, in the presence of a male—was forbidden. Unless you were *halal* to one another, of course! And if you were already married, what was the fun in dancing? The whole thing made no sense.

I had an idea, though. If we weren't allowed to shake our booties in front of all males, how about creating the major and class with all females? The Islamic rule didn't apply to the same sex being in one room. You could take your scarf off in front of the other females, so that should mean you could also dance in front of them. Why didn't they do something like that? Gender separation was applied on the buses, in classrooms, in prayer rooms, so why not create a gender separated dance class?

Of course no one else had thought about that, and the society in which I found myself clearly didn't care about my desires. So since dance was out of the question, entirely, I had to work on picking a major and passing the exams. I decided to be fearless, though, because even for someone like me, breaking down the culture wall was achievable!

My primary reason for passing the exams was to escape having to stay home all the time, doing nothing (watching the walls, anyone?), and being utterly unproductive, meaningless, and no fun. Who wanted *that*? I also want to get out into the world and explore. In fact I was driven to do so, in ways other than my one-time half-cut "hiking" experience! What better way of getting out of the house than pursuing higher education and its attendant lifestyle?

I noticed that most women in lower classes were expected to be excellent housewives, and if they pursued an education, it was a big plus. The combo of housewife-plus-education was a great one, but the women were still passive, and usually stuck with being a housewife even if they had knowledge to work with. Even when the kids were grown up, they still stayed at home.

On the other hand, women who had education and actually worked with their knowledge, potential, and skills fell into a different category in my book ... the respect category. They were the tops, and I loved them. I felt they knew their worth and acknowledged their equal status to the men around them. Of course the rest of the country didn't see it that way, and gender equality issues were rife, leading to difficulty for women who wanted to be entrepreneurs, artists, or CEOs of big firms. At least that was what it looked like. Women had second say.

All I knew was that I wouldn't be fulfilling my destiny if I just sat there and accepted that there wasn't a major for dancers, and that I had to give it up. Screw it, I would rather cut my wrists than do that. So I reverted to dancing in my living room.

But what was I to major in, if it wasn't dance? Biology, any kind of medical study, math, law, and any type of classes related to the law were scratched immediately, because I didn't have the patience for them. That didn't leave me with much, but I always like learning Italian ... so I thought I'd come up with an answer. Instead of going to a language institute and learning Italian, I told my parents I would be declaring it as a major (and was ready for the debate that came post-announcement, too, since my dad had his eye on me becoming a doctor!).

The strange thing was that in Iran, specifically Tehran, everyone was trying to teach a language and create a language institute. The funny thing was that some of those teachers didn't have a certificate or degree to teach; they would just spend a couple of years in the US, or whatever country, as a good citizen, and learn the language. Then, once they returned to the mother ship, they founded a Language Institute. But I didn't want to go there. So instead of going the easy route, I chose the alternate route: language studies in college (where the professors had to have some sort of degree).

"You're so talented. Wouldn't you like your name on a card as *Khanoome,* (Ms.) *Doctor?*"

"Dad, I could care less about what's printed on a name tag. The best name tag would be *Delkash the beautiful and great but stuck in this country!*" I said teasingly.

"Del, *jan,* I am serious. We are talking about your future," he answered firmly.

"I am too, Dad. I want to do what I want to do. What you want wouldn't make me happy. And that matters too, right?"

"But you have to think about it—if you *were* to dance, how could you make money?"

"Um … with difficulty, but at least it's what I like doing."

"That is what you'll say the first couple of months, then you'll shout out 'my father was right!'" he said with a smile.

"Let's negotiate! Let me study Italian literature, which I think I like but am not so sure yet, and see what happens…"

"Del, I don't know why you are so stubborn, but I don't want to push you, *azizam*. The more I push you, the more stubborn you are…" he said, with such a disappointing tone that I thought I would sink into the ground. But I went over and laid a big kiss on his cheek to let him know his wish would be considered, but with a .000001 percent. He cared, and despite his firm views and way of thinking, he would do anything for me. In the end, though, I did get my stubbornness from him!

He'd been an engineer back in the day, before he turned to entrepreneurship, so he naturally pushed toward a non-art major.

Doctors, engineers, and lawyers all ended up in my psychological dumpster, though; not because I didn't appreciate their value, but simply because there was no intellectual (or emotional) interest.

Well, I told myself, it was this or becoming a young, uneducated girl sitting in the house and waiting for some young, well-established guy to come *khasteghari* (the guy and his parents would come visiting to see if both ends approved, possibly resulting in marriage within a day, or a month). Super traditional, and that just wasn't me.

How dull would that be? And how dull must both the girl and boy be to tolerate such conditions?

I'd already told my parents that the last thing I wanted was to be *stuck* with someone. We were on the same page there, but with two different mindsets about *why* I wanted to attend university.

The thing was, I wanted to go to school the American way; the way I would have if I were in Brooklyn. I wanted to live life in my freshman and sophomore years—years that no one really studied anyhow, but focused on dating, having sex for the first time, and generally living it up. In Iran, that thought had to be hidden in the basement of your mind. God I missed Brooklyn and the life I'd led before my parents moved me.

All these pressures were making the 'rebel' part of my personality come closer and closer to the light. I'd been working to keep it hidden, to please my parents, but it was becoming a fight between being myself and being what Iran and my parents were expecting of me. And the country wasn't exactly doing its side of the argument any favors. I felt a shift developing in my personality with all the changes and social pressures around me. The first year of what I'd come to think of as the Inner Brooklyn Volcano was rising … and the lava was getting hotter by the second. The last thing on my mind was *studying*. I wanted to *live*.

Mina had given me some books that were inspiring and helpful, since I frequently expressed myself to her. Some of the books were untranslated, and I had no choice but to plow through the Farsi text. They were about overcoming different obstacles with love and developing your self-confidence while in a transition mode. One was a book from Deepak Chopra, which was translated into Farsi; I couldn't find the original English version, so I read it with difficulty.

132

I read it thoroughly. Another book addressed hope, understanding, and fearlessness, though Azin always reminded me that utter lack of fear was dangerous, as the emotion was a survival mechanism.

My idea of fear was somewhat different from hers. Instead of worrying about stepping out and being ostracized, I was worried about falling in line and living the rest of my life in the shadows.

One of my favorite books about love was by Leo Buscaglia, called *Born for Love*. The author was in fact popularly referred to as "Dr. Love," and I wanted very much to meet him ... until I found out he'd died in 1998! *At least, Dr. Love, you left something in your work for a lost girl in the wild, wild, Exotic East.* Reading his poems helped me overcome the darkness and bitterness of my current situation.

Thanks Leo ... many of your poems were my exact feelings toward the situation. The books, and writing my own poetry, helped me tame the anger inside, until I thought I could control it. I was angry at my parents, angry at the country, and angry at what Islam was trying to make me become. But I was starting to see that there might be a way forward, after all.

The books had ignited a romantic and passionate feeling toward writing poetry as a form of expression—something I'd never felt before. And this too gave vent to my inner turmoil. My life had been changed drastically with my parents' decision, and finding a way to talk about that—without having to rely on my parents or my friends—gave me a place to start planning.

I closed my book and notebook, eased back into my pillow-sack, and listened to the wind hiss through trees. Tomorrow was another day in Tehran … wasn't that right? Or could it be something more? *Shab bekhier,* Doctor Love.

After the spiritual moment had passed, I started filling out university forms to study Italian Language and Literature. "Go to university so I don't have to get married! Score!" I said out loud. I was fully aware that attending the Languages section of university was not going to be easy either, despite the fact that you didn't have to study math, biology, and physics for the *KonKoor.* The learning process would be a consuming grind. But it would be worth it.

Iran hosted a handful of universities, two or three of which qualified as excellent. In truth, I didn't really care where I got accepted. I would shut myself away with books and study for the chance to get out a bit. If that would get me out of boredom, I would welcome it!

The remaining months were brutal, though; while finishing up the final months of public school, I started studying for the *KonKoor.* I was a devoted—if not an enthusiastic—study slave!

My schedule became waking up at 4, studying until the bus came at 7, coming home from school at 3, and going back to studying. If I was organized, I finished my homework by 7, in time for dinner. Then it was time to start studying for the *KonKoor* again, until I finally went to bed at midnight.

I did insist on taking the occasional mini-break, but as far as going out even to answer the phone, well, my parents had taken an inordinate interest in covering that! "Thank you for the call, but Delkash is studying today." *What?* "Yes, azizam, she will be studying for the next couple of months until the *KonKoor*. No, you may not. What? How dare you take that tone with me! Maybe your parents should teach you some manners!"

Dead dial tone, and whoever called got the picture.

Anyone attempting a face-to-face meeting was met politely at the door, and promptly given their three-to-four-month notice. No friends, no mountain hiking until after the *KonKoor*—emperor's rules!

I was driven by the urgency to get into school, so swallowed hard and kept my nose in the books. What little free time I had was limited to family dinners on Thursdays (considered the Friday night in Iran). My new life was a dive from hiking and making friends to isolation with the books.

One of the biggest challenges was going to be the questions about and in Farsi. Rumor had it that some of the *KonKoor* questions weren't really testing your understanding of the content, but to make sure every detail *in* the book had been looked at. This went as far as an old *KonKoor* question about the birthplace of a long-dead publisher of one of the textbooks, or maybe what size jeans the guy had worn. In truth, these questions were *absurd*, but past test takers always made remarks that *any* kind of question was possible on the test. So I knew that I had to study everything in detail.

Since competition was rough, one question missed could mean you dropped behind five thousand other applicants. You had to know everything, and I understood that. So I was devouring the books, along with whatever Cliff's Notes I could find on them. I had to get into school, so I could get out of the house and into some sort of life.

And the exams were nationwide, so I was in competition with every nerd and propeller-head in Iran.

*

Then the big moment was finally there.

It was the night before the *KonKoor*, the test that would shape destinies, including mine. I'd done my best. Now I wanted to burn all my books and see what happened tomorrow. *Yes!* Burn them and leap over the flames while they crumbled into ash. My dislike toward the books was greater than I'd thought, but I was thoroughly sick of them, and couldn't wait to be finished with this test.

After all, had they not burned through these months of my life? And who knew what this might lead to? If indeed, in *this* country, it led anywhere at all. What could be the point of living here and being born female? It had to be—or at least was perceived to be—producing babies, and, depending on their husbands, grocery shopping. Being responsible for throwing the occasional family gathering ... and case closed. The man was the Big Cheese. It wasn't for me.

My cousin and I gathered around my mom's table to eat, laugh, and generally explore being relaxed (I couldn't even remember how to anymore) before the big test the next day. I felt so much pressure for the test, but kept telling myself it was a challenge to see what I was really made of. I wished I could talk with Krista and Bianca. Though I'd made friends in Iran, they weren't as close to my heart as the girls I'd left in Brooklyn, and right then—when my entire future seemed to be on the line—I really needed the support of my oldest friends.

Unfortunately, they were back in Brooklyn, probably having the times of their lives. I was certain they'd forgotten all about me, as I hadn't heard from either of them in some time. Probably too busy with boys or parties. Our only connection was the one or two pieces of mail we'd exchanged, as Internet in Tehran was either filtered or so slow that you were better off with the snail mail version.

But it would all be okay, I kept telling myself. Thinking about home just made me more frustrated, and closer to exploding. I was still trying to keep my temper—and frustration—to myself, but somewhere inside, I knew that we were heading toward an explosive situation. Going away to school could only keep me satisfied for so long.

Since my cousin Bahareh was also taking the test, we'd be in competition with one another. This was another complication; if she got in and I didn't, well, it would be a catastrophe. Both my parents would have a fit and suffer from MSS (Massive Shame Syndrome). Now, if she *didn't* get in and I did … my parents would be flying high, and everyone would be praising me for coming from a foreign country and still passing the test. It would be, of course, to my parents' honor, rather than my own. It was all about reputation.

Then, suddenly, 5 in the morning shrilled its alarm, and by 7 I was seated in an uncomfortable, wooden chair in a rundown high school that had a hanging wooden entrance door that I was afraid to breathe on, thinking it might fall away from the hinges. The chair creaked annoyingly with each shift of my aching buttocks. The exam documents were distributed *exactly on time* by a tall woman with fierce dark eyes and a rigid face.

Well, this is it. My make-or-break session ... entry to the unknown ... ticket to freedom or prison ... elevator to something or nothing ... heaven or hell...

Stop it already! No reason to drive yourself crazy!

While taking the test, my favorite cake treat, the Persian *Teetop*, was passed around. Yes! It was the best pound cake stuffed with chocolate cream; my memory of any type of Twinkies was slowly evaporating! The givers of the test were human after all, realizing how long the test would be and that its takers might perish from hunger and/or low blood sugar while filling out their Scantron sheets.

The best part of the entire thing (beyond eating) was irritating the test takers with the crackle of the cellophane packaging, and its effect on the others' laser-like focus. Some of them didn't even know a sweet treat rested inches from their scribbling hand, but I wanted another. *Would my neighbor even notice if I helped myself to her cake?*

I found—to no small relief—the test bearable and even dull, and close to my expectations. By noon it was over. *Wooh!*

Walking out of the depressing, worn-out building was beyond good. *What do I do now? Love, shout, dance?*

Before I could go anywhere, an aroma of flowers nearly overwhelmed me. As did the mere (but vivid) sight of trees, leaves magnified by my months of sensory deprivation. It was like emerging from a coma and experiencing the world's wonders anew. *Wow. How deep was I sunk?*

One thing rang true though: I was set to once more enjoy life...

The problem was, I'd been in Iran for about ten months, and still hadn't figured out *how* to enjoy life there. All I knew was how to insert Islamic serum in my mind, how important it was to have a good reputation, and how important family and family values were. These were my only survival skills. Everything was about reputation and how everyone else looked and accepted you. With that in mind, people would buy the most expensive cars and take expensive holiday trips just to keep a high-profile reputation. Keeping the reputation even extended to 60 million *toman* ($50,000) wedding price tags, with 350-plus guests, lamb-and-kebab catering, the best DJ in town, etc., all while putting yourself in deep debt!

But what did that teach me about life outside of Iran? Absolutely nothing. To learn *that*, I was going to have to get out there myself. Somehow.

Chapter 6: Back to Life!

After sharing and basking in the various congratulations on taking the test and having survived the epic study sessions, I wasted no time returning home. On the way, I thought about calling my friends and getting some adventurous stuff on my calendar. Even though the country was oppressed, rumor had it in school that there was so much going *underground*, and I definitely wanted to explore the nightlife, parties, fashion shows … and everything else.

Back home, I padded past my mom, who stood at the kitchen counter fiddling with fresh flowers bursting from a case like silent explosions. "Well, well. I've been thinking about you. Praying for you ... How did you do?"

I bent and sniffed the flower display, which included some of the most beautifully scented flowers, including red roses (the national flower of the mother ship), sunflowers, orchids, and gardenias (my mom's favorite), and the most wonderful purple tulips. Iran was *numero uno* in flower production, and anywhere anybody went or whatever occasion it was, we had fresh flowers. The trick here was to pick the colors carefully, according to the occasion, and this even included the birth and death of the holy prophets and other religious holidays. For deaths it was usually white, and everything else called for a rainbow of anything.

I bent and sniffed the display. "Nice! I did fab, but I'm exhausted." After saying what I said, I realized that my English accent while speaking Farsi was slowly melting away, though it was surely still there. Thank God, there was no sign of Farsi in my English. That remained untouched.

"I can imagine, *azizam.*"

"That was the longest-running study period that I ever had. Think it was because I had to read everything over and over *and* over again! Wouldn't wish that on my enemy!"

My mom softly chuckled. "In your world, 'you gotta run for the touchdown!' Go have a rest. You'll feel better."

Rest, of course, was the last thing in my whirling mind, but I played along. Eager to activate the plan hatched earlier, I was thinking of calling the girls and maybe Shahriyar, though he probably wouldn't remember me, even if we were to go through the hiking details! Then I remembered that he never even had a chance to give me his number ... all our communication was through Leila! Scratch that! I definitely didn't want to hang out with *her*.

I thought to put together a coffee shop date with some friends, though. I called Mina and told her to spread the word to Azin and Nooshin, their boyfriends, and whoever else wanted to go. I needed to relax, and this was my alternative to the soothing Brooklyn bike rides. My new 'ride' was going to a coffee shop with the religious cops showing up at any time to bash the evening! Party crashers.

I had to keep up the "worn-out" charade in front of my parents, as if I weren't going out to meet with someone I liked. *Yes. I'm a broken, post-KonKoor student in dire need of a breather...*

I knew my excuse would fly; but my demeanor must be its equal.

Later, I emerged from my room with practiced effort. "I'm going out to relax with some friends I haven't seen in months." *Nice declarative sentence. Solid delivery.*

Peering over a magazine, my mom said, "Oh. Good. Of course. When will you be home?"

"Before 9:30, maybe sooner." The correct answer was always "I'll be home soon," because committing to a time was impossible; what if we were having fun and needed overtime? *No big deal. Just a small, belated get-together with long-missed friends, dear parents.*

Incredibly, I turned and stepped out of the house without further comment from anyone. Now, like some exotic flower, I was ready to bloom and spread my adventure-*deprived* wings.

I had to exit the house with a vanilla and blah attire to let the folks know it was a regular, no-big-deal friend gathering of *all girls*! If they smelled any male involvement, my dad's protective side would arise, and I would be banned from going. Now, he was all *"You have grown into a beautiful flower and guys here are hungry to get a taste of you. Smell you like a flower and throw you to a corner…"* What did that mean? What if I wanted to throw a *guy* in a corner? I was the girl … I should be making the calls. Weren't my feelings to be respected?

The minute my toes—well covered in conservative shoes—stepped outside of the house, I changed the dull, white scarf into a sassy blue one, put glossy red lipstick on my bare lips, and slipped into some heels used only for strutting the runway at the Mercedes-Benz fashion show. Indulging in all this was fun, because I knew I would have to face both opposition and judgment if anyone saw me. But I didn't care. If the religious cops didn't see you, or if they saw you but weren't in a bad mood that day, you were in luck. And as far as I was concerned, it was worth the risk. I wanted to stand out!

I just wanted to do it without getting caught, by the religious cops or my dad.

This was too much thinking for just going to one coffee shop gathering. I felt like Bonnie and Clyde—the domesticated version. Still, I sprinkled some pepper and spice on the outfit, letting my inner self shine, and it gave me a rush of long-suppressed excitement, as though I was being stalked by the paparazzi. Outside, at least I could breathe without my parents watching my every move.

I knew the clock would soon strike 12; for me, that was when the moon stepped out of its hiding spot at 9:30. Everything would come to a finish before midnight! I had bypassed my parents, and now had to be wary of the not-so-cute guys clad in olive-green suits—the *Komiteh*—and the female version of them, the black-wearing *burka* women, aka *'black crows.'* They were the ever-vigilant, annoying "authorities" packing outright otherworldly questions and searching for a few easy bucks. Which I was willing to pay if they left me alone.

I would gamble on the chance of running into them, though, because the coffee-shop moments in Tehran were the best. It was all about experiencing friends and the possibility of making new ones. Sipping tall cafe lattes, fresh-made pineapple juice, or the infamous black Darjeeling tea (which also led to future tooth-whitening dentist visits), while nibbling on tiramisu, crème brulee, or ethereal Napoleon pastry … And the 5-star Iranian Zagat rated, top-selling potato chips, with melted mozzarella cheese and topped with ketchup and mayo!

It beat sitting at a desk studying Arabic—something I would probably never use in my life. Or filling gaps in my knowledge of the Quran—a book I might never read in my life, or might not *want* to read or understand.

Not far from the coffee shop, I laughed to myself, heels clacking away, recalling the somewhat elaborate scheme my friends and I had devised in case the "cops" questioned anyone. Not many options existed for getting away if these "cops" did hit us up. One was posing as a married couple and the other was posing as cousins. The best was cousins—that way we didn't need to present a marriage certificate.

The plan had to be understood by all of us, though, in the event of any individual being interrogated alone. That way he or she would have the 'right' answer. Right was having the same answer as the *other* person.

Was this complex planning really worth the considerable trouble? *Yes, it was!* Without doubt, yes! Planning around my dad was one thing, but planning around the religious authorities was a whole different ball game.

We all sat down around a few pushed-together tables in the café and shared stories of how we escaped the mammas and the papas. Everyone's strategy was different, and we laughed until someone revealed that their strategy was saying that they were going over to my house! That was not funny at all, because I would fry if my dad found out. Then she said she switched the last two numbers of our phone number around and that I should chill out. It made me think that we were as clever and devious as independent filmmakers. We *had* to be. Any slip-up would result in a major disaster. The authorities here didn't always play nice! In fact, they *never* played nice unless they thought you had money.

We talked and laughed as we had our food and drinks but, like all good things, the night was coming to an end, and we managed to get out of there without the *Komiteh* bothering us. I made it home by 10 o'clock, and that was okay due to the parental understanding of just how hard I had worked over the past six months in regular school and prepping for the *konkoor*. Eleven o'clock would have been fine too, but midnight would have been pushing it. At any rate, there was nothing to do in the streets at 11 o'clock after having eaten in Tehran ... maybe a stroll in the park, and that wasn't worth the risk.

Finally back in my dim room, I felt a wave of loneliness, and plucked a pen from the holder on my desk to write in my lined journal about all my suppressed feelings in a country I was trying to find a partnership with. This hide-and-seek game wasn't doing it for me anymore, and I was hungry to break loose ... to go to underground parties, have a relationship, start drinking. Going out of the house was a bit difficult since I knew I had my dad to deal with. But I had to find a way to do it.

Chapter 7: Girl, Accepted

On the day the test results were to be announced, the streets convulsed as if in protest. Every accepted, failed, humiliated, confused, carefree, nerdy, stubborn, religious, and happy-go-lucky student moshed and twitched and flew around waving newspapers in an attempt to locate their names among millions, to see whether they had a chance at higher education ... or in my case, a chance to do anything to escape boredom.

Newspapers rattled and crinkled back and forth between ink-smeared hands, from one grinning face to another pinched with grief, all in anticipation of finding their name in long blocks of tiny-fonted text—similar to fine print, especially that in pharmaceutical advertisements.

Some names were so alike they might give false hope to many, who thought they were accepted only to find out otherwise. But given the chaos, even several minutes of that would be good.

I maneuvered and weaved through the crowds, searching for a paper.

Usually they sold out by 8 o'clock on such an occasion, but I had on my lipsticked smile and pepper personality in hopes of getting a paper from some hipster (or hipsters) in case of an eventual hook-up. You never knew!

Being accepted or not accepted was, at this point, far from my control. Whatever was going to happen would happen, as no one on Earth could make changes to the newspaper. Some highly imaginative types might wish to pen their names in, but there was no covering up reality at this point. If you were accepted, the newspaper would have your name spelled correctly. If they didn't, it meant you were out.

Of course if someone's parent had died in the Iran/Iraq war, they were automatically in. With that, on top of all the competition, the chances were minimal. But those scores dictated whether you got into college or not. We didn't have interviews or essays or lists of references like the colleges in the US did. It was all summed up in one test. Forget calculating an average of all your strengths … just be a good test taker, and hope that only a few martyrs' children had applied that year, and you were in!

"Ouch! Hey!" Some idiot elbowed my back, and I wanted out of this mass of people, some of whom could use a bath or tic-tac, but I pushed forward to find a paper. Suddenly, a spindly guy dressed in over-sized clothes like a scarecrow came toward me, looking as if he was going to grope me, so I turned and nearly collided with an attractive young man with brown eyes.

"Well, hello," he said. "Need a paper?"

"I sure do…"

"Please, take mine."

I ripped the paper out of his hands, trying to be respectful at the same time. When I looked down, though, I had no idea how to make sense of the list—not to mention how to comprehend the different universities and their corresponding cities, or how it was printed and categorized! I only knew of the three main schools located in Tehran; Tehran University topped the list, and Sharif and Amirkabir University followed. These were the public, Harvard-type universities. Then we had the Azad Universities, which you had to pay for, but were a bit easier to get into and were scattered all throughout Iran.

The nice-looking guy wore an expression indicating that he hadn't been accepted, and didn't really care one way or the other. He smelled like lime oil. He gave me an impression of empty good looks, shallowness, and talking to an empty telephone booth.

Check out other targets, loser, I thought to myself.

People were still fighting over papers, and I moved over to lean against a wall in a doorway sour with rotten vegetables. Suddenly I found my name … What? Was it my name? Was I reading it correctly?? Delkash Amidpour? *Yes*—it was my first and last name, right there on the list of people who'd passed and been accepted!

Like flies to sugar, others pressed in on me to eye the precious paper, but I pushed them off and, after a few moments, found my test results too! *I was really in.*

Given the struggle to keep the paper, I wondered if cutting out the strip on which my name and results were printed might be a good idea—something to show off proudly if someone wrenched away the paper. Such accomplishment was how you made a name for yourself, or for your family.

I gazed intently at the results. Could it be real?

To no one, and to everyone, I shouted: "I've been accepted into *Persian* Harvard ... Tehran University!" People around me chuckled as I expressed my excitement among so many introverts, but I didn't care. I had done it! Hard and at the end, luxuriously sweet! Here I was, fresh off the boat from NYC, packing a heavy Brooklyn-Farsi accent and roughly one half the vocabulary of a Tehranian local ... and I'd easily (with lots of kick-butt studying) taken down considerable competition!

I grabbed a cab and ran to the house, arriving without any oxygen left in my lungs.

I ran in, shouting like a diva expressing genuine—even tearful—joy over my enormous accomplishment, and it seemed as though the mountain climb had been a sort of frontrunner of this success. A few bumps here and there, but I'd made it. I couldn't fit in my skin … and felt as if I had received my first Oscar *and* saved myself from marrying some guy in whom I had no interest.

A new road opened, heading past signposts reading 'University' and 'Higher Education'—uniquely spiced exploration, right here in Tehran. There was a proverbial saying in Iran: Due to being locked up, studying for months and months, you forget what you look like, forget how to shower and socialize. But after you get accepted, the rest is like "ash"—or literally, in English, the rest is a piece of cake.

Basically, if you could pass and survive this exam, you could survive anything. I was a commando, an Oscar winner, and a survivor.

*

My parents couldn't contain themselves either, and both were calling the family about how smart their daughter was and how I had overcome the difficulty of learning the ins and outs of these books, even being new to this whole system. My dad invited everyone for dinner at our house, which I thought was a bit of an overreaction.

But I got over it; he was so proud of me, and I was so proud of myself that I would have done almost anything at that point.

The family was even more excited than me; they had called their friends and conveyed the breaking news: The one-time Brooklyn girl—not even a year in Iran—had been accepted in one of the best schools in Tehran! My family was, at the end of the day, a great public relations firm, too. To my credit, they were right. I had arrived late in July, and now—a year later—was accepted into university. That was Cowa-bunga status.

My present for getting accepted was taking driving classes, and if I completed within a year, I would get a brand new car. It was nothing big—just a Renault 5, which was equivalent to an Iranian version of the Ford Focus hatchback. But it would also a part of my newly attained freedom. I knew I'd be able to swap cars with my parents soon enough.

*

The next day, my mom proudly took me to my first driving class. Before I walked out the door, the emperor kissed both cheeks and said, "You are maturing, my princess."

Was I? I had no idea! I floated through the cab ride, ecstatic about my future. And everything was in good shape until we reached the driving school and I saw the car and my driving teacher.

The guy was probably in his late forties, bearded, smelly looking, without a back tooth, and looked as if he was a sales rep selling condoms. His name was Mr. Abbassi. The place looked professional, but this guy didn't even look like he was licensed or a comprehensive driver. And he was going to be my teacher?

The car was a run-down Iranian-manufactured Peykan. After observing it, I found two reasons why they would allow this vehicle on the road: it was cheap and it ran (for the most part). But it was faulty mechanically and from a safety side it was weak. It looked dodgy to me altogether ... I could imagine that if I hit the speed pedal, it wouldn't work past 50 ml/hr.

"This is what we're driving?" I asked him.

"Get in, kid," he said, and pointed to the driver side of the car.

I liked his demeanor because it looked like he wouldn't take any bullshit. Good. Maybe he'd be a decent teacher after all. There was no instruction class beforehand, and we were just going to jump into the driving.

When we were both in the car, I noticed it had three foot pedals: speed, brakes, and something called the clutch, which was connected to the manual gearbox. Within five to ten minutes, he'd explained the rules of the road to me and *when* to use each pedal. He had the brake on his side too, just in case I forgot or decided to ignore it.

Before we started the car and rolled out of the parking space, he said, "Listen to me and you'll be a pro. The *deets* you'll learn on the way. If you learn to drive in Tehran, you can drive anywhere in the world, kid," he said dryly, half-looking at me with his own stamp of verbal approval. He had a FOBish mafia way about him, but underneath those shabby clothes I got the feeling he was one of the best instructors. The tough-love kind.

The first day was horrible! People in that country drove crazy, and the pedestrians could have cared less if they lived or died. All I had to keep focusing on were pedestrians crossing and the crazy drivers popping out from nowhere. The best part were cars reversing down one-way streets if they passed their turn point. You had to be aware at all times, and definitely know where the brakes were. In Iran, you probably needed two brakes and a bag of good swear words and hand gestures. The thumb was equivalent to the middle finger (I was a fast learner there).

Mr. Abbassi's name was Jamshid and we started to develop an unusual friendship. This was the gist of the friendship: Him pulling the brakes and me pressing on the accelerator, followed by an argument, which ended with him telling me, "There are no traffic rules in this country, so it's either my rules or the highway, kid!" So I backed down and let him pound the brakes as much as he wanted.

It turned out that he was a civil engineer, but couldn't find a good-paying job to support his family, and had turned to this driving school. When I told him my story, he just said, "Good luck! You have a lot of balls to come back to this country ... stay true to yourself, kid." I didn't understand what the last part of his sentence meant, but it felt to me as if he were speaking from a place of truth. Maybe that was why he had so much tough love—he'd learned the hard way.

It made me sad to see how smart he was, and to know that he hadn't been able to use it. Finding a good engineering job was tough in Tehran, especially one that could support three kids and a wife. He said the country was filled with unemployed engineers, and look where one of them was now.

That first day, he dropped me off and told me he would pick me up every day for that week, at 8am sharp, so I'd better be ready at 7:45am. He would leave if I was a minute late!

On the second day he took me to the main streets and highways, and ended with a nice lesson in parallel parking. He was fearless and had a no formula or rule for driving. I loved it. The only part I was afraid of was this steep hill that ended with a traffic light on top. Finding a rhythm between putting the car in first gear and immediately pressing the gas pedal, without the car sliding backwards into the car behind me, was a challenge.

"It's so hard!" I complained.

When I complained, he ignored me. "Oh really. Let's try that steep hill and see how it works out … that's my favorite place to

162

drive!" Then he would take me to the exact hill I was afraid of driving on.

I gave him an irritated look but got super excited as well, because secretly I loved the challenge. Soon after, I was Formula One-ing it toward the hill! I couldn't wait; I was a student driver anyways, so that was my excuse if I hit anyone!

The hill was six lanes wide and the end point of a highway leading to Vanak Square. The traffic light took two minutes to turn green, so the easy portion was keeping your foot on the brake and clutch while you waited. But when the light turned green the cars had to climb their way up. Now was the tricky clutch/brake/accelerator fusion that I had to master.

"The gas and brakes have a love/hate relationship, so it's either one or the other! Make sure you let go of one if you decide to go with the other. The clutch is a good friend and follower of the accelerator. You pick the speed and it follows. Once you're in first gear, forget the brakes and pound on the accelerator, but with delicacy. Treat it like a girl—soft and gentle!"

"Is that how you treat your wife?" I asked, smiling with surprise.

"Maybe," he said, and quickly closed his brows. That meant 'Obey, woman!'

The heat was building and the pressure was definitely on! This was the pattern:

-Brakes

-Brakes-Clutch-First Gear

-*Fast and furious!* (I forgot the part where I had to treat it like a woman.)

The car jumped forward and then we were flying like an airplane. If Jamshid's foot wasn't fully awake on the brakes, we would have crashed in short order.

"I said *softly*! What the hell was that?" he said.

"Jamshid, I *am* the girl who needs to be treated softly," I said with a soft smile and charm.

He gazed at me for thirty seconds and, without saying anything about the car, said, "You want to grab some freshly squeezed fruit juice in Tajrish?"

"For sure!" I said, my heart racing with remaining adrenaline from my first near-accident experience.

He directed me toward the famous juice stand in Tajrish Square, where we met a line two blocks long. "My treat—heads up in the car while I go stand in line!" he said, and jumped out of the car.

It was my first time to be in the car alone, and I was scared at the beginning, but put on some illegal, FOB-ish music Jamshid had in his car stereo, which was hidden in the glove compartment. To change tapes you had to do the arm stretch, and this could only be done if the car was parked. Not recommended while driving!

After fifteen minutes he returned with two big fruit shakes, a smile, and a great sense of humor. Don't know where he picked that up. We talked, laughed, and joked around and after another fifteen minutes, he said, "Ok, kid, start the car up. I have another student waiting. But hanging out with you is a breath of fresh air!"

A third person might have thought this was a mini-date and this guy is hitting on me, but he was really looking for a friend. Someone that was okay with his hidden stereo, and someone he could complain to without hearing a different version of the complaint back.

The class continued for one whole week in different parts of town, until finally we were done and Jamshid told my dad to sign me up for the actual test. "She can drive anywhere in the world, including England," he said.

The day of the test was another *KonKoor*-type feeling for me. Both parents knew I would succeed, but I was afraid. The Scantron written version of the test was a piece of cake, and for the second part and final phase, I was in the driver's seat with a lady who had thick, tattooed brows and heavy lips. She sounded as if she'd been brought up in the army. Something like Delta Force. I thought she might have been some kind of badass general back in the day when the Shah was around. Delta Force was pretty strict, and tested my road skills on a steep hill, parallel parking, and my turn indicators. Passing the steep hill was a breeze, thanks to Jamshid, parallel parking had a slight angle when I was trying to maneuver the car, but I got it in bumper-to-bumper without crashing into any of the cars behind and in front. The last test was just physically turning on my right indicator—a replica of the question in the written exam portion.

Right or wrong on this exam, though, I knew all driving rules went out the door in Iran. The only rule was to stay alive, and that went for driver and pedestrian.

I passed. I couldn't believe it.

Before getting out of the car, Delta Force said, "You just succeeded in one of the hardest countries to drive in—stay alive!"

I felt honored and scared both at once.

*

The time between getting accepted to school and getting my driver's license to actually *starting* school were interesting times. I decided to register in the Italian Language Institute that July to start slowly getting into the Italian mode and getting used to whipping my hands around as I spoke. The school was dropped from the heavens itself, or maybe the people there were from a different world. It was heavily connected to the Italian Embassy in Farmanieh in Tehran, and this was the first time I encountered "brothers" and "sisters" seated in the same room—a real fusion. At times, I wondered if this institute was paying anything to a religious entity to allow the mix, but I never figured it out. We just wore scarves and *manto* in class, while everywhere else would have required a *wimple* as well. I thought that the owner of the institute must have had high-up connections to get away with it.

Class seating was as such: the guys sat in the back, or to the left, for a subtle conformity to separation. The girls formed their own flock. This loose interaction (at least in the public) was so much like high school back in Brooklyn, marked by shyness, rebellion, and awkward exchanges: "He *looked* at me" or "I am going to wear my gray wimple or silk scarf with my new pink gloss ... tilt back my head and ask questions in class to get his attention." To the instructor that meant you were paying attention; to others, it meant, 'Let me hear your voice ... is it delicate? Sexy? Provoking? Annoying? Keep on asking ...' When that was the goal, there was no such thing as a dumb question!

And so the story continued ... everything was ridiculously different in every institution. And I loved it.

I used my almond-shaped eyes over a cheerful, arresting smile and charm—weapons that I knew could attract anyone my way. Even with the New York, Brooklyn-accented Farsi, my confidence put those other negotiable qualities on mute.

Sitting in for my first class, I slyly glanced at two guys in the back. Probably late-teens, I thought; one wearing a long pink un-Polo-like tee and (hopefully) unconscious of how it conjured comparisons to the Pink Panther. The other sported a badly shaped goatee. I surmised that these two must have been from downtown Tehran, but had paid a shitload of money to be sitting in this class. Or they were just rich peeps with *no style*!

Registering for these external classes was pricey in Tehran, especially since they were extracurricular activities and connected to the Italian embassy. To register, your savings account had to be full, or you had to be working hard on your networking abilities. People went to great lengths to get into those classes.

Our teacher had a special spice and twist to him. Yes! First of all, he was a man, and it was the first time I was seeing one teaching me since my days in high school. They were indelible as ink. I liked him a lot, but it looked like they pulled him out of a Michelangelo Museum in Italy, or from the ancient lanes of Capri. He was definitely old school, but had this singing accent and very easygoing manner. An example: if someone's *scarf* slipped in class, he did nothing in the way of chastisement. He didn't even care ... he was a good teacher *indeed*! He was an Iranian Italian guy who spoke graduate-level English and Farsi, but with an Italian accent. The accent had Pavarotti-like grandeur. He wouldn't scold you for being naughty or wearing inappropriate attire. In other words, he was *not* a member of the religious green-uniform-wearing commandos!

The guy was so cool that I didn't even ditch any of his classes. As soon as I walked through the Institute's doors, everything was in a European mode—a newly found cultural comfort zone for me. The guys were cool, the girls cooler, and the teacher the coolest! The people there were nice and warm, and I started slowly opening up to the people I met. Most of the staff were Italian as well, and everyone acted as if we were in Europe rather than Iran. Being there felt better than being in high school or Tatbighi.

At times, I didn't understand their conversations, but felt close with them in other ways. The girls talked about their boyfriends openly, skipped classes when they felt like it, smoked and laughed and generally were carefree. They were obviously the upper class Tehranians, and not so traditional. They also appeared not to care about many of the problems confronting them. These things had all seemed taboo to me in a country like Iran, and seeing the women acting so freely was truly a dream come true.

Bits and pieces of the culture were being revealed to me with every class or social interaction that I had. I was a coin being flipped, swimming into the deep end of the ocean, traveling to Antarctica, driving cross country from LA to NY, going on a blind date to discover the guy is a family friend!

"What are you doing today?" asked Elham, a girl I'd recently met, who sat behind me.

She was a year older than me, petite, and was already a freshman at Azad University in Tehran. She was studying English Literature as her major and was coming to this institute to tidy up her Italian. Like everyone else, she wanted to get out of Iran, so her plan was to apply for an Italian student visa, head to Rome, and become a director. She was doing all her work through the phone-connected Internet at home, which disconnected every two minutes! But she wanted it so badly that she didn't let that get in her way.

"Going to Franco's class. We have a test coming up..." I answered.

"Sounds like a good idea, but all the mini-tests are rubbish except for the big test at the end of the semester. We can always cheat on these, and cheating is a good idea," she said with a wink.

A funny thing was that Elham was Jewish, but I didn't know anything about her until we became close friends. Another completely accepted secret was that there were many Jewish families living in Iran. She told me they were a minority, but because of all that had happened to the Jewish community in Iran, and everyone fleeing after the revolution, she didn't tell anyone her religion ... that is, until she trusted them. Also, people in Iran would quickly label her as *Johood* (Jewish), and would automatically have preconceived thoughts about her. Since I came from the US, and seemed more liberal, she felt safe in sharing her secret.

Elham was great, and had an awesome sense of humor. Coming from Brooklyn, I was totally accustomed to this and her dry Jewish humor. I felt like she and Elaine from Seinfeld were sisters.

*

Days passed, and my friendship with Elham tightened at greased-lightning speed.

We called ourselves The Duo, and spent long hours together in mutual witness of every little event. Sometimes she was the reason I went to this class! My sole priority was to drop by class with the new car the emperor got for me, pick up the girls, and circle the infamous reputable street called "Jordan"—one of Tehran's liveliest streets, abuzz with chic cafes, restaurants exhaling garlicky smears of fried food, art galleries, florists, bakeries, and expensive real estate where many embassies kept their playgrounds. And, in a very Tehranish way, this "night-life" was far from any you might experience in other countries.

Aside from all this chicness, Jordan was loaded with hot guys! As Elham described it, Tehranians would drive their fancy cars up and down the streets, making U-turns as needed so as not to be eliminated from the hunting game, or from getting the other (usually male-stocked) car's phone number. To outsiders, Elham noted, it might appear as if these cars were lost and in dire need of a GPS system. Looking deeper still, they might wonder why 90 percent of the thumping, laughing vehicles were filled with chic, made-up-to-the-max girls redolent of exotic perfumes. Or strikingly handsome, jaw-dropping guys! Maybe there was a reason why there were no bars—because there were too many hot peeps! This was the game and everyone liked to play it. So according to her, depending on which car (and which revelers!) might pace us, we would exchange numbers or peel off to dimmer side-streets for quiet conversation … maybe even get invited to some underground party. In short, it was the best situation for those looking to do something on a Thursday night.

The street itself was named after Dr. Samuel Jordan, founder of the American College in Tehran (later becoming Alborz High School), but was now known as Africa Boulevard—a name no one ever used. Jordan was *Jordan*—not the country, but the happening hotspot. It was an upbeat place to meet good-looking, upper class, wealthy Iranian boys and, in some cases, girls.

At times when the *Komiteh* demanded you pull over, you definitely had to have your excuses prepared, and ready for instant use. If you didn't, you'd have to face the end of a really fun night!

One night I decided to visit my aunt, and on the way stopped to pick up Elham for a quick cruise in Jordan, since it was on the way. I decided to take my dad's new Peugeot to attract attention, since my Renault 5 wasn't even comparable to the other cars there (and didn't have any air conditioning). I drove quickly to Elham's so I could blame imaginary traffic if I were to be late to my aunt's. Racing along the streets, scarf tied against the wind's greedy fingers, I thought I was in an old Hollywood black and white movie.

Once we got onto Jordan, I knew, we'd attract attention. But if anyone had to make the first move, it was the guy, or he would lose the opportunity for conversation or flirting. Elham's beautiful green eyes, black hair, pony-tailed inside her scarf, and clear, polished skin inspired guys to do the extra circles required.

Whether driver or passenger, our situation was win-win. Elham could understand and speak Farsi better than me, so—if necessary—could fill in any conversational dropouts or blanks. We got along just fine, and were always a big hit on the street.

Now, exiting the freeway, the new Peugeot growled like a glistening black tiger, nosing toward the street's thrumming crowd. Windows down, we blasted our favorite music, coast-to-coast smiles bright with the fearless passion of connecting. It was the same girl power that had connected us from the first day.

"Here, turn here," said Elham.

I braked, spun the steering wheel, and made a U-turn.

This was followed by many more; a seemingly timeless stretch spent watching a showroom's worth of purring imports: BMWs, Mercedes, even the new Toyotas—a big deal indeed! Bursts of flirting in between had us giggling.

Then abruptly, a horn blared beside us, and a swarthy guy in a black Patrol shouted, "What's your name?"

I smirked. "How's that *your* business?"

Struggling with divided attention, the guy grinned. "Well, our cars are right next to each other. I wanted to make sure—in case we collide—that I have some insurance information."

How clever! Just leave it to a Persian guy to bring his savviness to the table.

"Do you drive that badly?" I asked.

This intrigued him more and led to another U-turn as Mr. Good-looking continued battling against the road. Then the light turned green. The Peugeot was already in the lead, its polished form mirroring neon.

They should have just made the street into a big, long, unending one. The U-turns and the red lights slowed down our communication, and it was hard to pick up where we left off!

"Did you look at him!" shouted Elham. "He looks so in-control and like a man ... one of those who knows *how* and *what* to do with a woman."

I shook my head with motherly regret. "He's just like the rest of them—looking for bait. He should put his fishing rod back in the water, 'cause this fish is toughie, babe." Somehow, though, I doubted we'd seen the last of the Patrol guy.

But another U-turn and we hit a traffic jam. I pursed my painted lips together and slapped the dash. *"No!"*

Some fool in a tobacco-brown BMW, apparently going for a tight turn, had hit the bumper of the car in front of his, and now everyone was stuck. *Ugh!* Just what I needed with so little time. I still had to drop Elham off and drive to my aunt's home before the emperor made the dreaded check-up call.

Crap...

Of all things, there was the annoying green Honda, its driver famous in Jordan for picking up chicks and basically having one-night stands with them (per the gossip queen herself, Elham). He was just ahead of us now, and starting to look our way, but was then distracted by another girl. He muttered something, and I watched him struggle to conjure some question weighty enough to demand a reply.

All at once he found words, but his target closed her window, signifying complete dislike. I glanced at Elham, laughing, and noticed the Patrol guy's car crawling beside us. Our gazes locked.

No conversation, no trivial exchange, could equal those fierce, probing eyes, which tried to penetrate into my very soul and its secrets. *If eyes are the gateway to the soul,* I warned myself, *then his must swarm with desire ... and who knows what else?* A strange sort of ... recognition? It surged through me, quickening my heartbeat. This must be communication ... the man feeling, caressing, the muscles of my inner being.

And in that solitude, a moment of peace against the traffic jam's harsh reality, I knew the Patrol guy had felt a moment of connection, too. And he was going to use it.

"Do you want to get out of this knot?" he asked, sundering the silence.

I sensed levels of intent in those few words. *Nice way to pick someone up and take advantage of the situation...*

The look—and form behind it—were pleasing, but I roiled with tension over the constraints of time and consequence. I had places to be; did I really want to mess with this guy right now? I paused, thinking, and then felt someone pinched me.

"Hey," Elham said, "get with it. He asked you a question."

I drew a deep breath, exhaled slowly, heart hammering at my ribs. I needed to find a way out of this, and quickly. Was I interested enough to surrender my name and number? I wasn't sure, but I knew I didn't have time to sit around thinking about it.

As if anticipating this, Patrol guy grinned, easing the force in those hypnotic eyes. "Follow me through this block," he said. "But be careful. There are many dead-ends in these streets."

He accelerated then, deftly angling his car in front of the Peugeot.

Here I go, I told myself, barely questioning this newfound trust. It felt right. He'd probably help me if I drove into a nasty ditch ... wouldn't he? Or was I putting too much trust into his good looks?

Exciting and a bit scared, I followed him.

Chapter 8: Hero of the Night

What did I just see? Some powerful energy, to be sure.

Elham must have known I had butterflies fluttered in my stomach; she could probably see it in my eyes, though I was too arrogant to admit it.

No ... I need to connect mentally before allowing any feeling to brew, let alone start shakin' in the knees!

"Snap out of it!" I said firmly to myself.

Turn after turn, the streets kept getting narrower and steeper, as if we were driving along the edge of a mountain. I had no idea where we were going, though I could see the freeway in the distance, cars speeding toward the future. Where was this guy taking me? And if I didn't like it, how did I get back to familiar territory?

Abruptly, the other car's brake lights flared red. It slowed, then pulled off onto the shoulder. I was forced to stop to avoid collision.

"What's he doing?"

In truth, though, we both knew what he was doing, and the butterflies in my stomach suddenly became even more active.

The guy opened his door, sending a swirling dust devil off in the wind. He climbed out and stepped toward us.

My 'butterfly' status: They were crashing into one another now.

Elham giggled, but immediately snuffed it. "Here he comes…"

Then he was there, and leaning down by my open window. I caught a trace of cologne, and he gazed at me as if he was inspecting lamb shanks. "Do you know your way home from here?"

He smiled like a hopeful wolf, as if anticipating a 'no' from us.

I inhaled sharply, and pressed my lips together as if in reaction to some insult or inappropriate joke. Elham caught this and

182

was quick to respond, before I could say anything inappropriate. I was furious that this guy had led us on in that way; we'd thought we were coming out here for one thing, and now he was just sending us on our way. The nerve!

"Yes. Yes ... and thank you so much. We're in such a time crunch!"

I split my attention between the steering wheel and this strikingly handsome cad. "Thank you" was all that came out of my mouth. I didn't want to get caught looking at him again. Not after I'd been so wrong about his intentions.

I'd been caught looking at him once, and that was plenty, thank you.

I thought now only about my dad's ensuing phone call, and getting to my aunt's place in time.

He grinned, then, and everything changed. "Well, no problem. And here's my number, in case you ever *do* need directions."

He produced a slim gold pen and scribbled on a business card. "My name is Arash." He locked his dark gaze on me, as if in fear of losing the moment, and Elham put her hand on my arm. She knew trouble when she saw it.

For a moment I was hypnotized, then took the card and gave him another "Thank you." My vocabulary basket was suddenly empty, and I only knew this word. But maybe it was for the best.

I realized he was staring at my hands, which—aside from my face—were my only visible flesh. He just stood there, staring, and I wondered suddenly how any girl could avoid falling for him. He looked like money and underground parties and probably knew all the cool people in Tehran—the ones who really knew how to party, rather than hanging out in coffee shops and drinking pineapple juice!

I felt as if I'd fallen into some sort of daze, and couldn't get back out of it.

Then Elham snatched the card from me and dropped it into my bag, knowing full well that I would mull it over endlessly, and end up not calling him. I never did. If I stayed here, though, and had to face him, I might end up getting myself in trouble.

He stood straight, ran a finely muscled hand through his hair, and nodded. "Okay, then, I'll hopefully see you later."

He turned and stepped back toward his idling car.

Elham gave my arm a light slap. "Hey! Let's get going, unless you want to sit here looking all night. If you go for him now, you know you'll get in trouble. He's just a playboy."

I smiled wistfully. "You're right, he does look like a playboy. And like all the other leeches. They see a hot girl—or in this case two hot girls—and *bam*! Lasers shoot from their eyes and from south of the border. If you know what I mean!"

"You like him, and you know it," she said, laughing. "Maybe you should give him a chance. He saved us from going down Komiteh Lane, after all. God knows what they might have had in store for us down there! Why don't you give him a call?"

I smirked, shaking my head. "I get it, I get it! Point taken. I promise to look into it!" I said, as if I was swearing before the jury. I checked around, and eased the car back onto the road. "Now let's land you home. This piece of metal and I should be somewhere on the opposite side of the city, like at my aunt's house by the golden phone. The emperor will be checking my status any minute now.

Giddy up!" We both laughed at this reference to *Seinfeld*, and away we went.

I understood exactly what she was talking about and knew that I would eventually surrender to the urge to call Arash, the so-called hero of the night.

*

After dropping Elham off on the corner of her street, I peeled off toward my aunt's house. Good thing the car was a Peugeot, and could handle speed better than just about anything on the road. The Peykan could move fast, but God forbid you needed to put on the brakes at the end. You'd have a personal Armageddon! Those cars were impossible to stop. Taxi drivers had Peykans, but young people completely declined to drive them because they were so dangerous.

Thanks to my quick pace, I arrived at my aunt Elahe's just in time for the telephone call the emperor made to check up on me.

"Hi! I'm here!"

Both my cousins, Ghazaleh and Bahareh, were there too, and automatically added up my dad's car and my bright scarf to realize that I'd been Jordan cruising. I didn't know them well enough to share boy talk with them, but suspected that it took one to know one ... so we were in the same boat! That said, I still didn't want to tell them what had happened with Elham; that way I'd be safe from any loose lips sharing with my aunt. If it reached my aunt, it would be only milliseconds until it reached my folks. *Trouble!*

We had dinner first, consisting of an hour and a half of storytelling, laughter, and enjoying Persian-style lasagna, which my aunt prepared in a pot instead of a Pyrex casserole for oven baking. Rather odd, but delish! So good, in fact, that I got the recipe. I admired anyone who cooked outside the box and didn't limit their techniques and palates to what they were told or how they were raised. That was real creativity. My aunt had fearlessness and courage, applied to everything, including her cooking!

I loved the food, dessert, and mingling with the cousins. It was happiness flavored by actually sitting at the table with family in Iran, which always gave me a sense of connectedness, forgiveness, sacrifice, and generosity.

After dinner came the Persian tea hour and, of course, the emperor chose this time for round two of the check-up call. Was this simply because he didn't trust me?

"Hi, *khoshghel khanoom*," he said. "Are you having fun? Did you park the car somewhere safe?" That was a superb greeting. That meant my secret at Jordan hadn't leaked … yet!

"Dad, your car is safe. Along with its diverse cousins, parked on the same street! And we are having a fab time, so please don't worry!"

"Great, *azizam*. When will you be coming home?" he asked quickly.

I smelled that question from a mile away, so gave him exactly what he wanted to hear; although since I was at a trusted place—my aunt's—he wouldn't have objected had I said I wanted to stay the night. After all, this was a trusted family member—they were blood related, and she would be reporting *everything* to him, without the slightest error.

"Whenever you need the car, Daddy." Persian fathers liked attention and respect, and having you throw the ball in their court.

"If you want, sleep over at your aunt's and come home tomorrow morning. It's your aunt, so totally ok. Do you want to?" he asked.

"I'll take it!" I said happily. I preferred being away from the parents for one night, at least.

"Okay. Well, drive safe tomorrow morning, and always look to your right and left when making *that* turn!" He always had to say that, just to make sure I made my turns diligently!

"You got it! And good night," I said, relieved that he hadn't suspected *anything* or heard about me coming late to my aunt's.

I don't know why I had become so fearful of my dad finding out. I came from the US and wasn't scared about anyone seeing me there, so why was I so scared in Iran? The pressures of society there made me worry about it, though; I didn't want to think that I was conforming, but subconsciously, I was still trying to fit in. Especially for my parents' sake.

Back at the table, we shared tea, fresh pastries, and watermelon slices. I really enjoyed getting closer to the cousins, despite some lingering cultural and language barriers, which seemed

189

to drop away in actual conversation. Perhaps this was testament to the depth of the familial connection? It seemed they had the same type of difficulty I was facing, with the traditional parental leash buckled on.

During our tea-hour, Arash kept popping in and out of my mind. Not that it surprised me. I knew my parents would have told me I was too young to be thinking about that sort of thing, but I wanted to explore. But I'd have to be really brave to actually call him. The country's *Komiteh* added to the fear of my dad finding out, which went on to the fear of a neighbor finding out, added to the fear of the neighbor across the street finding out, even though it was nobody's business. It was my life! But all those issues were so interconnected that I had to think about everything.

On another note, strategizing made it fun. For now, just for now, I chose to ignore this and focus on the antics of my two cousins.

Even after my aunt left for bed, the night continued, as it did with many Iranians after dinner. It was prime bonding time. For the first time, my cousins began opening up, and I was beginning to see what they were like outside of family and school. For the first time, I got to see the secret side of them—the side they kept to themselves, to keep it out of family gossip!

"Did you see him?" Ghazaleh was asking her older sister in front of me.

"I did," Bahareh replied faintly. "But only for the duration of the class I ditched, so not long. He is wealthy and good looking, but I don't know if he wants to get married."

I casually regarded Bahareh. She was pretty! Any guy would be lucky to marry her. But what was this—my goody two-shoes cousin sneaking out to meet a guy? I'd never expected that!

Her late dad came from the western part of Iran, called Kermanshah, which I had never seen. I knew it was a city of mystics, whose people were very happy and upbeat. I marked my mental geography map with an X on that city, which I wanted to explore when I could go there without my parents checking up on me every five minutes. If people like this family lived there, it would be a place to see.

"But you won't know that," Ghazaleh was saying, "until you go out with him again. I do like the way he talks on the phone. Especially when I say *wrong number* and hang up on him because Mom is sitting next to me ... haha!" She couldn't stop herself from giggling.

"Does aunt Elahe know about him?" I asked.

Bahareh shook her head. "Nope. If she knew, there would be no going out alone, and we don't want to even go near *that* point ... that means the old woman *doesn't trust you!* I mean we are friends, but I still keep this stuff away from her."

She gave me a level gaze. "I know you're new to all of this, but Iran is totally different from *Am-ree-ka* (that's how she pronounced it!). Parents here don't approve of boyfriends, and going out to dinner with them, or even going to the movies, so we do it behind their backs. Not that we want to lie, but we do want to explore and just have fun. Are you seeing anyone now?"

"No." I said firmly. Still didn't trust them. I didn't know them well enough yet, even though I went to school with Bahareh.

Anyway, I was telling the truth—I *wasn't* seeing anybody.

Getting a phone number from someone didn't mean I was seeing

them! Deep down, I knew I was going to contact Arash. But that still

didn't mean anything was going to happen. Maybe I wouldn't like

him.

After talking some more about Bahareh's male prospect,

though, I realized that was the problem: In this sort of society, how

could you know if you really *wanted* to date somebody, let alone

want to have sex with them? If a girl were to have sex, and her

parents found out, there was a 95 percent chance she would be

crucified or put out to join the homeless. Or she'd be forced to marry

the guy. And what if she hadn't liked him?

The conversation, however, didn't get to that point. Mostly it

focused on building a plan for a second-round meeting with this guy

my cousin was interested in. After a few more hours of talking (and

occasionally using Super Hero strategy), the plan was set. The

strategy consisted of Bahareh taking her big (huge and giant) bag

(holding makeup, a funky scarf, and shoes), and changing in the

parking lot or grocery store down the block. The plan had obstacles, but not to worry—even that was calculated! She only took one scarf, because she didn't want to be seen with the same scarf she left home with.

Since my aunt wasn't supposed to know, Bahareh's date time was when she ditched her English class, which was on Friday mornings. In order to prevent any leaks or getting caught outside, she assigned Ghazaleh the role of secretary that day. Since the English Institute contacted parents to inquire about absent students, Ghazaleh would sit by the phone and fake reading a book that was supposedly more than five chapters long. If she needed a bathroom break, she would have to unplug the line before she walked away. She couldn't simply unplug the phone for the whole morning, in the event that someone called and got a three-hour-long busy signal.

Poor, ill-fated Ghazaleh had to wake up early on her weekend to help Bahareh out with her date! But she seemed fine with that, and happy to help her sister.

Bahareh, after the date, would have to downgrade to her original appearance, wearing a *wimple* instead of the colorful, short, edgy scarf, accompanied by her ragged black sneakers. She also had

194

to delete any suspicious perfume scent, and put on her nerdy glasses to appear as if she'd just received the Harvard Award for Great Academic Achievement.

Since Bahareh and Ghazaleh were pros at this and always planned ways to get around their parents, their plans always worked. When they didn't—rarely—there would follow months of silent and caged limitation in their house. That made them extremely careful.

And gave me many ideas.

*

I went to sleep that night thinking about Arash, and the way he had managed to break the ice and speak with me. When it came to guys in Iran, I put layers of self-made brick walls in front of me. This was because I'd been warned by the Tatbighi girls that lots of single men in Iran wanted a way out of this country, and would see my green card as their ticket out of the joint. Some of them just wanted to get to the Land of the Free, where they would find opportunities for growth and making their own decisions. Many of them wanted to get away from the forced Islamic society. And if it meant forcing a girl with a green card to marry them, so be it.

I wanted a boyfriend, but that had made me overly cautious.

So I decided that if I were to call Arash, I would mention nothing about my green card and simply note that I learned English at a very young age at the Language Institute. If he asked which language institute, I would say it was called Brooklyn Dodgers, and that the owner ferried his way toward the States in hopes of a better future.

The next day, I went to summer class just to see Elham and have a girly chitchat with her. We had a *kebab* sandwich together from the place across the street, and talked.

"So, have you been in touch with the Patrol guy?" she asked.

"Nope," I said, devouring the next bite.

"You know you like him. You might as well have a little fun!"

"I agree, I *think*...."

"Yeah. He looks like a *man,* and he looks fun. Let's prank call him, at least."

I merely nodded, as though I was considering it. Prank calling was a norm in Tehran for girls who wanted to play around and have some fun without any repercussions. The guy would pick up and the girl would blow air and hang up after causing some confusion. Or the guy would pick up and the girl would flirt, hoping she could get into his mind. The last had multiple outcomes. Sometimes it didn't mean anything. Other times it meant the beginning of a relationship.

I just wasn't sure I was ready to take that chance.

We strolled to the back of the school to look at the beautiful rose garden, where the trees between buildings and the parking lot would shield us. Unless cameras were hidden somewhere, no one in the buildings could see or hear us here. We were free to do whatever we wanted.

Elham immediately dug out her cell phone. "What's his number?"

While telling her, a chilly rush of uncertainty and—I had to admit—anticipation sped through my heart.

"We're just going to have a laugh, you dork!" she went on. "And you know how to bring that out of a guy with your feisty personality! Just act like yourself—joke around, but step on that tail to let him know there are boundaries he can't cross! He should be a gentleman!" she said firmly, but with a smile.

I knew, somewhere in the back of my mind, that I was headed into hot water … but who cared?

Elham handed me the cell, and I took it and pressed it against my ear. "*Alo?*" I said, almost in question, as if I was wondering if a person, animal, or alien was on the other end.

"*Alo, be farmaiid,*" replied a strong but sexy male voice, using the formal Persian expression for: "Who is this, and please say what you've called for."

I steeled myself and paused for a moment, then suddenly found myself rambling. "Have you heard the new Arian song, just released?"

Where had the words come from? Barely familiar with the band, I knew only that they were one of the few Islamic Republic-approved boy-girl groups, with super-sizzling guys in the band. They actually had sold-out concerts! But the girls in the band had to sing with full scarves and *wimples*. And since they were singing with the boys, you couldn't hear their individual voices. *Yup, keeping the mystery of which female voice is heard—another weird factor.*

"No, I haven't ... what's the name of it?" asked the manly voice. I thought the owner of the voice must know that I was the lost girl from the other night, but he still didn't know my name.

I swallowed hard. "It's called *The Hero of Jordan on a Dark Summer's Night.*"

It sounded like he was smiling, though it barely surfaced in his voice. "Who did he save?" A certain charm and energy could be heard through his voice.

"An excellent driver." Surely this was better than "Two scared girls in need of a GPS or better knowledge of windy Jordan streets."

He gave a soft chuckle, then said, "I see. This great driver, does she have a specific name other than 'excellent driver'?"

"That she does."

"Well, is her name as pretty as her eyes?"

There we go with the flattering sweet talk, and impulsive conversation specific to Iranian guys! They knew just the right amount of sugarcoating to add, and when to add it.

"It can be. Depends on the eye of the beholder."

Elham loved the back and forth, softly giggling and lip-synching to say this, say that, although I had to brush her aside with a serious glare. I didn't need her distracting me right now.

But he had to be enjoying this, too. "The beholder's eyes saw many beautiful things, but because he respects excellent drivers, he would like to clearly hear what her name is."

I swallowed again, liking the direction he was going. He was being a gentleman, and that was more than I'd actually expected. "Delkash. But also know that not all excellent drivers have the same name."

"Did you find your way home all right?" he asked, changing the subject.

"Yes, it was fine. Did you?"

"Difficult, but I managed to find my way," he said with a chuckle.

"Okay, good. Then be sure to check out Arian's new song. I have to run."

There was pause, then he said, "Can you give it to me so I can listen to it at least?"

I knew the map he was following because I had the same compass, but didn't mind going along with it. "You don't want to purchase it? Me giving it to you could be called piracy, and hard-working artists could suffer." I said with a smirk.

Now we both were flirting metaphorically, and I could tell he wanted to ask me out for a date. At this point, though, I wasn't sure how Iranian couples connected or what the dating protocol was. Going to his home is completely out of the picture, but where could we meet without the *Komiteh* sneaking up on us?

A home, of course, we would have closed doors. But a lot could happen behind them, and I wasn't about to take any risk with this guy. I barely knew him.

Then he spoke. "Let's go to Vanak Mall. They just recently opened the coffee shop downstairs, and no one really knows about it."

This reassured me that I might be in good-but-still-questionable hands. "Where? I don't know Tehran very well, and if you could—"

Elham quickly signaled that she knew the location. A famous joint, actually, she mouthed. The fact that I knew nothing about it emphasized my lack of Tehran social travel. But I pushed on. "Actually I'll find my way. I can make it at 5, but can only be out for an hour." I thought I could go during my Italian class and afterwards I'd just go home. It could work ... fingers crossed, toes crossed, arms crossed, legs crossed...

"Good," Arash said. "I'll see you there and ummm ... don't forget the tape, Ms. Excellent Driver."

"Oh, I'll definitely bring you the single." I giggled with flirtatious glee, and ended the call.

Elham stood close, having quietly laughed off and on, and thoroughly enjoyed eavesdropping. "You guys have perfect chemistry and make a good couple. A couple who annoy the hell out of each other and laugh at the dullest, most boring things with a grain of salt."

I shook my head and stretched to smell a rose. "Such an Iranian-man expert. Aren't you supposed to be an Iranian-Jewish expert?"

"I am, I am, *ghorboone hameghi beram*. I adore them all!"

We were both going through hoops of giggles, but I felt a slight chill when something occurred to me. "It's so *hard* to date in Tehran, and I'm not going to understand even half the stuff he says. And on top of that, he'll hear my Farsi accent and know I was raised somewhere else and then will question where, and basically be my slave because he'll want a bite of my green card! These question marks will repeatedly pop into my head..."

"Everyone dates in Iran and everyone knows that everyone dates. It's no secret. Your parents even dated!" she pouted back.

"That might have been in the Shah's time, but not right now, with all the *Komiteh* guys thirsty to make some money off me."

During the Shah's era, there were no religious or Islamic restrictions. Ladies went out without a scarf, wearing nothing more than minidresses, Iran had the best cabarets and bars, and the same kind of concerts as in the west. Nobody with *wimples* on stage! After the revolution, when the government turned religious, women—and particularly teenagers—had to deal with a whole new set of restrictions. Dating wasn't acceptable, and having sex before marriage would end in catastrophe. That's why fashion shows, parties, and alcohol all became hush hush. But for an adrenaline junkie like me, that meant that those things brought additional excitement … and so I decided to play the game as well.

Elham rolled her eyes. "Listen, even the *Komiteh* guys have crushes, but it's a process and they flow with it. Just play the game and have your radar up when you go outside."

"Is this the part where I say 'What would I possibly do without you?'"

"You could say that, but you could always treat me to the blood-red beets in Tajrish Square."

We left the garden, and I hailed a cab to take us to the Square. I'd heard a lot about Tajrish Square and the yummy roasted beets they sold on the streets. Tajrish was in the northern part of Tehran, and one of the city's busiest transportation hubs, so there were plenty of people there, selling food. The smell would make you drool, or so they said. It was the equivalent of New York's Union Square or Columbus Circle. The market was similar to the one in downtown Tehran, but due to its up-scale status, it carried vegetables not found in other supermarkets. One of those, at the time, was broccoli—an extraordinary, pricy vegetable available only at the Tajrish market.

I was excited about my coming date, and quickly agreed to explore this new part of the city with my friend, to celebrate.

*

The following days were extremely long, as I got ready for my first date in Tehran, with a random guy who spoke a language I could only partially understand. Still, I was excited.

And of course the whole concept of strategizing made it even more exciting.

I took a big bag and filled it with what I needed, as I'd learned to do from the pros. My heart pounded, but I was excited to see Arash, and knew I was headed toward a little adventure.

I kissed the emperor goodbye, and left the house as if I was just bound for my class.

Although I never wore much makeup, I applied some eyeliner and mascara in the cab. I'd managed to get a cab by myself, and didn't have to worry about being crowded or fondled by the other passengers. Or the driver himself! And soon I found myself at the mall, which, to my surprise, resembled a shopping center in the Big Apple itself.

Out of the cab, I caught pools of fragrance in the air, especially freshly *kebabed* corn on the cob, with its smoky sweetness. There was the hustle-bustle of people walking, talking, and bumping into each other without paying no attention, taxi drivers looking for bait, street vendors hawking goods, hoping for a *toman* (Iran's monetary frequency) or two, and colorful fruit kiosks.

Walking, I saw stores bearing actual brand names, while others were small, privately owned boutiques carrying exports from Turkey, Sweden, China, and more, all at highly inflated prices. Local people's salaries could be lower than that required to purchase certain items in these stores!

I approached a fine marble stairway—very chic—leading to an area of newly opened shops downstairs: furniture stores, Internet cafes, *manto* shops, a pizza place, and the coffee shop Arash had

mentioned.

I felt tense and a bit afraid, and all of these senses heightened

as I headed down the stairs.

How come girls always have to get antsy?

My face flushed hotly with apprehension, and suddenly I felt

as if I couldn't speak. All because of someone whose last name I

didn't even know.

My hair flowed freely from the back of my scarf (it was ok if

your hair was long and it stuck out, as it supposedly didn't make any

man horny), and without any hair showing in the front, I knew my

big brown Middle-Eastern eyes were in the spotlight. I pulled the

scarf toward my face, afraid it was going to fall any moment, and

suddenly heard someone behind me. "So you found it all right, and

didn't need a navigation system this time?"

There stood Arash. The date version, with dark black hair

brushed back and hazel-colored eyes with a smile all their own. We

were standing at the bottom of the stairs, looking right at each other.

My mind flushed with thoughts. *He's so toned, manly, and athletic.* But what was I to do? This being Iran, there could be no handshake, kiss, or knowing smile in public, so I nodded and gave a native hello: "*Salam* back."

"I thought the young are supposed to say 'hello' first."

"That's when the older ones don't make the initial smart-ish comments."

He nodded slowly, as if digesting the elements of a complicated joke. "*Salam*, Delkash Khanoom. Should we go inside and grab something to drink?"

"Is this place safe, or frequently interrupted by the *Komiteh*?"

"It's safe. They still haven't noticed it, so it's not on their radar yet. If they *do* come, there is a back entrance to the café and we could go out from there. The guys are my friends."

"Okay."

I felt as if I might be arrested at any moment for being in public and talking to a member of the opposite sex. But what if I were only asking directions, or where he purchased his shirt? Would that be considered a felony?

Inside, we chatted for a while and slowly became somewhat comfortable together. He didn't seem to notice my accent or, if he did, he didn't care. I didn't go into great detail about my life, but did list briefly my likes, dislikes, and where I went to school.

He spoke fluent Farsi, was degreed in engineering, but had made his way into business, joining the family's real estate company. They had escaped to London during the revolution, and his father had become increasingly wealthy in privately owned real estate. His father—Mr. Hossein Sarraf-Zadeh—was also a well-known architect who had returned to Tehran fifteen years after the revolution to serve his country. He had returned with incredible wealth—a fact surely recognized by the government and many in that specific industry in Iran. It had made him a powerful man.

I realized he had no accent to his Farsi, so wondered if he spoke English. But we continued to speak in Farsi. "So now you have graduated and aren't really pursuing engineering like the one million guys in Iran who are engineers. How do you spend your time?"

Our order was ready, and we paused to get the food: An alcohol-free pineapple juice cocktail, plus the famous chips and mozzarella treat, plus a high-calorie, high-cholesterol dessert impossible to turn down, even by high-end fashionista *manto* girls. I couldn't resist; it was better than Brooklyn pizza!

"Where was I?" Arash said. "Oh, we are building the new hotel on Vali-Asr … And it is taking a long time to build. It's not like anything else in Tehran. We have to bribe our way through a lot of avenues with the government, but hopefully it will open in two years." He gazed deep into my eyes. "And what are your plans?"

Caught almost by surprise, I said, "To become a choreographer ... but that is a completely closed door in Tehran, so I have no idea what I will be doing."

Right after I said it, I realized I should have kept my mouth shut. He intuitively knew, at that moment, that I was *not* from Iran. Girls born and raised here would never give that answer. Typically, the response would be doctor, engineer, or let's-see-what-happens, which usually fell into the marriage category. Never would they express a desire to become a choreographer, because they wouldn't know that existed, or wouldn't want something so out of bounds. That was a huge insult to the parents, who would never in a million years accept that. He probably had a bunch of question marks already maneuvering around his head.

"Do you dance regularly?" he asked.

I didn't know if he had figured me out from the start. A typical Iranian guy would think I was out of my mind, or living in a dream. That type of art was illegal in Iran, unless you were taught privately or in some underground studio.

"I did some ballet a couple of years back," I said, swallowing that the location had been Brooklyn. "But do it now at home with dance videos."

"You mean the satellite?" He chuckled.

"No," I said wanting to wrap up the conversation. Either he was becoming a smart-ass or was dumb. "Listen to this Arian single for now ... I'll question you about it later." I had to rush to a whole new world, but for now I wanted to get away so that I could think.

"Do you want me to drive you home?"

"That is the *last* thing I need—to be caught in a car with you!"

He gave a dejected shrug and picked up the tape, wondering perhaps what might be recorded on it.

I stood. "And please listen to it until the end. Don't say I didn't tell you so."

"Yes ma'am!" His velvety voice made him sound like some dashing knight.

I thanked him for treating and was ready to jet off, but noticed that his downcast eyes looked sad.

"Can I have your number?" he asked quietly.

"Why? Are you saying you would like to see me again?"

"Yes ... that's what it sounds like." His eyes weren't sad anymore, but were begging me to say yes.

I recognized at that moment that Arash was a typical Persian playboy. But he also seemed to be very respectful of me, even though he was in his mid-20s. He flirted without pointing to anything sexual, and kept within his boundaries ... at least that was the energy I received from him. I thought at that moment that he had a caring personality. Perhaps there could be more to this after all.

"Well, I have your number so let's see what happens." And I left the coffee shop as if I were Cinderella obeying the fairy godmother's wishes and dashing for a pumpkin carriage.

Chapter 9: Arash to the Max

My pumpkin carriage was actually an elegant Peykan cab. It also served as my mini fitting-room while I erased all traces of makeup and transformed myself back to an innocent schoolgirl.

The driver observed this transformation, and like the nosy taxi hack he was, blurted: "*Dokhtar Khanoon*, does your father know where you were?"

Nosy civilians! What's it to you? Just do your job! But obviously I couldn't let it get out of hand, in case it somehow made its way back to my parents. So I replied, "*Bale Agha.*" It meant 'yes, mister,' but with a tone that meant *none of your business, just drive.*

That night, I thought about my encounter with Arash, and how I had enjoyed it. I wanted to call him from the living room phone, but my dad would focus on me and wonder who I was speaking with. So that was definite no-go.

Instead, I waited until the next day, when I planned to venture out and buy a cheap secondhand phone from the telephone-fixer, and use it to call Arash at night. Iran had a no-return policy on any merchandise brought from any store, though, so if the phone didn't work, I was stuck with it. Nonetheless, it was a chance I was willing to take.

The first time the phone rang, Dad was out and Mom was gossiping with the neighbors on the front porch about who was seen leaving the house across the street, who got married on the other block, or divorced—the usual chit chat between neighbors.

The jangling phone twisted my nerves and before it could ring again I grabbed it.

"*Befarmaiid,*" I said in a controlled but very delicate tone.

"*Salam, Delkash.*"

Right away I knew it was Arash. This both shocked and excited me, because it meant that he'd managed to track me down.

"*Salam.* Hey, how did you get this number?"

He responded with a low chuckle, and I felt myself flushing. Had he called Elham to get my number, since I had used her cell phone last time? That would be the only way for him to reach me.

Then it hit me. The tape! I had recorded my phone number on the tape, and then completely forgotten it. It had been such a bright and brilliant idea, though—mimicking a serious breaking-news update voice to record my telephone number at the end of the tape I had given him. Now I remembered telling him to listen until the very end. He had listened ... attentively! And he'd reached the prize at the end.

I'd just forgotten all about it in my excitement.

I laughed but firmed my voice. "How did you like the single?"

"Great. It was great, a Grammy winner for sure. The production was amazing," he said flirtatiously.

"I know. That's how we roll!"

We both played the flirting and clever game pretty well. There were girls in Iran who became doctors and some that married them. I was none of these, though. I was in a category of my own, and that meant I was allowed to flirt with the guys that might become doctors, and still become one myself. Or something.

"How are you?" he asked.

"Good. But I can't talk for long…"

There was a pause, then he cleared his throat. "One of my friends is throwing a party in Shahrak Gharb on Thursday night. Could you come with me?"

Wow! Shahrak Gharb is like Beverly Hills relocated! Is he asking me out?

I didn't know much, but got the feeling this could be an introduction to Tehran's underground community—all the parties everyone talked about, but which I had never witnessed firsthand. I wanted to explore and understand what this was all about. And I had heard that lots of stuff happened at these parties. Lots and lots of stuff. Risky? For sure. I thought I might bring Bahareh along. Then again, I still hadn't developed a deep trust with her. If she came, she would surely find out about Arash; and even worse, that I was going out on a date with him. Then, if she delivered the story to my aunt, it would go straight to my dad and I would be in the gutter! The emperor would start monitoring my every move, and I'd never get to do anything! Still, I wanted to go with someone I trusted to get me out of there if I needed it, and she would be a good ally.

It was time to take the leap and finally start trusting her.

"Well, I don't know your friends, but would love to come. Can I bring a friend of my own?"

"Who?"

Was that a tinge of concern there? I wondered quickly if he'd thought I meant another guy, and smiled.

"Just my cousin..."

"Of course. Do you want to go over to your cousin's, and I could pick you up from there so we all go together?"

"Sure ... or we could go there and meet you," I answered, hoping he would counter.

After a pause, he said, "I will pick you up from her house. And don't worry about the *Komiteh*. You know, you can always pay them off—they are money hungry!"

Wowzer! Protection from a dude in Tehran! Feeling secure from the *Komiteh* would be the best thing in the world, and if he knew how to get around them...

I hung up, incredibly excited. This was my time to see the underground community in Iran; see how everyone really partied! Was it hip? How was the music? The drinks, the girls without *mantos*, the food ... the drugs? There were so many unanswered questions in my head.

I knew Bahareh was a sure go, and as long as we were going together, all we had to say was that we were going to my friend's place for an all-girl party. I pictured it as a shower sauna, reading 'Ladies Only' at the entrance. What could be easier?

I heard an impatient clicking on the line, and realized that Arash was tapping his finger impatiently. "Okay, let's do it that way. Whatever you want."

I gave him her address, and warned him to be punctual. There wasn't much of a buffer to fall back on. I would have to get to my aunt's place on time, and we'd have to get out of there before anyone got suspicious enough to stop us.

After saying goodbye and hanging up, I realized I couldn't wait to see him. I felt very playful talking with him, and suddenly goose bumps were spreading all over my body. I felt like he was giving me something, but had no idea what it was … a new perception of life, perhaps? A new understanding? Whatever it was, it felt warm, and I hugged it against me with open arms.

*

The black two-door Patrol pulled up, and I saw Arash eyeing me in full force. He probably wanted to see how I looked without this *manto* and scarf, and had been counting the seconds until he got to. It wasn't like I was going to bed with him, but it sure felt like it at that moment.

Bahareh looked hot, and I wondered if maybe she was a good catch for Arash's buddy. I would gamble the cash in my father's checking and savings account on her returning with more than five hot guys' phone numbers and also a husband if they had a chance to speak with her.

Smiling at that, we climbed into his car and off we went.

Aside from my brief introduction of Bahareh, not much was said. Excitement and some tension were in the air. We arrived fashionably late, which is why all Iranian hosts say that the party is starting two hours before it actually does. The house, like others in the Shahrak Gharb area, was like a villa. Stepping into the foyer, I thought I had entered an alternate time. The girls there looked fresh from a photo-shoot with Fashion Week, one prettier than the other, each wearing a painter's palate of makeup and cutting-edge attire. It was indistinguishable from any American West Coast party, or even the part from *The Great Gatsby*. These people were high on life and drinks!

I had taken clothes over to Bahareh's place to change, and we'd told her mom that we were headed to her friend's birthday party. That way, when we walked in with dressy attire, she would know why. Since I had gone to my aunt's, first, I was covered; if my parents called to find out where I was, she would tell them the truth … the version of it she *knew*.

Now I wished I'd had some better clothes to wear. The girls and guys were both fashion savvy, wearing *Vogue* wardrobes. It was as if they had gone into Carrie Bradshaw or David Beckham's closet and borrowed their wardrobe. It was fearless, chic, and contemporary fashion for the girls. They all had an attitude about them, and the dresses were all about sensuality and passion. The tops so flirty and the bottoms … some were tight skirts and the rest short and cut out to the tee! They were all beautiful, and their bodies were perfection.

On the other hand, the guys were all dressed in Armani, and attractive, with six packs up to their throats. They were incredibly sexy. And Arash was at the top of that list.

Guided by Arash, we moved deeper into the house and its bumping, thumping beat, through a *mélange* of perfumes and colognes and oils, and the constant aroma of food. Despite the chaos, a warm atmosphere of fun and cheerful mingling prevailed. Clusters of people chatted and laughed and danced, getting to know each other. Some were speaking Farsi so fast and using so much slang that I just nodded and didn't try to get it.

"This is a great turnout!" said Arash. "More than I thought would show up."

We all noticed how a number of male celebrants patted Arash's back, or even gave his shoulders a friendly tap. I learned later that these were all his frat buddies or colleagues-turned-frat buddies! Arash appeared to be the big, popular cheese ... a role he loved, I was sure.

We moved on, careful to avoid collision with others caught up in conversation or dancing. The place was packed, and my eyes kept getting hooked on the extremely handsome and refined guys. I'd never seen so many in one place.

Bahareh was slowing getting into the groove of the party, too, and her little conversations here and there were revealing more of her friend side and how she lived her personal life. It was a side of her I'd never actually seen before. She was flirtatious and fun and had respect for herself. I didn't know if she could keep that respect with the amount of drinking she was doing, but she was on a roll. At the same time, I noticed she also stood beside me in case I needed her help with the language, or was left alone. *My wing girl.* If I'd known that I had that sort of security in my cousin, I would have started hanging out with her a lot earlier!

I felt we were both in the same boat as far as relying on each other in times of trouble, and our potential for a friendship was finally coming into the light. We both wanted to live our teenage lives despite strict Persian parents and this oppressive society. It was something that bonded us together, and made us each other's best allies.

Suddenly someone approached from my right. "What do you want to drink?"

Arash introduced his bud Ali, who was also the party host. I had no idea what sort of drink to ask for, so improvised. "A glass of Pinot Noir, please."

Bahareh giggled.

Arash turned and said, "They aren't really wine connoisseurs here, *azizam*. They go by the drink type—wine or vodka."

Bahareh snickered. "Or *aragh saghi!*"

I was taken back. The literal translation was *doggy sweat*, but what the hell did that *mean*? I made sure I kept a neutral expression. Arash noticed this, admiration clear in his eyes, because I think he too (in his post-return-from-London days) had been subjected to this

224

ruse. It looked like he respected me for trying to figure things out in this land of mystery and intrigue. My gut told me that he'd figured out, by that time, exactly what I was: a stranger in a strange land.

Then my wine arrived, and I forgot all about that. This was my first time having a drink, and it was in this overly religious country, where I wasn't supposed to do anything! The feeling was two-fold: having alcohol on top of the mindset that I was in Tehran rather than in Brooklyn. I was exploring life, but in a completely different way than I had imagined. I was numb but happy. *Add that to my teenage free spirit.* Tehran didn't allow drinking at all, so there was no legal drinking age; a person just had to decide for themselves when they were going to start breaking the law and imbibing alcohol. Well, for me, the time was right then. I took it and forgot about New York's drinking age of twenty-one and up.

Arash stepped away, toward some guy who was waving at him.

I seized the moment and cornered Bahareh. "What the hell is *arash saghi?*"

"Relax. It's an alcoholic drink. Cheap but potent. Iran's version of American moonshine, but distilled from raisins."

"Really? Should I be afraid of losing my eyesight and going brain dead if I drink?"

"Not if you stick with the wine … whatever it is. You probably don't know this either, but wine and all alcoholic drinks here are sold underground, or on the black market—another reason why not everyone is familiar with wines. It's not like we have cellars and wine-producing vineyards here!"

"No. But doggy sweat? That's just gross."

She shot a casual glance around her, not wanting to be overheard. "Oh, that's just a reference to its nastiness. Lots of people distill *aragh saghi* at home, and it can be disgusting! Here you just get used to it, especially when the underground inventory is hard to find…"

I wrinkled my nose as if sniffing something rotten. "And how do you know about wine cellars and the various types? Hmmmmm?"

Abruptly the music blasted, and Bahareh shouted: "Leave it to the movie guy ... he is the best, although he needs to upgrade his stock from Betamax to VHS!"

I was lost. Movie guy? I just gave a goofy grin and jumped over my confusion.

Bahareh didn't seem to notice.

"We'll watch one together some time when you're over at the house," she said.

Was she talking about actually *movies*? She'd learned about *wine* from *movies*? Not that I should have been surprised; how else was she going to learn about it in a society that had outlawed it?

As soon as Arash turned back to me, though, I decided to use that very excuse. "To be honest, it's from movies that I know about Pinot Noir. I've never had a drink before!" I didn't want him to think that I knew too much about wines, because that might have led him to realize that I was from a foreign country. I didn't think it was very effective, but half of my voice was lost in the music anyhow. Get an *E* for effort, but Arash just nodded and grinned sarcastically as we took our glasses.

So there I was, having my very first toast with Arash and Bahareh. Breaking every rule in my US head of *when* to drink, and rules here in Iran about *what* to drink, I took my first sip. It was both delicious and liberating. It was with the cousin I was developing a friendship with and the black Patrol guy that had the hots for me. Always a first time for everything, and I was excited to be breaking rules. That moment was a special one, for so many reasons, and I put it away in my head as something to remember.

I noticed Arash paying full attention to me as he drank to the toast. He was observing my every move. Oh God! He wanted sex!! Or was I imagining it? Was I being too dramatic, thanks to my overprotective parents and the thoughts they'd put into my head?

Bahareh, who I noticed was becoming protective of me, took his look in with slight discomfort. "So, how do you know all these people?" she asked, shoving herself in between us.

Arash grinned. "Oh, school, parties, going out ... some of them are just guys you see as you drive up and down Jordan, Ms. Bahareh..." he pointed out sarcastically.

I could see the joke in his expression. He loved pushing buttons, and he clearly knew that he just pushed a big one. *"And your point?"* she said right back.

"No, I was just referring to traffic and shopping centers that everybody comes in and out of ... you know. You people watch while in traffic..." *But you never pay attention to the cars racing up and down Jordan,* he said implicitly. He smiled quickly, but he was so charming that I had trouble feeling annoyed at him. Even Bahareh smiled a bit at that.

Still, I felt Arash was getting to know me faster than I was getting to know him, and it made me a little uncomfortable. He was very familiar with his surroundings, and me—well, I was still a virgin in every way you could imagine. But I didn't think that made him respect me any less. He didn't think I was the type to just stand around, laugh, and act stupid. He was going to have to work for my affection, and he knew it.

I brushed my hair off my shoulders and glanced away to the party. Some of these girls certainly know how to dance. Shaking it like that with their hips and shoulders and sexy turns. The guys all drooling like dogs as the girls rotated their hips slowly, almost inviting the thoughts I knew the guys were having.

The girls basked in the attention, completely aware of the power they held.

Then Arash stepped closer to me, and I could smell his cologne. "Do you want to dance?"

"Sure, but I doubt you can keep up."

He flashed that bright smile again. "I'll try my best."

He had no idea what he was talking about. During my practice in front of the TV, I'd come up with my own fusion of hip-hop and Persian belly dancing, and I knew how to shake it. The formula was simple: Feel the music and let it guide you. No matter what it told you to do.

"Hey, that's erotic dance, woman! Are you doing it intentionally?" yelled Bahareh, as she danced only with her hands.

"I'm not doing anything that my body doesn't want to do!" I shouted back, laughing.

Arash couldn't stay still and moonwalked his way onto the dance floor with his own set of moves. At one point, he turned salsaish on me and, for a few moments, I had emigrated to Cuba.

Grabbing space, he flung me left and right with the rhythm of the

Persian *gher* (beat). Whether Persian, Spanish, or South African, I

thrived in the moment. Here I was at my first Iranian underground

party, not caring whether I knew the language, its slang, or culture ...

every turn, each move, liberated me more and more.

Abruptly, the music shifted to another tempo.

Everyone shouted: *"Baba Karam!"* Literally, *Daddy Karam*

... another big question mark for me. I had no idea what that meant.

We cleared the dance floor. Everyone took a hat from

somewhere, although not all wore one. But my question was on why

they were all suddenly dancing like *men*!

"Are they *gay*?"

Bahareh gaped at me. "Huh?"

"And what is up with the lip-thing? Look! That one guy is

moving his lower lip back and forth like he's imitating a Joker. It

looks like he's about to start bawling or something. And with the

arms out like they're going to punch the other dancer in the face.

Why?"

Bahareh burst out laughing and I couldn't control myself either. I didn't know if I was laughing with Bahareh at my comment or at something else.

"No, crazy, this is a type of dancing called *Jaheli*. They are imitating *jahels*—ignorant people. It's just a dance style where they have fun, and it's sexy ... it goes back in history, and is taken seriously."

"Must be the last page in a history book, because I don't find anything sexy in a woman moving her lips left and right!"

God, learning more about this culture every second.

Arash, hearing my hearty laugh, smiled broadly. He joined us, and I quickly changed the subject. Intently focused on the dancers, I asked, "Why do 90 percent of the girls have bandages across their noses? Is that like being part of a *nose* club?"

Bahareh shook her head, but Arash took over the convo and said. "Nope, this is a status symbol and a real one ... nearly everyone in Iran has had a nose job. Look around. Do you see an eagle nose in the bunch? And some don't need a nose job because their nose is perfect," he added charmingly, suddenly kissing the tip of my nose.

I could feel myself blushing red at this unexpected affection, and turned to scan the room. He was right; everyone out there had perfect noses, which matched their facial structures exactly. Frankly, they were beautiful. This culture was definitely sophisticated and complex, but with a measure of insecurity. Not all was as it seemed.

Arash nodded, as if keyed in to my thoughts. "Do you want to see the real Tehran?"

I took in how close he was standing to me, and wondered what was going on. "What do you have in mind?"

"Follow me."

Bahareh and I stepped after his lead, climbing stairs that opened onto a den-like space on the second floor. Bahareh, my wing girl, wasn't going to let me go alone with him. Instead of being annoyed, I loved her protective side. Besides, I didn't really know him either. Though I liked him, and liked the world he was showing me, I didn't know if I could trust him.

Upstairs, the architecture was striking: marble floors and luxurious curtains color-coded with French and Italian-style antique furniture. Another section of this floor had been designed to recall

Iranian, or maybe Turkish, history. Stunning Persian calligraphy was spray-painted across the walls in quotes, proverbial sayings, and even single words, which evoked whispers of ancient civilization and their mysteries. In the corner sat a loveseat with plenty of pillows for relaxing.

"Out here," he said softly. He led us outside onto a terrace overlooking the city. The city where I was born—the one I had left behind, and now returned to. The arresting view strengthened my connection to its beauty, culture, and history. It was alive with light, scent, and sound, and the Milad tower shimmered like some otherworldly jewel. This conjured pure compassion I never could extract from any book or conversation with an Iranian in some foreign country. I didn't like it, but I was connected to that country, and it called to my heart.

Beside me, Bahareh sighed. "Wow ... talk about breathtaking. This is beautiful."

Silence cloaked the three of us, and Arash fixed his attention on me. Shyness rained on me from hair to toe nails. I could feel that he wanted to get closer, touch me, and feel my skin. Above all, I think he wanted to just look at me, though, because he was gazing into my eyes. It was overwhelming and I felt luminous passion vibrating in my soul.

He was absorbing me and I was being fully absorbed. Maybe he was wondering why I said such weird stuff, or maybe he thought I was the hottest dancer alive. I hoped it was the second. I wanted him to like me as much as I thought I'd ever wanted anything in my life.

Continuing to look at me he asked, "What do you think?"

"This is *the* Tehran that we see in the news…"

"Yes," Bahareh interrupted, "but this is also Tehran from Arash's friend's house in Shahrake Gharb." She giggled at that, and I almost smiled with her. She was right: Part of the reason it was so beautiful was because of where we were, and what we were doing.

"The city has layers of spirit, and even with all its red flags, it's so emotionally powerful and happy," I said, feeling connected to a home other than Brooklyn.

"Wow, that's deep," Bahareh said. "Let's go softer next time, cowgirl!"

I could sense that Arash wanted to be alone with me, and I wanted the same. There was no getting rid of Bahareh, though, and for the first time all night I started wondering how to get away from her. Talk about a third wheel.

We talked a while longer, until I realized it was pumpkin time and reminded Bahareh that we had better get back to the "ladies' sauna," where her mom was scheduled to pick us up. This put an obvious damper on Arash's spirits.

To his credit, though, he drove us back to the spot we needed without complaint or argument.

While exchanging goodbyes, he asked me if I would call him tonight, with a serious gaze. "What do you think?"

"Well, if I can I will. I don't know the situation at my aunt's house."

The ever-eavesdropping Bahareh snuck Arash an optimistic look, implying that she would take care of it.

Everything had gone as planned.

Afterward, we chatted about our first party together, the adventure of it, the sheer fun, and the phone numbers Bahareh got from a bunch of the guys. None of them had realized that they were all hitting on the same girl, evidently, which we found hilarious.

I was starting to see a whole different side of my cousin, and I loved it. She was totally different from what the outside world and my outside girlfriends saw. She was the same age as me, with the same circumstances, and a family member, and more importantly, she understood me. She was helping me build bridges with so many unknown factors in a mystery country that I was trying my best to understand.

"So what do you think of him, girl?" I asked.

"I think he had a good head on his shoulders, and is respectful. Much more so than the other guys at the party. You know, the *aragh saghi*-swilling ones acting like frat-boy Casanovas…" She had definitely seen *that* part. "But be careful. They are all respectful at the beginning. Play your cards right, girl."

"I don't get it. Why is it always a game? Why can't we just go with the flow and watch what happens?"

"Del, things are different here. When it comes to guys, you can be playful, but also have to be careful. Some have the opportunity to leave the country, but others have to make money. It's not the easiest thing, nor is living with our parents. They can drive you up the wall!"

She started to take off her makeup, and continued. "So since Iran isn't fun and doesn't have lots of opportunities for people like us, we try to somehow make it work. One way is to get married!"

"Ouch, with any schmuck?"

"Well, one that could give you some security and is not an A-hole. You know, a guy who knows your worth."

"Isn't it like that everywhere? Same thing in Brooklyn. That is just common sense."

"Yeah, but there is no way out for us here, and this is an easy way out. And it's a way to get folks off your back. So it's a bit more important than it would be in Brooklyn, don't you think?"

"You seem like you have your facts straight ... and that's a compliment."

"I hope so. Iran has lots of talented, smart, and hot people, so either they use their brain to get to a better country or, with difficulty, find a way out through the marriage route," she said, pulling her upper lip to the right side.

I was shocked, but fully absorbed this. She was like a Tehranian cultural encyclopedia book for me. She knew what she was talking about.

I was fairly certain, when I thought about it, that some girls—if they tried—could get out solely on their brains. Bahareh was smart where it mattered, and had earned one of the highest scores on the *Konkoor*, but my acceptance had slimmed her show time attention substantially. In my defense, I was new to this country, and hadn't realized what would happen if I competed with her in that arena. But now she was sharing her knowledge with me when it counted. And it sounded like she was just going to try to marry a nice guy and count on him to see her for what she was and take care of her as much as possible.

"What do you want to do with your life?" I asked.

"I'm going to study civil engineering, but my real passion is fashion."

"Hey ... that rhymed. Haha."

"Ha, so it did. Here, let me show you some of my designs. One day I will start my own company ... no idea when that day is."

With that, she stood and walked toward her closet. Returning, she flipped through a fat notebook. For a while we perused professional-quality sketches of coats, dresses, and accessories. Bahareh knew her way around pastel pencils and ink, and I was impressed at this—a real plan, with real talent. Maybe she wasn't counting on the marriage ticket after all.

"It's a bit difficult," she said, "to start anything now, especially for girls and especially in fashion. So if we really really want it, we have to go through lots of frowns and opposition until we get to a little peephole of opportunity! You know what I mean?"

"You're so talented, though," I said, gazing at her drawings. "Hey, you could even do designs for *mantos* and scarves ... that would be cool too."

"I know ... I know, but I'm not into that as much. If these don't make the runway *then* I will tackle that sort of thing!"

I loved her enthusiasm and perseverance. Some would easily give up the dream, but it looked like Bahareh had the guts to move mountains. I hoped she made it. And I started to think about the fact that I wanted to do that with my dancing.

Suddenly I realized how exhausted I was, though, so I climbed onto the bed and burrowed in.

"Okay ... well, sketch away while I go to bed, woman!"

"What?" Bahareh dropped the notebook. "No! Arash is waiting for your call!"

"I can't call him from here! Aunt Elahe would execute me, and probably you, for being a facilitator!" I laughed while tugging the blanket closer, trying to keep it muffled.

"They're asleep. As long as you keep your voice down and don't get overly excited, nothing will happen."

"You sure?"

Bahareh rolled her eyes. "Couldn't be *surer*! Now call, and good *night*!"

I dialed the number as she gave me a sharp smile and switched off the light.

Arash—no slacker—picked up on the second ring. It sounded like he had tormented himself, counting down the minutes to again hear my voice. "*Alo…*"

"It's me," I said softly. "Were you expecting someone else at 12 o'clock at night?"

He chuckled. "No one but you. I'm glad the wind blew my way tonight."

Ok, so he was a charmer.

"Did I wake you?"

"No. No. I'm usually up doing work for my father. Glad you called. I was waiting for you anyway, so how could I go to sleep?" He said this so flirtatiously that if I was still at the party, I thought, he would have kissed me and glued himself to my lips.

"Didn't think I would be able to, but here I am."

So this time I did most of the talking, opening up to him and becoming more comfortable after the party. I even started flirting back with him … and who could blame me, it was midnight!

We talked for five hours straight, until the morning light glowed in the windows. It felt like we were developing boundaries, respect, and unconscious intimacy, but I didn't reveal anything about my life in America. I was still scared, and didn't want the relationship to be built on artificial pillars. Intuitively, I felt that he had sniffed something out and was waiting for me to confess, but I didn't think our first real conversation was the time for that.

Toward the conversation's end, he asked what I was doing tomorrow.

"Class, class, and um ... well ... maybe talking with you?" Shyness surged through me, and I feared how he might respond.

"Well, good luck on the class parts of your answer, and don't forget to call anytime during the day ... *azizam*."

Wow, he was taking this to another level. I swooned. He'd just called me darling!

Suddenly that five hours felt like five minutes, and I didn't want to get off the phone. I had to, though, or we'd be caught. And then we might never get to speak to each other again.

"Good night," I said, reluctantly hanging up. The only thing that made it any better was knowing that I'd get to talk to him again in a few hours.

I officially had my first boyfriend. And I was mad for him.

Sliding back under the covers with the phone under the blanket with me, I could see Bahareh sleeping in peace, and thought what a strange but enchanting world it was. I was glad to be exposed to it, discovering it slice by slice. But for now, it was bedtime. I needed to look as if I hadn't been up all night, and that meant sleeping.

Chapter 10: Movie Guy

The days passed, and my telephone conversations with Arash increased to twice daily. My hours were filled with class and friends I had made everywhere, and—more importantly—the fine-tuning of my mind. This part had to be done right!

Arash, on his way back from work, usually picked me up from college and dropped me off at home. He was twenty-seven years old, and worked in Farmanieh, close to my class and house. He ran the operations and management section of his father's real estate firm, and being bi-lingual, was also trying to expand the business to Dubai. Lots of businessmen in Iran tried to have a hub there; the profitability was huge in Dubai since it was like the New York City or Hong Kong of the Middle East.

Sometimes we would hit a coffee shop, where I sipped Nescafe and Arash gave a bottle of wine—labeled as pineapple juice—with some cash on the side to the shop owner, to pour into a kettle. Then we would have some warmed wine as well. Leave it to Arash to get around the system and know how to get his way.

He had gotten comfortable with me, and we enjoyed spending time together. There was never a dull moment between us, and so the relationship boat moved forward. Sometimes when I didn't understand situations or was baffled by others, I would flat out flood him with questions and he would tease me crazy while answering them. I still didn't explain anything to him and he never asked, but I figured he knew all about me and was just being a smartass about it. Sometimes, out of the blue, we'd start communicating in English for no reason, and then laugh about it. We would have the occasional argument, but it always ended up in even more teasing on both ends. We never took anything too seriously.

He didn't want to get married, and neither did I, but we were having an awesome time together. I was barely nineteen, and he was twenty-seven.

Even so, I resisted his numerous invites to his apartment in Farmanieh. The big F neighborhood was fancy-shmancy, and in the northern part of Tehran, about fifteen minutes from our house. It wasn't that I didn't trust him, but I wasn't ready for more. After all, I didn't yet know what to do with my life, didn't know why I selected what I had selected for college, and didn't know how things would go in this ivy-league university with Iranian nerds. How was I supposed to decide on what I wanted to do with this guy?

There was one thing I knew for certain, though: Even though I sometimes wanted to run away, this mysterious country fascinated me!

*

One night, when Bahareh's mom had gone with her girlfriends to Shomal in northern Iran, Ghazaleh was out with her friends, and Peyman was doing his own thing, Bahareh saw an opportunity and invited Shaheen, a guy she had met at Arash's party, and I to watch a movie together. She loved to socialize and party when her parents were away.

I first thought it must be some censored, Islamic Republic-produced movie ... the ones they sold here in bookstores, altering the branding of distribution houses to make it appear simple and educational, and taking out all swear words, sex scenes, and scenes where a woman might be wearing tight or exposing clothing. Nothing too westernized or contemporary, and definitely nothing steamy or hot. Legit stuff. These films were absolutely drained of anything interesting. If we were going to be watching something like that, I wasn't interested. Still, I decided to go, since she'd invited Arash.

After everyone arrived, we poured some drinks and made sure there was enough for everyone.

Then the doorbell rang. "Expecting more guests?" I asked.

Bahareh stood and shot me a mischievous glance on her way to the door. Her boyfriend, Shaheen, watched her walk away, looking her up and down as she walked toward the door. Arash glanced at him and said loudly, with a chuckle, "Hey ... *cheshmato darvish kon...*"

Metaphorically speaking, he was saying *keep those eyes to yourself, you dirty bastard!* And I loved him for it. He was still the respectful guy I'd thought he was that first night.

In shambled a tall, muscled guy wearing phony Ray Bans and carrying a suitcase roughly the size of a large TV. It must have been crammed with kilos of souvenirs, or clothes enough for a three-month trip. Despite this, he handled the case with authority, no doubt benefiting from his own bulk. His fine-carved moustache would have been the envy of any butcher, and his shiny, styled hair was portable advertising for the gel company.

Oh no, I thought in a swirl of fright, *should I run out of here?* He was probably a drug dealer, from the looks of it. A million and one thoughts ran through my head until the guy set down his burden with a thump that shook the floor. *Who in the world is this guy? And why is he selling drugs with such confidence?*

Frankly, I felt sick to my stomach, and couldn't imagine Bahareh involved in this kind of stuff.

I stood by Arash as Bahareh approached the guy and asked, "What do you have new for me today?"

Beneath the black shades, he grinned, stretching that mustache. "Lots of stuff, and you will love it!"

I clenched my jaw in suspense, and watched the guy unlock his anchor of a suitcase. He must have loads of drugs, going by the sheer size of that thing. I didn't want to be too judgmental, so waited while he fumbled with the 1970s-era artifact.

"At last!" he shouted in triumph, opening the thing.

I couldn't believe it. The case held an amazing quantity of videocassettes, both Betamax and VHS. So *this* was a movie-guy … possibly *the* movie guy! Delivering the latest-and-greatest to your doorstep.

"Just received the newest movies yesterday," he said. "So they're fresh. Fresh off the boat, or FOB-*ee!*" Something like laughter gurgled in his throat. To me, this immediately increased his greasiness rating to five stars. How did he get access to all these movies? Who gave them to him? Most of all, why were they still using Betamax?

I glanced at Bahareh, who said, "Delkash, you know the good ones, so check out the titles and pick some out. I'm horrible at this stuff!"

"Um ... okay..."

I scanned the labeled cellophane offerings—a riot of colors and genres. Comedy, Romance, Drama, Horror, Suspense, Documentaries, and in varied flavors of Chinese, German, Russian, and the newly released American films. *Wow!* They were priced relatively cheap: 500 *tomans* per VHS, equivalent to 25 cents. Uncensored and straight off the shelf of any foreign market. I couldn't believe it.

It was cheaper and more convenient than going to the movies, and you had your own personal delivery boy, with no delivery fees or tips included! This greasy guy made a living from this stuff, and even had a wait list taped to the lining in his suitcase!

I admitted to myself that even the suitcase was interesting, probably dating back to when Iran was the Persian Empire. It sure smelled ancient, but its contents were new and uncensored. Being able to watch blood, or romance, tight jeans, tank tops, and push-up bras made all the difference, compared to the normally blacked-out or otherwise edited Iranian version.

Arash leaned over the suitcase while the big guy watched. "Hmmm ... Let's have a look…"

He helped me choose some movies as I complained about the Betamax tapes. "Those are real *old*, you know."

Arash gave a slight nod. "Yes, but at least you see the whole movie, rather than a thirty-minute butchered version!"

We both giggled, fingers poking through titles. Finally, we had five selections: four American, and one Swedish. This was a cosmopolitan journey, and everyone wondered where the Swedish film stood (but didn't really care, because we would probably start with the American ones).

Arash took the bill and Mr. Greasy slapped shut his case and lugged himself through the door while we gathered to watch the first movie together. My first movie with Arash, and it would be a complete two-hour ride with only silence between us, with the movie doing all the talking. I wanted to move close to him, and knew that he, who I had met only a couple of weeks earlier, had the same intention. I would never make the first move, but I hoped that he'd make his so that I could allow it...

In the back of my head, though, I knew Bahareh would get protective and fill the space!

"Wait a second," she said, and brought down the curtains so her nosy neighbors wouldn't invade our privacy. "Okay ... all set to go!"

That particular problem soon solved itself, as Arash sat down beside me, sliding his arm across my shoulders and—for the first time—gazing into my eyes at such close distance. The movie watching was a great excuse for closeness, and though he had wanted to take me to a local theater, we'd never be able to be as free as we were here inside a house.

I snuggled against him, planning to enjoy this movie, and these intimate moments. I could feel his mind flashing with thoughts and images as our bodies got closer, and felt his heat growing stronger. Like most men with toned, muscular physiques, he was a girl-magnet and knew it! I sometimes wondered why, when he could have anyone, he had chosen me. But then again, I knew what a catch

I was! I was a whirlwind of confidence, and that was completely different than any other girl in my circle. I liked to think that it was what attracted Arash in the first place.

"Okay, lovebirds," Bahareh said, not without compassion. "Let's watch."

The movie was actually copied from some theater, with poor resolution and sound that dropped in and out. At times, babies could be heard crying in the background, and audience members bumping and shuffling, probably getting up to use the restroom. These people certainly were not dues-paying extras in the Screen Actors Guild. If only the director knew this was the end result of his efforts, surely the Oscar nomination would be trashed! *If* there was to be one!

This turned the movie into a comedy, earning frequent laughter from everyone. At the end, no one knew even what the story had been about. Had some famous actor like Brad Pitt been featured, no one would have noticed!

But between the gathered friends hummed a good, light energy. Although the movie had not been a hit, the whole concept of the mustache-guy, his tremendous suitcase, and the Betamax cassettes generated plenty of laughter, even a sense of bonding.

I stood and stretched. "Does anyone think the other movies will be better?"

"I will take a wild, educated guess," said Arash as he stood. "And say 100 percent *not!*"

Turning, he again found himself near me, and I felt he wanted to indulge in my lips, and to forget about the unwanted companions … be in the moment.

"You never know," Bahareh said, heading for the kitchen. "Sometimes the guy filming has a better seating position, or maybe some babies have already had their bathroom break!"

We watched the second movie, which wasn't much better, and soon it was time to say goodbye. I didn't want Arash to go and, from his expression, he didn't either. I could see that he wanted more time with me, but that he liked our little group. "Bahareh," he said, "if it's okay with you, why don't I invite some friends over, get some *kebabs* to barbecue and some more drinks? Call it a mini get-together…?"

His eyes pleaded for a *yes, of course, Arash*! He knew I would decline any suggestion of going to his place, because of the emperor's checkup calls to my aunt, but he must have thought he could get around it if Bahareh said okay.

Back from the kitchen, she considered the notion. "It's a good idea, but we really should keep it down. The nosy neighbors could tell my parents, so if we make sure no one finds out, you keep to yourselves going up and down the stairs, and park far away enough to avoid suspicion ... I say, let's party! But don't forget to do it with a *shhhhhhhhh*!" She cracked up. She loved secret parties, being secretive and strategizing. It was the kick to her life!

"I agree!" I shouted with a giggle.

I looked at Arash and saw that he was staring right at me. He was reassuring me that if that's what I wanted, then that would be happening tonight.

"And I second that," said Shaheen, who was trying to get closer to Bahareh for a big French kiss. This *clearly* allowed him more time to get it.

The guys agreed to make a stealthy run for supplies, and were relieved when Bahareh mentioned that they needn't buy charcoal because her parents were stocked. There were even chicken parts marinating in the fridge. *Leave it to a Persian mama to leave the house with ample food in the fridge for her chickees.* After the two set off, Bahareh and I freshened our drinks (I was becoming a pro in this) and began preparing side dishes to accompany the chicken *kebabs*, and were mostly successful at not laughing too loudly. Mostly.

Within twenty minutes, Arash and Shaheen returned in a rustle of bags and clicking bottles, stepping gingerly as if through a minefield.

"Hey," Bahareh said. "What took you so long?" And cracked up because she thought she had made a sarcastic comment.

After a few moments, the spontaneous mini-party was underway, and anyone invited would surely accept the invitation. The smorgasbord consisted of illegal drinks, alcoholic drinks, hard-core drinks, and protein. That was all we needed. The main drinks were vodka and cranberry juice, plus yogurt dip and chips,

Mortadella, and a main dish of just barbecued marinated chicken. The up-to-now quiet Shaheen insisted on tending the coals and grilling the meat, and did so like the *chef de cuisine*! He sliced a few roma tomatoes, brushed them with olive oil, and threw them on as well.

But the best addition to the night was the company.

A friend of Arash's dropped in to play some Iranian oldies and new songs. It wasn't long before an informal choir got going (so much for keeping quiet!), chanting familiar songs and some we didn't know so well, but there was a sustained sort of harmony flavored with smoky barbecue and laughter.

I felt like I fit right in, and it was terrific.

Everyone was sophisticated, and discussions ranged from Iran's economy to fashion to the new skiing *piste* they were inaugurating in Dizin this coming winter. We teased one another, but no one took anything personally. This was very close to the Jewish and Italian humor I had experienced with the girls in Brooklyn.

"Check it out," someone said, waving at a girl cradling a guitar.

Standing in a corner, she gestured soulfully while strumming, her long, pale fingers fretting with passion's precision. Rich, warm chords mesmerized the group, and some rocked gently in their chairs or even from the floor. This was my first time witnessing an Iranian girl playing the guitar. Nothing irregular or bad about it—a girl who liked the guitar and played without her scarf, and sang at times. Simple art, and food for the soul. It just wasn't something you saw in Iran, though.

Throughout the night, I sat beside Arash, but had no difficulty connecting and laughing with everyone invited. All the boys knew we were dating, so out of respect, kept their distance. I took comfort and security from his affection.

After dinner and some more guitar, we opened a poetry book and started reading from it. I never had heard such poems; some parts I understood, while others eluded me. The reader gave off a vibe of hardcore mysticism and spirituality. Then, finally, I could see the book's cover: *Fale Hafez.*

"Why are we reading this book?" I whispered to Bahareh.

"This guy Hafez was a famous poet back in the day. His poems told of connecting to the beloved, or the 'tongue of the invisible.'"

"Oh."

"Usually we make a wish, then say a little prayer and open a book he wrote called *Divane Hafez* to see if the wish comes true."

"Why not other poets? What makes him the man?"

"Because," Arash interrupted, gazing into my eyes, "he communicated deep spiritual experiences, and is a genuine mystic, in love with his Beloved…"

I was taken by surprise. Arash was so quick to answer this question, and on top of that I'd never heard Mr. Jordan Playboy (or so I thought) speak like this.

"His poetry is like a *dua*, or prayer," he went on. "And he wrote poetry expressing love, spirituality, and protest. Today many use his sayings as proverbs. So, Del *khanoom*, when one wants to know answers to their destiny, they consult Hafez."

I felt Arash so near that I thought he must know everything about me, burrowing through my soul with that penetrating gaze. At once my doubt melted away. I wanted to tell him how much I enjoyed being with him ... tell the truth about my life. All of it.

"By any chance, are you trying to indirectly communicate something to me?" I asked quietly.

He narrowed his eyes, as if figuring some complex equation. "Why would you think that?"

"Because you are..." I trailed off, and glanced away, knowing I wanted him just as bad as he wanted me.

He sustained himself and paused, hoping the moment would not end. His body energy was getting intense, and I felt he wanted to reach out, grab me, and wrestle with me. I knew I would eventually surrender to his kiss, but I wasn't ready yet. His sexual energy was going through the roof, and it was all just ... too intense for me to deal with.

The clock rang 1 in the morning, then, signaling that midnight was gone and it was time to leave. Everyone ignored it, including Bahareh, who carried on chatting with and enjoying her invited guests. This mirth and music went on until somewhere around 3, when the party hit one of those quiet pockets.

At that, people began checking out, gathering whatever they'd brought—food not included—and saying thank-yous and good-byes. I pulled Arash to the hushed, dim corner and asked if we could speak before he took off. I wanted to tell him the truth—that I trusted him, and that I enjoyed getting to know him.

"Arash…" I began, swallowing hard. But my Farsi wasn't working too smoothly in the conversation. He realized that and jumped in.

"Did you enjoy yourself?"

"Of course! Did you?"

He grinned broadly. "I always do when I'm with you…"

"Smart guy…" I joked with a wink.

"Or so it seems to some. Do you want to continue this dialogue in English, or should we switch channels?"

Did he want to speak in English because he thought the Institute did a fabulous job teaching me, or did he know? Why had he asked that? I froze. Oh my God … he did know! And now he knew why I'd been covering it up! I felt like crap.

I stood there, poised and solemn. "You know?"

"From the very start. You know your answers and questions are not those of girls who grew up here. No. It's obvious—at least to me—that you were raised in a different culture. But you should know that I don't care because I am *not* after your green card." His posture told the firm truth of this statement, and his eyes were so innocent. "Look, I know you are scared because lots of guys want to get out of this country somehow, and hooking up with a girl with a green card is the easiest way. But you know, or maybe didn't, that I was raised in London and already have a ticket out ... that is, if I *wanted* it."

"So..."

"So I don't need to trick you and act like I'm head over heels for you and your family, or pretend to love every joke you tell!" he ended with a chuckle.

I remained quiet, unsure how to express myself. Words weren't working at the moment, but I enjoyed hearing what Arash had to say and wanted to hear more. Still, I had to ask: "If you aren't acting, then what are you doing?"

"I'll tell you. Simply being ... and enjoying every moment with you."

"And your intention is to *not* take advantage of me, right? Because, as I recall from the girls I've spoken to, that is another issue girls have to deal with today."

"Listen, the fact that you're asking is another indicator that you are *not* from Tehran's world! Girls here play the game and you're asking me if I want to have sex?"

"Umm ... right. So *do* you?"

For the first time, he looked away. "Whenever you're ready ... have I ever touched you or asked you for more?"

He was right—in all the time we had spent together, he hadn't even kissed me. Or was he laying low until he got what he wanted? A strong urge told me to throw these thoughts heard around the block and at school away, and just be me, and relish my time. I smiled, knowing Arash could talk with me without being pushed. We had evolved as an amateur couple until this moment of truth. I could finally, completely be myself.

"By the way, I think my jokes are funny." I had to add that.

Tension drained from his stiff stance. "Of course, of course … but to an extent."

Stepping closer, he looked into my eyes … and leaned down.

He lifted a hand and tenderly held my chin toward him. This was the guy I could be comfortable with, who had opened my heart without looking at my breasts (from what I knew). He stirred butterflies in me, and every moment he infused me with life.

"Okay..." I said, closing my eyes letting him know I was ready for him. I didn't know to what extent I was ready, so I let him roll the dice.

His lips brushed mine, warm and gentle and soft, and I kissed back, abandoning myself to this exquisite man, this delicious moment. Our kiss was small, long, and suspended time … it was the first time I had tasted someone who brought new experiences into my life. New emotions were rising to the surface, passing delicate spaces in my soul and filling them with passion.

I opened my eyes and ended the kiss softer than a midnight sigh…

We stood smiling at each other, a mutual recognition of how right it felt, and then I looked back into the room. This was my life. My life. I was going to seize it ... and I didn't care how or why anyone else lived theirs. Even in Iran. Even in taboo-land.

I turned, and Arash gazed at me like I'd just given him the key to glory.

All at once, my worries, thoughts, and doubts about coming to Iran, struggling with the language and culture, seemed distant and inaccessible.

And for now, they were.

Chapter 11: Lost in Translation

For me, discovering Iran was fun. I'd been there for a bit over a year, and now I had some friends, and connected with every one of them in a different way. Some understood me, and others didn't have the slightest idea of the changes going on inside. But who cared? I was enjoying both worlds, sweet and bitter at the same time.

Sometimes after our Italian class, I would venture out with Elham, and at other times I would spend time with family and get to know them. My dates with Arash had become bi-weekly, usually after Italian class. He always had cash on him if the *Komiteh* approached, and I was frankly getting used to being ultra-careful outside. We would either go to dinner or just have a *majoon* in Tajrish Square, which was every fruit blended with dates or honey or a variety of nuts. We talked, exchanged ideas, laughed, made fun of each other, and conducted ourselves with one foot in Farsi and the other in the ocean lingo of English. Fin-glish or Fars-glish—it came with no instructions other than that we both understood what the hell the other was saying.

At times a question was cut in half by any word that filled in the blank. That word might have even been Italian! It didn't matter, as long as we were communicating.

My meetings and talks with him had to be kept on the down low, and I had to skip out on some classes or leave after forty minutes of class to make it happen. And the calls caused me to lose lots of sleep and turn into an insomniac. I didn't care. I was young and carefree and spending time with someone that I cared deeply for.

My mom kept asking boyfriend questions to gather data about whether I was doing anything under the rugs. She was a good spy. But if she knew, then my dad would definitely know, and then I would be under the radar. So I made sure she never got a whiff of what I was doing.

There was a time when I was on the phone with Elham, telling her about our date, and the emperor picked up the phone from the living room to make a call. He overheard a tiny bit of the story. The next day when he asked about it I said I was telling her about a scene in a movie I had just watched. Since I didn't have a long list of lies on my record, he accepted that and went on with his day. My list of lies was actually long, but as long as they were kept hidden from the parents and the family, I was doing just fine.

Strictness led to lies, which led to moving forward in my dating life.

Arash and I moved through the days hand-in-hand (when I put my hands over his in the car—yes, a risk!) and sometimes lip-to-lip, when we could squeeze in a kiss in the darkness of the night and car.

One night, he asked if I could go out with him to the movie theater, and I (developing the courage to step out with my boyfriend without fear of being spotted by family or the *Komiteh*) said yes. My cover-up and white lie was that I was chilling with Bahareh at a coffee shop. Her cell phone was turned off during my movie time.

Her cover plan was that she was spending time with me, while in reality she was out in a coffee shop with Shaheen. We fit each other's bill.

That night, Arash and I went to see an American film in the theater. The theater was packed, and a line had formed for popcorn at the concession stand. The majority of people stood outside on the sidewalk, where a vendor sold fresh walnuts floating in saltwater-filled jars. The vessels didn't look dirty or smudged, and if they were, the public seemed unconcerned and within minutes had depleted the stock.

Arash and I joined in on the fun and bought some walnuts, which were dumped into a plastic bag. Six freshly salted walnuts in a plastic bag for 500 *tomans*. That was nothing in dollars! It was 75 cents! I could buy the guy and his jar with my allowance … but then again I had Arash, so I passed on that portion.

We headed inside and got seated, and I dug into my walnut bag. The crunch wasn't annoying, as everyone gnawed on some snack—including sunflower seeds, which were impossible to enjoy without being cracked open. Nobody minded. This wasn't New York

City, where any intrusive sound would provoke head turns, sometimes hostile glares, and whispered threats here and there from the ultra-sensitive.

I crunched away. "It's a good thing no one's giving us the look. We're making quite the noise!"

Arash nosed my ear and whispered, "They are doing the same thing," and gave gentle kisses with soft breathy chuckles.

The air was close and scented with hot popcorn. The film was surely American with famous actors, although dubbed in Farsi. "Oh, I've seen this before," I whispered.

The dubbed version, though, was nothing like the movie I had watched in the US. I listened carefully, picked out words and phrasing that was mistranslated and badly edited into the wrong places. This gave the movie an absurd, unintended twist.

First, I thought I heard them wrong, but other than the voices being completely off and the affectionate words cropped, some slang terms were so poorly interpreted they made no sense at all.

I couldn't help it. "This is translated wrong! It changes the whole meaning of the scene," I said, laughing.

Arash started laughing while pointing at the crowd. "I wanted you to see this whole mess, not necessarily the movie!"

I simply couldn't stop giggling through this drama-turned-comedy, especially when the screen suddenly went black. "What is up with the black?"

The audience shouted in unity, clapped, blew out enthusiastic wolf-whistles. A few completely lost it, cackling and rolling in their seats. I had never seen such a thing.

"What on earth is happening?"

Arash had to shout over the convulsive laughter. "This is the censored sex scene, and everyone knows it because everyone has a movie guy! They're making fun of it, like when you know but don't know what's happening. When they think you're stupid, but you have it all figured out."

"Why aren't you joining in on this home run?" I laughed, setting aside the empty walnut plastic bag.

"You go get her! She's a hottie!" screamed some guys from somewhere in the theatre.

Someone across the aisle said, "Atta boy! She was beautiful, wasn't she?" The crowd roared on a soprano note, fading when the next pathetic scene unfolded.

I shook my head. This was easily the most ridiculous, hilarious picture, next to the mustached guy's collection at Bahareh's house. Everyone there knew the movie's plot, scenes, and how it ended, but still they chose to gather here in this theatre, re-watch it, and eat dirty but delicious salted walnuts. Strangers building memories together.

I doubted the effect held up for screenings of Iranian-produced movies, but as far as these mistranslated, poorly dubbed foreign jobs went, they were like comedies. Perhaps funnier was that the entire audience knew this, but nonetheless paid for a few inevitable laughs. Wow! This society bonded in very weird ways.

Inching closer to Arash, I scratched the back of his head and murmured, "Thank you for bringing me here."

"For you, anything…" he smirked while stealing a small kiss. We lingered in the intimate darkness.

Many in Iran would probably label our kiss or our date as a right or wrong, Islamic or sinful. But for Arash and I, this was a temporary suspension of mandatory discipline in order to enjoy ourselves whenever, and however, we could.

*

The day after the movie, I woke up to get dressed for class. Elham and I planned to grab lunch at the famous charbroiled burger and pizza place in Vanak, then head on to the Institute.

Gastronomy in Iran should be made a science ... that's how good the food was! Every restaurant I went too made me want more, and though I'd always tried to keep my calorie count low, that was a part of myself that I had to let go. I couldn't resist the food.

Elham drove her mom' s Iranian-made Renault Pars (assembled from the French manufacturer's parts), and since it didn't have air conditioning, the heat outside could have burned through our skin. To compensate for this lack, Elham's brother had installed some sort of engine, or compressor, in the trunk, proving himself a highly skilled technician and problem-solver. This improvised AC system, by way of a long nozzle, pumped cold air from the trunk into the car.

When I first saw this contraption, my jaw dropped; it was truly unbelievable, and out of this world! "What in the world of science creation *is* this?"

"Take a wild guess," said Elham with a smirk. "Compliments of my genius brother!"

Elham's brother was the sort of guy who never went to school; in fact, I think he had dropped out of eleventh grade. But he excelled in figuring things out through trial and error. He had once aspired to be a NASA engineer, and probably would have made it, had he not dithered and fooled around so much, leading to marriage at eighteen. He still nurtured ambitions of leaving Iran and going to Texas to pursue his dream of flying to the moon.

Now, back from the moon and into reality, he was a gifted mechanic and ran his own shop. It was busy all the time and brought in good money, and he had a wife he adored. So, career-wise, he was happy, though I don't think his job did him justice and used all of his potential. Installing a homemade AC unit in a stick-shift car whose

275

small engine barely turned its own wheels was genius. And it saved our butts anytime we went anywhere.

"Let's get in and get going!" I said, sliding into the matchbox-shaped Renault. "I'm hungry!"

Elham squinted in confusion. "Where are we going again?"

"You know, the famous charbroiled burger joint in Vanak! I've heard so much about it, and it's time to indulge in something different from Chelo. I'm tired of crusty rice. So *bezan berim, andiamo, vamos.* Or, as Kramer would say, giddy up!"

At that, we drove wickedly into the wild, wild, streets of Tehran, where driving was as art.

After a good drive with the music competing with the roars of the AC, we pulled up to the charbroiled place, where the smell made me start doubling my production of saliva.

"No," said Elham, with her mouth wide open.

Already a line nearly a kilometer long had formed, which, despite moving quickly, seemed only to get longer. That wasn't fair. We were in starving mode!

Okay, I thought, someone had to wait in line. "Why don't you stay in the car," I said, "and I'll get the pick-ups ... maybe we should have called and ordered a week ago!" I said, pissed but still hungry.

"Wait. Let's see if we can find a friendly face, that way we can just cut in instead of waiting for who knows how many hours! Gimme a second while I browse..."

Even though I was very hungry, I thought that approach would be kind of rude, barging into the middle of the line smiling and signaling to people behind you. No, that was lacking in etiquette. If I were standing there and someone tried to pull that on me, I would object ... possibly loudly, and file a lawsuit!

Elham hit the brakes. "Wait here! I just saw Ali..."

"Ali? Who on earth is Ali??"

"The guy from Jordan. You don't remember, as usual ... I think Arash fogged up your brain so much you can't remember anyone else!" She jumped out of the car.

Her greeting was very warm, and awkward at the same time ... well, at least in my eyes. Simply a *Salam*, eliminating a hug or kiss.

I sat watching, dreading what might happen next. Would she offer Ali money to buy their food? It sure was beginning to look that way, and others were noticing with hostile stares. Here we went, I thought. She would insist that he let her pay, and he would insist that he pay instead. It would go back and forth for some time, until finally she gave it up and said that he could pay this time, but she'd pay next time. It could go on for ages. God, it was embarrassing.

Before long, though, Elham trotted back to the car, grinning. "Ali has invited us to free burgers and pizza! *And* now we are spared standing in line and roasting in these *wimples*, and missing class in the bargain!"

"But we should pay them back, girl." I said, kind of confused.

"They are treating Del. And when a guy treats, you accept!" she continued giggling.

I didn't get this concept, but it didn't matter anymore. I just decided to wing it. Since Ali had extended the invitation and Elham had accepted, we had to sit and eat with him. The food was heaven. Flame-broiled burgers and pizza baked to crisp perfection in a brick oven. Stuff this delicious, I mused, ought to be advertised in Vogue, and served along the models' runway in Paris! It made the world go round! Forget Brooklyn, this was the cheese!

Partway through lunch, Elham leaned toward me and whispered, "Eating this is better than sex!"

A comment typical from Elham, who was likeable and hilarious, and created from her vivid imagination.

I managed not to blush, but did softly giggle. "Mmmm-hmmm, girl, you just may be right!"

Ali chewed his pizza, oblivious to the topic. "So," he said, blotting his mouth with a napkin, "where are you guys headed now?"

"To an education institution," said Elham with a chuckle.

"Yes," I chimed in, "that is precisely our destination, in our elaborate Oscar-style *mantos* and *wimples*." I had to hiss some laughter at my own corny statement.

Ali looked at us, back and forth, as if trying to decide something. "I say you skip class and join us."

"Two questions, Ali Joon," I said. "First, join you where? And second, who is us?"

I felt somewhat conflicted. There might be danger here ... or maybe just another round of good times. It was funny how danger and fun times were turning out to be best buds in Iran.

I also thought of Arash, who was supposed to pick me up from class so we could be together. I didn't want to get dragged into something without him knowing.

Ali sat up straight, assuming a casual air. "My dad just bought a villa out in Lavasan, and we're all headed there in an hour to escape the pollution and make *kebabs*, drink, and get a little fun times in." Even more upbeat, he said, "C'mon, it'll be fun, and you won't regret it!"

"Well, I have a boyfriend," I said. "So if he's down and doesn't have to work, I will ditch class and join in the Lavasan fun!"

I didn't want to ditch Arash, though I totally could have. I felt this security with him and I think I respected him and liked him to the extent that I wanted him to know. Ali wasn't bad and his friend was hot, but Arash was my beau.

Plus, my parents would think I was in class, so I didn't have to worry about being back for a while.

I was getting to know myself fully, now. I knew that I liked Arash, and I knew that I had to keep some details of my life from my parents. Maybe they too were afraid of the system too, and I was protecting them in a way. What they didn't know wouldn't hurt them, and it would keep them from worrying about me too much.

"If they join, then I'm in too!" popped Elham.

So the fate of this near-future plan was left in Arash's hands.

Ali studied us with apparent composure, as if he had all the time in the world. "Okay," he finally said.

Elham leaned toward me and whispered, "We could have gone, you know. Arash doesn't have to know *everything!*"

"But we barely know these guys. Who knows what we'll be stepping in to? Anyway, I also want them to get the picture that I have a boyfriend, so hands off is the name of the game!"

It looked like boys and girls did a lot of jumping around with one another in Tehran—everyone flirted with each other, and it took a while for two to become exclusive. I know I respected Arash, but on a totally different note, he was also fun to be around. I wanted to keep that.

"Fine," Elham said. "Call him." Her expression said that I had to do it, or she'd count me as no fun.

Ali stepped away in search of something to drink, and—I thought—to give me a second. I picked up the phone and dialed.

Arash answered in a matter of seconds. Elham probably thought that he'd be the typical Iranian man and say no to everything, but she was wrong. And it turned out that I was completely wrong as well.

The call went on for nearly twenty minutes, with plenty of nods and smiles and mm-hmmms on my end. Ali sat sipping some frosty-looking concoction and watching carefully.

Finally, the call ended. Cutting to the chase, I gave Elham the Cliff's Notes version.

Stunned, she said, "You mean he didn't give you a flat-out *no*? Didn't shout 'How dare you even talk to or have lunch with another dude'?"

"What are you talking about? Woman, we are not living in the fifth century. He said, 'If you know him, go and have fun. But *do* you know him?' I mean, we're going somewhere with him, and Arash is right—I'd rather not be afraid. Besides, if you're crazy for Lavasan, Arash has a villa there, too. We could all go on Friday, and I could tell my dad that I'm at your place. I'll head to my aunt's first. That way we've got another house to go to if anything happens, and Arash can go with us. Of course I would be lying again, but my aunt always goes out on Fridays, to the mountains. So it'll be tough for him to call and check on me."

Ali, finished with his drink, was visibly getting twitchy about the whole thing.

"You sure we could make it Friday?" asked Elham. "Things happen and the parents twist and turn with their decisions. What if your aunt decides to randomly pay a visit to her sister, and then you have to stay, and we're stuck in the house!" She laughed, but half of her tone was completely serious. She really wanted to go, and was afraid that I was going to screw it up with my new plan.

"*Boro ghomshoo,*" I said with a chuckle. *Get lost!* "It'll be a piece of cake, and we will—we *shall*—get out," I declared. "Sorry Ali Joon. *Merci* for lunch and umm …well, the cut in line!"

We all stood, and apologized for not being able to make it today (*and be their girl toys,* I thought in my head). I felt as if we were part of a secret BF and GF society, formed to guard against public (and official) disapproval. He seemed all right, though. He didn't bite.

I knew Lavasan was gorgeous, and also knew it was home to the rich Iranian crowd, with their servants and new Mercedes Benz sedans, and similar to Los Angeles' Calabasas, Bel Air, and Beverly Hills combined. I was excited about seeing this. Who knew what I'd find there?

Back in the car, we drove toward our class. It was refreshing to have a little adventure like this. It was unpredictable and totally out of the blue. What if Arash had joined us and we had ended up in Lavasan in a complete stranger's house! No rules were the name of the game in this country. No rules except for the emperor's, which we kept ignoring for the one goal of having fun.

*

That night in my room, I went under the covers, pulled out the secret telephone, and called my secret boyfriend.

Fortunately, my bedroom was situated far from my parents', because my laughs and naughty flirts weren't always so quiet. One loud answer and the cops would awake, or at least start to get suspicious.

The conversation wasn't as long, as usual, but plans were set.

Strategy: On Friday, I would head over to my aunt's, with a little white lie (how every other girl would always label it), and would change directions along the way. Arash would pick me up two blocks north of my house. Then we would grab Elham and be on our way. The only additional point we had to take into perspective was the *Komiteh*. I told Bahareh to have an eye out in case my aunt and the emperor were to touch base but she said it was unlikely for her mom to even hear the phone while she was out climbing.

In a sense, Elham was a third wheel. But she didn't care—she couldn't marry a Muslim guy anyway, and it was hard to find someone Jewish in the crowd in Tehran. They usually kept quiet among all the Muslims. So she settled for simply having fun, and we got along very well and enjoyed our time together.

So, armed with a bag full of smiles, chips, yogurt dip, raw chicken and meat *kebabs*, vodka, and blasting DJ Bobo-style music, we drove into the sunset headed toward our one-day vacation.

Chapter 12: Living Large in Lavasan

I was excited to spend time with Arash and my best buddy, Elham, in Lavasan—wherever it was. The twisty road threaded through a landscape filled with fascinating sights and a symphony of aromas. The car entered a hundred-yard stretch redolent of fresh green grass, then a low spot swirling with stony bites of dust. Bursts of flowers—crimson, lemon, white, and violet—adorned the earth, and trees reached fruit-laden limbs over the road as if luring the travelers with apples, white berries, and apricots.

The intense heat was kept mostly at bay by the cranked-up AC unit. Arash brought watermelon seeds to munch on, and I observed that nearly every soul in Iran seemed to be into sunflower or watermelon seeds. People took them everywhere, whether watching a movie, driving, or having dessert after dinner. Often, the seeds *were* the dessert! It could be listed under side dishes and dessert on a restaurant menu at the same time.

Abruptly Arash braked, stopping the car in the middle of the road and gazing straight at me. Oh!! How I wanted to have sex with him when he looked at me like that!

I looked back, thinking he might be crazy, or was hesitating to say we were out of gas. "Ummm ... this is the road, *azizam*," I said, thinking maybe I was missing something.

"I know, silly ... but look at those sour oranges and berries hanging from those trees!"

"Oh yeah! This is going to be fun!" said Elham.

After a few moments of gazing out the window to connect the dots, I saw what they were pointing at. They were acting like temporary monkeys lusting after a mid-road snack! "I know what you're going to do. Isn't it illegal?"

"Nothing is illegal in this country!" Elham declared. "Get out! They're calling your name!"

I giggled. "Yeah ... what could they *possibly* be saying?"

"I want your *sex*!" And at that, Elham cracked up.

Arash pulled the car onto the shoulder, and they both climbed out. We, meaning my boyfriend and I, strode through the tall grass toward the white berry tree. Waving away a cloud of buzzing gnats, Arash appeared to dive headfirst into the ground, with his feet thrust into the air. Handstand time!

"Look at you!" I cried.

In a show of amazing balance, he twisted his body and faced me. "No, I'd rather look at *you!*"

Not used to such "free" displays, I felt a rush of fear. Maybe if I were in Brooklyn I wouldn't feel this scared, but then again, these two monkeys were jumping into these trees as if the rule was to take other people's fruits and be happy you did it! Well, flexibility's arrow hit me through the heart at that point and transformed me into the same monkey.

Arash's handstand came to an end and he brought himself back to his feet, panting with effort but grinning.

"Jump, climb, and start eating!"

"Just like that? What if the neighbors see us?"

"Then we split!"

I stepped toward a *toot* berry tree, heaved myself onto its bulk, and climbed faster than I thought possible. Halfway up I stopped and inhaled the intoxicating sweetness of white mulberries, which literally bled sugar. "Hey, these are delicious."

Not even thinking about pesticides (don't even think they were used here!), I plucked a sticky bunch and gobbled them—an explosion of heaven in my mouth. They were as good as any piece of fruit I'd had there. I plucked another pungent bunch and savored it, unable to stop.

Arash viewed this spontaneous feast for a few seconds, then decided to intervene. "Okay, okay. You'll spoil your lunch!"

This went nowhere, and he was forced to pull me down by my jeans leg.

Elham had already scaled a *Shatoot* tree as if it was second nature, and perched on one fat limb, munching the purple berries as if she owned the orchard.

"I know you like them," Arash said, "but we have somewhere to get to!" Laughing, he shook his head.

In a *toot* trance, I said, "They were ... so ... good. Where can we get some more?" This sounded like a priority to me at that moment.

By the way, *toot* means *berry* in Farsi, and the word after explains the million and one *toots* we have in Iran! White, red, dark red...

Arash waved a hand before my face to induce normal blinking. "They sell some up the road, but let's grab some sour oranges for the *kebabs*. They work well together ... wink," he said, accompanied with a physical wink. *Must really taste good*, I thought. The comment sounded like a sexual one, and I definitely took it as one. Now I really wanted him.

Back on Earth, I said, "Wait, are you sure they won't arrest us?"

"Again with the fear?" joked Elham. "Get a grip, woman. They will join in the fun ... nobody will call the cops for eating a berry or two. Or should I say, in your case, two hundred! Besides, they're dangling over the streets. Someone should maintain their trees better."

Meanwhile, Arash had moved like lightning, and jogged up to us with at least twenty *narenjes* (sour oranges) bouncing in his bowled-up shirt. Back at the car, he dumped these into a bag and eased himself into the driver's seat. Peering at me again, he grinned broadly as if to tell a funny story.

"So ... how did you like it?"

I clapped once, jarringly loud. "Let's repeat on the way back!"

Elham hooted in triumph. "Yeah, girlfriend! At last! Finally the Mafia side is lurking out! You're getting out of that right-or-wrong-or-sinful mode. This stuff is not a big deal here. Even if the neighbors found out, they would probably give you a bowl to harvest in."

Arash put the car in gear and we drove off. For twenty minutes or so we recharged, while basking in the echo of our fruit-picking gig.

Finally Arash slowed. "Here we are…"

He nosed the car into a sandy entrance that looked as though it might lead to some deserted shamble of a house, but opened onto a parking area serving a luxurious Spanish-style Villa. A dream home for sure. It might have appeared deserted from the outside, but it was breathtaking in design, surrounded by a U-shaped garden bright with flowers, tomatoes, and grape vines, and watched over by white, black, and red mulberry trees on the inside. The villa had accents of Andalusian (or perhaps Italian) porcelain, and an iron stable-style door added a humble rustic charm. The airy house gave off a dreamy magic, as though it had stood here forever. It would have been perfect for some Lifestyles of the Rich and Famous-type TV show.

"Look at that," I said. "The outdoor patio should be featured in *Meditation* or *Um Magazine.* Just close your eyes and breathe in the freshness..."

We opened the doors and got out of the car. Arash stretched his arms over his head. "The only thing I'm breathing is your perfume." He shot me a teasing glance, then leaned down and kissed my neck—a wet kiss that refreshed my skin.

"C'mon," Elham urged. "Let's go!"

Officially parked now, we unloaded our goodies and strode through the incense of flowers and fruit to enter the villa. Once

Arash opened the door, I marveled at the work of great minds and architects. The interior held a scattering of art objects from Paris, Spain, and Italy. And the garden could certainly rival any in Holland.

Natural light glowed across white marble stairs, tiled walls, wood-and-glass combo floor units, a Persian framed carpet, and a grand piano polished to infinity. And this was just the beginning! Balconies opened onto a stream bobbing with watermelons, cantaloupes, and honeydews, which were corralled by a big rock.

"Why are those melons in the water? Won't they float away?" I asked loudly.

Elham rolled her eyes. "Well, Ms. IQ, that's why there's a big rock keeping them from escaping. Besides, touch the water. It flows down from the mountains and is very cold."

"Thanks for the enlightenment Ms. *Know It All!*" I fired back sarcastically.

Arash had invited eight or nine others and they arrived a bit after us. They seemed like tourists in this villa. They were staring at its Zen-like spaces, some gazing at its art, others at the house itself. After about half an hour, everyone was drinking, eating, and enjoying the mini-vacation. I was surprised by everyone's warmth and never expected to visit this villa and mingle with people so hip, fashionable, friendly, and easy to converse with.

Best of all had to be the uncomplicated comfort of sipping wine on a patio with Arash and Elham cracking jokes, with the boundless blue sky stretching away over us. Ah ... this was Iran at its finest.

I took a sip of wine, and turned to Arash. "Do you come here a lot? I mean this is better than all therapies combined—herbal, aroma, or otherwise. Never knew this even existed in Tehran!"

Tehran was hot, dry, and polluted, with cab drivers driving crazy. There was so much noise that you could hardly hear the vendors on the street shouting the prices of the products! Each day, ten million souls made their way through this city's crowded streets. A drive across Tehran could take as long as the journey from Montpelier to New Hampshire, with Lavasan nearly invisible in the background. I'd never have thought it was this beautiful.

Arash smiled and stole a kiss. I guess I was being cute, in his book. I couldn't be sure what was going to happen with us, where we'd end up, but he was opening my heart bit by bit.

"Picture time!" shouted Elham, shattering my reverie.

"I need some rouge," cried one of the girls nearby.

"Here you go," said Elham. "Use mine."

This piqued the attention of yet another girl. "Can I use it after you? Mine is inside and I don't feel like getting up."

The cycle continued, until those in need all wore the same shade of lipstick, having passed it from one to the other. I wondered why none of them seemed concerned about catching some disease. Count me out—I'd go with whatever was left on my lips after kissing Arash, drinking, and eating.

I didn't care, and the picture was taken as a keepsake from this first visit to Lavasan, where I took advantage of sitting beneath the sky, watching the sunset with someone who accepted me for me, and enabled me to feel safe. It was so surprising to feel safe without the *wimple* or scarf, and be with Arash without being judged or arrested by the *Komiteh*.

I was different than the other Iranian girls, and I knew that Arash saw that, and appreciated it. I saw myself as real and easy going. I didn't need a ton of makeup, and didn't go out of my way to dress up … I was who I was. Maybe that was a trait I brought back from Brooklyn, where you had to be yourself or you wouldn't survive. Girls in Iran wore so much makeup, and it made me think that they were trying too hard to impress the guys. Maybe I had too much confidence.

Everyone else treated me like I was some sort of alien, though they wanted to understand me. They wanted to understand the US *through* me. And I was an open book! Nothing to hide except that in my book, there was nothing wrong with talking about sex. In fact we'd had sex education in school (and some had sex in school!), and I didn't think there was anything wrong with knowing about it.

That was only part of what attracted Arash, though. When I asked, he told me that it was mostly because I made him laugh. Guess that was where the Jewish/Italian sense of humor kicked in. He was right—not all girls in Iran had a sense of humor. Elham was a diamond in the rough, for me. Arash accepted me for who I was, and not through some other lens, including the US citizenship—the golden pass for lots of peeps in Iran.

And maybe I liked him for the same reason. Most guys in Iran—or at least the ones I saw—were sex fanatics, or trying to use the chick for something else. That was what happened when you grew up in a society like that. But Arash was respectful and fun and understood me, which was where I stayed sane. I never needed to explain anything to him, or lay down any rules, and that made me absolutely comfortable.

When I came back to reality and glanced at Elham, I saw that she was on the phone. She whispered that it was my cousin Ghazaleh, and I could tell from the look on her face that we had to get back to Tehran. I was a bit scared to find out about what the phone call was about, so I didn't ask. I just knew we had to be back fast. The three of us ran out to the car and got on the road.

*

We got on the road shortly after sunset, the clouds blushing crimson, violet, and gold.

The ride was quiet, tinged with both warmth and a little melancholy. I hadn't been ready to go, to let go of the freedom we'd tasted, but I knew that the phone call to Elham meant we were out of choices. People were asking after us.

We dropped off Elham with whispered goodbyes, and drove on.

After a short while, the car pulled over to the curb at my house.

"That's odd..." I said, staring at the house.

"What is?"

"Our lights are never off."

"Well, go up and see who's home, or what happened. I will hang around here. Or ... Del, are you scared?"

I narrowed my eyes. "You are so funny. Of course not! But wait for my signal before you leave!" I brushed my lips against his, reluctant to climb out. "I'll miss you..." I whispered seductively.

Then I was running across the sidewalk. I mounted the stairs, slipped my key into the lock, and opened the door. "Hello? Anybody home?"

The house stood empty.

This never happened, and it was unheard of on a Friday. Especially unheard of when I hadn't arrived home and the folks didn't know where I was!

I rushed into the kitchen, and could see a scribbled note attached to the refrigerator: 'Aziz Joon in the hospital, come to the hospital, we are all there ... Was worried about you. We will talk later. Dad.'

Shoot ... did he know I lied? How? Had he spoken with my aunt? I was screwed, and even though this was bad to say, I was glad my situation was temporarily being ignored because of another situation. I didn't know how my father would react if he knew, but I was getting nervous! The last thing I needed in this caged country was another *cage*! I brushed the thoughts into a drawer in my brain for the time being and focused on getting to the hospital.

Then anxiety surged coldly through my nerves. This was my grandmother, my blood, the only one in the family I could potentially just let loose with and not worry about a thing. She was well traveled, kind, and protected me from my parents. At one point—the first time I'd talked to Arash, at my aunt's house—my father had evidently been calling that very line, trying to get through. He'd known I was there, and continued to call for hours, always to get a busy signal.

He'd known right then that I was there, and that I was on the phone. Or at least he'd suspected.

Then my grandmother had stepped in and told him that actually, I *had* been on the phone with her. Telling her about my night, and talking to her about some things I'd worried about. We'd talked for five hours, right through the night, she told him. She'd covered for me, and saved my butt. And I'd never forget it.

Why? Maybe she protected me because I was cute or the far-away granddaughter? My dear Aziz Joon...

Tears burned in my eyes, but I knew Iran had top-notch doctors ... at least that was the word on the street, though the medical system itself sucked.

Thank God Elham had heard her phone ringing. I felt as if my dad's note must have been on the refrigerator for hours, and immediately dialed his cell. What if something had already happened? What if I was too late?

After a few seconds, he answered and assured me all was well, and said that I ought to go by for a bit to see Aziz Joon.

"But how could this have happened? She's still very young …" I knew this was beside the point, that anyone could be hit by misfortune, but I couldn't understand how she'd fallen ill so quickly, and so seriously.

He said that she'd had a very sudden heart attack and, after calling the ambulance, had waited for an eternity for them to arrive. Then, when they finally got there, they'd taken her to the wrong hospital! I was shocked at that. This was a human life they were dealing with, but no one gave a rat's ass in that country. Even if you confronted the driver, he would have barely apologized, or said that he'd done his best. No one was responsible for their actions in a situation like that.

I hurried out of the house, jumped into Arash's Patrol—he was still outside and playing games on his phone—and we sped toward the hospital.

"Wow," he said, "what a bungle!" He seemed unsurprised that the driver may have made a mistake. "This stuff happens here, sometimes often," he said. "Liability is kinda different in third-world countries, but at least the doctors make up for it." Still, he drove as quickly as he could, seeming to know that I needed to get there as fast as I could.

I was furious, but my grandmother was alive, and for the moment that was all that mattered.

As usual, the highways were crowded, so we took side streets, only to arrive at the hospital to find the doors blocked by a motorbike dropping off its passengers.

Livid, I cried, "I don't believe this!"

Normally the bikes carry one or two riders, but I could see what resembled some stage magician's trick, a wind gust blowing up the female passenger's long *chador* to reveal four kids underneath! Not counting the male driver, it was a full-blown family. How could the bike take so much weight? Stranger still, how were those rumpled kids geometrically arranged one atop the other? A real achievement, calculating the setup and hiding it under the *chador*!

"Tell me you saw that!" I exclaimed. "It was like an optical illusion."

Arash rocked in his seat, trying not to burst into laughter. "Oh wait! There's room for one more kid."

"What?"

"Believe me, you have not seen the power of these motors and the power of that *chador*, babe!"

Babe? That was the first time he called me babe, and with a British accent. This was a relationship shock for sure. I suddenly felt closer to him than when he called me *azizam*. But now wasn't the time to fret over it. I had a grandmother in the hospital, and I had to get to her.

I jumped out of the car, telling Arash I would call him "secretly" tonight. Or maybe not, because I might have to linger with my parents at the hospital. If my dad knew I had lied, the restrictions would begin as soon as I got home.

Only time would tell.

I passed through the swishing entrance doors and headed for Aziz Joon's room. Once I found it, I stood in the doorway, peering in at the flock of people gathered around the bed. My heart sank. Now I fully understood the term 'cacophony,' because here it was. Multiple conversations in progress, plus a barrage of questions posed in various ways, with much repetition at my grandma. I pitied the woman in the other bed, who looked anesthetized, or worse. But at least she wasn't having to listen to all the babbling.

I stepped into the chaos, and waved at Aziz Joon, my mom, and Dad, if they even noticed.

"Salam, Aziz Joon," I began. I was immediately drowned out by the others.

"Didn't the doctor have his beeper on?"

"Why?"

"*Mage mishe?*" (How could this happen?)

"So, you have asthma?"

Everyone was asking questions at the same time, and I wondered how they expected her to answer them all. No one permitted her room to breathe or time to talk, and I could see from her face that she was still in semi-anesthesia mode. The whole thing sounded like a confused interrogation mixed with crazed paparazzi who'd left behind their microphones and had to shout.

I snuck closer, observing that the husband of the knocked-out lady in the other bed now sat beside my mom. He had slowly gravitated toward the action-packed side of the room, maybe to grab a pastry or be part of this chaos.

The room was filled with fresh flowers and pastries, much fingered and crumbled. I remained polite, learning that Aziz Joon was tolerating her guests. Some were family, some friends of hers, some friends of my aunt's, and the fugitive from the other bedside!

Aunt Elahe, Kamran, Ghazaleh, and Bahareh were all there, as well as some of my distant cousins, who were vacationing in Turkey and Cyprus (I had forgotten their names). They had evidently hopped on the first plane upon hearing the news. Everyone had dropped their lives and conflicts to rush to my grandmother's side, and I felt the love and warmth in that gesture. My father's family in New York were great, too, but this was a different quality of love. Sincere, trusting, and compassionate. At that moment, it lit my heart—the pure reality and joy of it.

Abruptly, though, some distant family member leaned so close to me that I was assaulted by the rancid breath, and wanted badly to reach for a potent mint. Worse, I couldn't even understand half of what the woman was saying, and I feared asking her to repeat anything because I would pass out and require hospitalization due to another reeking breath! All I did was nod politely, as if confirming whatever was being said, and quickly turn away to avoid further questions.

Finally, I made my way over to my mom. "What in the world is this?" I asked so confidently (I hoped) that I completely pushed my absence earlier in the day aside.

"Yes ... all these flowers, pastries—I haven't had a single one—and family ... although I know they should be leaving soon. Oh God, I'm getting a headache."

"I don't doubt it, but imagine what Aziz Joon is thinking!" I said, not caring if the others heard me. That was a tad bit too much for someone who was half-conscious and just had a near-death experience. I hoped they'd all go away soon and leave her to rest. She looked like she needed it.

Suddenly a nurse swept into the room, her curves enough to shut the entire male population up.

"Okay," she said, her voice half-sensual, "visiting hours are over."

Another way of saying, 'Beat it, people!' And I was glad to see them go.

Now was the time to say goodbye, which would at minimum add another ten to fifteen minutes: A round of kisses, followed by declarations of "Hope she gets better" three or four times back and forth between them, then—on the actual way out—repeating that refrain to everyone still in the room and to each other...

At Aziz Joon's side, I lightly kissed her, then smiled. I could see the reflection of her love smiling back at me, so pure. Looking in her eyes, I felt a particular beauty, and, even in a room this crowded, knew the same love and beauty thrived in everyone's heart. They were all here for her, after all, and though I thought she loved me better than most, I was glad they'd come.

Regarding her sweet, slightly troubled expression, I asked, "Do you have a dry mouth from all the explaining you did tonight?" I giggled, but knew it was difficult for her to talk. She was beat.

With a small grin, she said, "Next time, I am going to have a board displaying Frequently Asked Questions from all these laymen-citizens-turned-professors tonight!"

Seeing this animated sarcasm tugged a giggle from me, and noticed that Ghazaleh was laughing too, in the distance.

"So, what question should I ask that hasn't already been tossed at you. What do you need?"

"How about the questions the nurses ask one another while changing my serum? 'So where did you get your eye tattoo?' or 'I might highlight my hair blonde, what do you think?'"

"Ha! Glad to see you haven't lost your sense of humor." I felt even closer to her then, knowing that she could joke at such a time.

As I bent over to give her a kiss, my dad signaled that we had to go. It was time to go face the music about my absence. Stepping out, I glanced over my shoulder, and saw her eyes moist with tears, and her lips smiling at me. If she could have helped, she would have. But I thought I'd be able to handle things on my own.

I left the room, hoping my dad wouldn't bring up the day, and was also planning how I was going to call Arash. But my dad would probably stay up reading his newspaper to make sure I went to bed ... or just keep the newspaper covering his face so I would think he was awake, and behave myself.

"How was today?" he asked after I shut the car door.

"Good," I said, trying to sound neutral. I never lied to his face, and didn't know how to.

He looked at me and I knew he knew that I had lied. At that moment, the world came crashing down. I hated lying, and now I was a liar. Why? Because I had gone on a fun excursion with my friend and boyfriend! Ugh!! My father was my best guy friend, and I hated to betray his trust. It wasn't like this in Brooklyn, where I'd been able to do things with my friends, and hadn't had to find ways of doing it behind my dad's back. It was this stupid environment that forced him to be so protective, and so forced me to lie. Domino effect.

But here, he had to worry about how people would treat me, and how they would judge him, and we were both forced to follow rules we didn't like. This was one of those times when I wished I was in my bedroom in Brooklyn, rather than here having to worry about these things. I didn't want to disobey my parents. But I had to do it, if I was going to have a life.

Still, how was I going to explain that to him? Even if he understood, would he be able to get around punishing me?

"Dad..." I began, and looked at him.

Suddenly, he looked at me and cut me off, saying, "Let's talk tomorrow. Today was too long of a day. I didn't expect this from you."

Silence cut in between us, and neither of us talked all the way home. When we arrived, he brushed his teeth and went right to bed.

I had messed up, but it was my right to go out and have a good time. If my dad had been able to stand up to society, and let me do what I wanted, I wouldn't have been in trouble. Shouldn't he have been able to say that it was my life, and that he wanted me to live it the way I wanted? Shouldn't he have been protecting me, rather than following some stupid rules that neither of us believed in?

I went to bed, but though I was tired, I still knew I had to call Arash and let him know what had happened. We began our normal conversation, combined with teasing, flirting, talking about our days, and lots of sensual innuendo. I was getting good at it, thanks to Arash! He eased my fear and told me to just be truthful.

"Iranian fathers are very strict because lots of guys are scumbags," he said.

"So does that mean you are one of them too?" I asked quickly.

"Hmmm, well you do have a point," he laughed. "Don't think I'm just a good boy all the time!"

"Well I'll let you know when you are transforming to a bad boy, so you can clean up your act, pronto," I said in a sensual tone.

"Deal…"

"G-Night," I said. "With a wet kiss."

"Wet kiss back," he answered, and I closed my eyes, stepping into a dream world.

Chapter 13: The Interview

In Farsi, we have a saying: "Play, play, with the beard of the father also play." In my opinion, it meant don't pull the tiger's tail, or, in other words, don't go looking for trouble. Now I was in the hot seat at breakfast in front of my dad. Going to school in the US and living there for fifteen-plus years had not taken the traditional Iranian out of the man. I was the prisoner, about to be grilled!

"Why did you lie to me?"

"Why do you say that?"

"Don't get smart with me, Del…"

Just the fact that he used the short version of my name meant he only knew about the lying, and not Arash. So that was great, and meant I wasn't in as much trouble as I'd thought.

"Why weren't you with your aunt, and with Elham instead?"

"Because you would have opposed if I told you I was with Elham and going to a barbecue."

"Why would I oppose? If I knew this girl, her parents, and the rest of the people that were there, I would let you go. I don't want to imprison you and tell you … you can't go," he said softly. "Listen Ms. Know it All, Tehran is a dangerous place if you deal with the wrong people, and I just want you to be safe and have fun."

"Dad, I didn't know half the people at the bbq, but I knew Elham, and she is a good friend. You can't have total control over everything!"

"What if one of the people at the party would have taken advantage of you?" he said.

"Someone would have to invite that possibility. I don't hang out with rapists, Dad!" I snapped back.

"I don't want to argue, but I have to be firm. Next time, you tell me. Even if your mother doesn't know, I have to know! I want to know the exact location and people, and want to speak with Elham's parents to make sure we are both on the same page when our daughters go out!"

He looked at me and made sure he was understood by looking into my eyes. I felt a rebellious feeling coming over me, shouting, 'I will decide who is good and who is bad! I will decide if I want to go or not!' but kept my mouth shut, knowing he did have a point. But so did I.

"I will, but I also need you to trust my judgment! I can decide if I should go or not!"

"Yes, you should, beautiful, but know I am protecting you." His tone went down then and my rebellious feeling shrank and surrendered. "Guys are guys, Del Jan, and there are people of all walks of life in Tehran. I love you." And he kissed my cheek and left the kitchen for a meeting he had to go to. "Call your mother at the hospital too. She slept in Aziz Joon's room last night."

"Got it…" I said. I picked up the phone and called Arash first. This was an ideal time to speak with him in the daytime, now that Pops was heading out for a meeting!

He picked up and was surprised to hear from me, but I told him to keep near his phone, and that I'd be calling him again in a moment.

After those five seconds of talking to Arash, I called the hospital and acted like the first time I'd dialed, I'd hit the wrong number. That way—in case my dad had heard me on the phone—I had a story prepared.

My mom picked up and told me Aziz Joon was doing awesome, and that she would be home later on. That was perfect, I thought; I could talk to Arash and then slip out of the house for a 'make-up class for Italian.' Another lie. I'd been lectured by my dad not thirty minutes earlier, and already I was planning how to lie again. I knew right then that I was losing my innocence. And I didn't regret it.

It was my life, and I had the choice to decide who I was going to see, and where I wanted to go. I was the one who had to live with it. I just had to find a way to make my parents *accept* that.

When I heard the door slam and my father's car engine roar down the street, I knew opportunity knocked.

When I called, Arash picked up immediately.

"Just spoke with mom and Aziz Joon is fine," I said. "She's coming home today."

"See, I told you the doctors are the best here."

"Actually I think my grandma just got lucky. Your ambulance drivers are idiots!" I said, laughing.

The joking exchange went back and forth until the story got boring.

Arash, drained now of laughter, confessed that if something like that happened to his grandma because of a derelict ambulance driver losing his way, he would probably kill the man.

I laughed at that, realizing that I'd felt the same, and felt even more connected to him. Word on the street was that a girl must remain a virgin until marriage, but I didn't understand that, and didn't agree with it. Why couldn't a girl explore her sexual side with her boyfriend? Why did she have to save herself for—if her parents had their way—the first and last guy she ever talked to? There was nothing distasteful about getting close to your boyfriend, and as long as a girl wasn't a slut—or making porn videos!—why shouldn't she be allowed to do what she wanted, with her own body? But in our culture, even *having* a boyfriend was frowned upon! The whole sex and virginity notion had so many rules and regulations ... and I didn't think anyone really believed in it.

Wasn't that the whole point of life? To live intuitively and organically? It was terrible to think, but I was starting to believe that religion laid down the law there, and kept people from reaching God in a spiritual sense ... which should have been the main point of religion. Instead of using it for spirituality, though, the government used Islam to make rules for people about how they lived.

So my question became this: Were my parents limiting me because of this Islamic law (I'm sure my dad messed around before getting married!)? Or were they limiting me because of what my family would say if they knew I had a boyfriend? *Or* would my parents have thought it was okay if I had a boyfriend in Brooklyn, and had just changed since we moved to Iran? We left a bit too soon for me to figure the last one out! This question would remain a mystery, but my gut told me that it would have been the same story as now. Only now, I saw it more clearly because the law was actually on their side.

In the meantime, the laws in Iran were encouraging me to think outside the box, rather than inside. My rebellious side guided me to watch the sex scenes in movies, and rewind them more often, just because it was illegal. I had no intention of sleeping with Arash until I was ready, in any case, but I wanted to know that when the time came, it would be *my* choice, and not someone else's.

"By the way," Arash said. "I wanted to tell you something."

"Yes?"

"I have some inside scoop from one of my friends working in a TV station..."

"And what in the world does that have to do with me? But please do share."

"Well, there's a guy I know. A sports reporter. He told me the English section is looking for a sports intern, and you speak fluent English and are charismatic and have the time and energy now, so why not give it a shot? It sounds interesting."

I nearly fell over. "What? That is out of the blue. No way!"

"What do you mean?"

"I mean, what will they think of me? What if they do a background check?"

"And so what if they do? This is an *internship*, not a job!"

"Well, for starters I am not religious the way most newscasters on TV are here. And anyway, I would suck! I have never done that stuff before!"

I was glad that no one was home to hear me, because my voice had become louder than I intended, with excitement and shock. I could hear some fright in my tone, too. I felt a wave of energy, thinking about the internship, but was scared about what would happen if they found out I wasn't religious. I'd done a lot of things that were against the rules—what if they did a search and found out about all that? Would it all come to light?

"Again, so what? Then you would suck, but give it a try. If you get the internship you can say 'Arash said so,'" he joked, but in a serious voice.

"Always the charmer, aren't you?" I said, knowing that I was already excited and convinced. It was going to be a risk, but it was such a great opportunity that I knew I wouldn't be able to pass it up.

The background check was a worry … but hadn't I just been saying that I wanted to live for myself and make my own decisions?

"I'm just so different from the other women on the station," I said, voicing my concerns. "What if it becomes … a problem?"

TV newscasters in Iran had a specific dress code, and that didn't include Victoria Secret Angel bras or the men wearing the new J Crew look. I didn't think I would fit in even, and I knew it would mean more pretending. More lies. But I wanted to see what this new world could show me, and I'd do anything I had to.

"How am I going to fit this into my Italian class schedule?"

"Stop asking all these questions and just dive into it. If you don't get it, that means your class schedule doesn't fit into it. "

I decided to believe him. He didn't do things the way I did; I was organized and he just winged it. But he was a successful businessman, and maybe that meant he had better intuition than I did.

I agreed with his offer to connect with his friend, and move forward with the interview. But first I had to tell my parents, and hope they agreed.

*

"I am so proud of you for making this decision!" my mother

shouted.

My father had the look that read: 'This is my daughter and is

going to be famous one day.'

Which meant that I was in. But I hoped they realized that it

was just an internship.

"Yeah, so I thought since I have some time before college

classes start, I should see if this is a path I want to explore with an

internship."

"Brilliant! I know you will reach high places, beautiful!" said

my dad. "By the way, who gave you this idea?" he continued.

I blanched. I hadn't even considered *that* part of the story. So

I said the first name that came to my mind. "Elham."

"A good girl," said my dad. "Helping her friends out and

trying to help them find their way. I really like her ... so thoughtful."

Elham was scoring points and getting credit on behalf of

Arash, but I had no problem with that since it kept me out of hot

water and meant that I could see her more often. More Elham credit meant more Arash time too, since I could use her existence to go out on dates with him. My God ... one simple lie was making a monster out of me!

A couple of positive things came out of this, though. My parents thought I had already become a celebrity in my not-yet-determined internship status, and Elham received the gold star from my parents. Both of which meant more freedom for me. If I could get the internship, it would mean even more latitude for my adventures.

*

I had no idea what to wear, was a bit nervous, and had no idea how my prospective internship supervisor would view me. After all, this was the country's national broadcast agency, and it was federal. No one could be more likely to be strict about my hair showing, brows trimmed to perfection, or an inappropriate smile than their fully loaded Islamic black-*burka*-wearing crow sister department, otherwise known as the HR office. I was just going to have to look and act the way I felt I should, and leave the rest up to fate.

323

After getting my attire on, I ventured out.

I cabbed it up Vali-Asr Street, the longest in Tehran. The heat was terribly oppressive, but the driver refused to switch on the AC, and my *wimple*, formally arranged and tied, stuck tight to my head. God, how could women work like this? I had an important internship interview, and all I could think of was how uncomfortable my clothes were!

Finally, the cab driver said, "I will turn the AC on, but the fare will be doubled."

Is this guy out of his mind? The AC was part of the car, right? I could smell him sweating, so I knew he was suffering too, and probably praying that I'd ask for the AC. And in this heat, with this traffic, I was going to do just that. I would have paid triple.

On arrival (grateful to soon be out of the reeking, hot cab), I took a quick look in the mirror to make sure that even the roots of my hair were covered.

Picking up on my nervous fussing, the driver said, "They are not that bad. Don't worry. They are human, after all…"

I managed a flash of a smile and answered softly, "*Merci.*"

The driver wasn't a bad guy after all, and I brushed away my previous negative thoughts about him. But he would probably run the AC until getting another passenger, and then make *them* pay extra to have it. That was just the way of the cab drivers there.

I paid the double charge and climbed out, anxious to get into my interview.

*

At the main entrance, the security check took forty-five minutes: fifteen to confirm I was registered, and then the next thirty to do a top-notch security interview to make sure I was who I said I was.

After stepping slowly through the scanner, I was subjected to a body search by—of course—the dreaded black crows. Although they didn't find any guns, ammo, or swords in my bag, they did find an old mascara and lipstick.

"What are these?" demanded one black crow.

Why do you care? was my initial answer, but I quickly swallowed and replied, "A mascara, and lipstick."

"Why do you have it in your bag, *Khanoom*?"

325

In this case, *Khanoon* was an annoying way of saying *Miss*, and it reeked of a lack of respect.

Um, because I am a mature female and might need it, I thought, but dared not say. "No reason... it was left in my bag." I used a low tone, hoping to sound very low key, as if it really didn't matter

"These items will stay with us, as this is not a makeup-driven environment," one said with a fierce, dark glare.

"Okay."

I wondered suddenly if these women had ever rebelled, or missed male attention. Had they ever had fun in their entire lives? What made them want to work in this sort of job, anyhow?

They urged me through security before I could say anything else, and I was on my way, leaving them and their sad lives behind.

I couldn't help my genuine curiosity about them. Did the crows ever make love? Or feel cool seawater caress their toes? Smile at the sunset, or have a glass of wine under the stars with the man who pleased them? How did they make love? With sheets in between their legs? Obviously they were open with and supported one another, enjoyed each other's company ... but I sensed that they had also been caged. Or maybe it was due to poor education or simple lack of social awareness, and they'd never learned that there could be more out there.

I put that away, though, and tried to prepare for the interview. How hard could it be? I decided it was best to remain calm and centered, listen, and not rebel against the interviewer in the event of disagreement, which was my usual route. I wanted this internship, and the experiences it offered, which meant I had to play nice. For now.

Striding through the building, I found it surprisingly well designed, even tasteful, unlike some other government or city buildings, with their bland colors and anonymous, often dehumanizing interiors. The place hummed with quiet efficiency; subdued conversations, various clutches of workers drinking tea (the coffee equivalent in Iran), running back and forth with tapes, and a few four-by-four patrols prepping for shoots. All regular stuff you would see in any TV studio, except that some women wore *burkas* and others long black *chadors* in addition to *burkas* and *mantos*. I wondered how they survived, even with constant air conditioning.

A few stood outside smoking cigarettes. Normal stuff. Nothing to be afraid of. So far.

A flight of stairs led me to the International English section besides the Sports unit. I knew the people in Sports were considered the cool sorts, laid back, and it appeared to be true. And all the guys were hot! I approached and they glanced up from work with surprise on their faces. Even my formal attire couldn't hide the sparkle in my eyes. Here was a chance for them to flirt with me, step over their regular borders, as if we were all ready to grab a drink and drop some coins in a jukebox.

Either it was my effect, or these men were feeling similar to Alcatraz prisoners!

One man stood, beaming a smile and obvious interest. "Can we help you?"

I halted. "Yes. Where is the English sector? I am here for an internship interview." I hoped that sounded as delicate as intended.

Did women in this department even talk? Later, I discovered they do, but without much eye contact.

"Please, sit here." He indicated a chair. "Let me grab the individual who can help you better. I believe this is the first time they are running an internship."

He smiled with such a courteous and charming face, and his voice so sensual and noble, that I immediately liked him.

I sat, and from my comfy seat I saw that the office equipment appeared new, the furniture modern and high quality. Some of the guys still gazed at me hungrily, and I thought that they needed more young girls in the office, to balance the employees and keep the guys happier.

At the sound of footsteps, I turned. And here stood my interviewer, smiling as though at a familiar face. He greeted me quietly, and led me to a space not too far away.

The dialogue began in Farsi, and transformed slowly into English. I maintained an even, candid line: No, I had not done any journalism or reporting; nor conducted interviews using these methods, and on top of that my major in college was Italian

Literature! The only plus I had going for me was my fluent English, with no Farsi accent. I spoke and knew very good English, and that could help the reporters in correspondence and communications.

Honestly, in English, I thought I could be hired as their replacement! But that was another topic.

The interview was short and flowed smoothly, yet oddly did not include the usual questions: Does this qualify for college credit? What do you plan on pursuing in the coming years? He didn't even describe the internship. He ended with: "You come from the US and would be a great help to the staff. The rules here might be different from what you are adapted to, and this is also the first time we are running an internship. The people are okay here, just keep up with the team and don't talk a lot. The head director is educated and brought up in the US. He's full Iranian though, and is buddies with the Islamic HR head, so you don't have to worry about much!" He smiled toward the end, as if he was telling me that in this section, everyone was more relaxed than they were outside.

What a mouthful.

We stood, and the interviewer added that someone would contact me if I should get the internship—almost as an afterthought. In fact, this sentence was the only part resembling a well-rounded interview.

I thanked the man for the opportunity, but reminded myself not to shake his hand. Just say good-bye. On my way out, I noticed that the room was full of applicants wearing heavy-duty *burkas* and *chadors*, with a few girls sporting full-blown moustaches and leafy eyebrows. They were all in line for the interview.

I thanked the guys that had helped me, and they bid me goodbye with a please-stay-longer-we-need-estrogen-in-the station look.

I couldn't help but giggle.

It occurred to me that, had I been stuck into the box of 'applicants,' it would have meant a big, bold, red 'no.' But I'd been different from the start, even in how I arrived, and it had shown in my attitude and demeanor. I wasn't as fearful as the other girls. In other words, I didn't give a shit if I didn't get the internship, and it had shown. Plus I'd come with a personal recommendation that I didn't think anyone else had had.

In short, I'd stood out, and I thought the position was probably mine.

So now, I had to find a phone. I asked the sport guy if I could make a phone call. He showed me the closest phone and whispered very softly, while looking in a completely different direction, "The phone lines are all controlled." Then, assuming a different tone, as if he was saying what he was saying from the beginning, "Dial One, and then your number."

Immediately, I understood what he meant: The phone lines were watched. This didn't surprise me; I expected that they had personnel cameras recording everything as well. People were watching our every move, and storing the information for HR, in case they ever needed it.

Plucking the phone from its rest, I dialed Arash's number and, when he answered, said, "Hi, Dad. Could you please come and pick me up? Yes. The interview is over."

Surprised, Arash didn't immediately grasp that this was role-play, but must have caught on, because he chuckled.

He cleared his throat. "Yes, *dokhtaram, hatman*." *Yes, daughter dearest, coming.* He choked back laughter.

"*Merci*," I said, trying to keep my own laughter inside. Actually, everyone was trying to keep it inside, because they read between the lines. They were all around my age or a bit older, with the same outlook and frame of mind. They looked charming, naughty, and fun. But they all had a difference with me: They were making money and needed their jobs. They couldn't afford to acknowledge what I was doing, in case they got in trouble.

They had to earn, and had metaphorically sold their souls to the company to get and keep their jobs. Act stupid, eyes locked onto the computer screen. Keep your comments to yourself ... it was just like working in any other large company across the globe.

Then an alarming thought popped into my mind: Where the hell were we supposed to meet? No! I couldn't believe neither of us had mentioned it! We got caught up in the role-play charade, and forgot about the particulars!

A rendezvous in front of the TV studio couldn't happen. There were cameras all over and this kind of relationship was illegal.

Suddenly lightning struck, and I knew what I had to do. I darted out of the station, my mind racing.

*

The restaurant where we habitually met was—fortunately—close by. I decided to just wing it, hoping that he was smart enough to figure it out when he couldn't find me.

And then the waiting began.

I ordered my favorite mini-pizza: the *makhloot*. Far from your normal Italian pizza, this Iranian-created mutant smorgasbord came topped with sausage, bologna (*Halal*-type, since this was the Islamic Republic), bell peppers, onions, mushrooms, corn, and—if desired—practically any other vegetable, organic and otherwise. The toppings were so densely applied that they overloaded the crust, which seesawed when picked up! The whole thing was probably worse for you than any traditional Brooklyn slice.

I loved it!

I hoped Arash took long enough for me to finish my pizza. I didn't exactly want to share it.

Chapter 14: Hired

After about forty minutes of waiting and munching, I heard a voice behind me. "I knew you would be here!" Arash grinned and blew a kiss from afar, savored the warm aromas of meat and cheese. He stepped closer, and halted at the table. "How was the interview?"

Trying to handle the loaded pizza, I said, "I have no idea! It was not as frightening as I had imagined ... the people were just normal."

He observed my obvious enjoyment of the meal, and gave a wise-guy smile. "They accepted you."

"What?"

"You heard me. And by the way, *tarof nakoni han!*"

It was just like him to joke around by invoking the Iranian system of sharing-but-not-really-wanting-to share. I knew he must have talked to his friend (and the main connection), and now he was the oil greasing the wheels of business in Iran.

I nearly choked. "Are you serious?"

He nodded. "Your first internship, with the Islamic Republic of Iran Broadcasting."

I pushed back into the chair, as if moved by the power of the words themselves. It was so surprising that just because I spoke fluent English they had hired me. I wasn't even in college yet, and there was no such thing as college credit, either, even if I was studying Broadcast Journalism! The disconnect left my jaw hanging!

I was scared, excited, and wanted to jump across the table, grab Arash, kiss him, and loudly give thanks to the Lord. It was just an internship, but the fact that they had accepted me as opposed to all the other girls—who were dressed more religiously—baffled me.

He stared at me, his eyes adoring, and I started to blush at the attention.

"You made all of this happen. Such a big shift, and a new experience. Exciting, and frightening at the same time. I mean, I am a gal that doesn't even know what she wants … the only thing I knew I wanted was to become a choreographer!" I said, giggling. "Then studying Italian Literature to get the folks off my back, and now interning in Channel 6 in Tehran, Iran! This life is a roller coaster!" I continued. "But you will be rewarded according to what you have done, dear knight!" I said this in English because it sounded weird in Farsi.

"What? I love rewards!" he said with sincere charm.

"Rewards are always better when brought to life, rather than stated with words." Flirtation changed my voice and brought me to more giggles. I knew I was rambling and being silly, but with the good news fresh in my mind, I didn't care. Through Arash's efforts I had secured a high-profile position, and I wasn't even nineteen yet!

I still couldn't believe it was real. "Do they pay anything, do you think?"

"Who cares? This may open up some career path doors, since you have no idea where you are headed!" He said this laughing, and I agreed.

Arash sat down for a slice of pizza, and joined the fun. He was supposed to be working, but wanted to share the good news and spend some time with me. He was surprised I had called him from the TV studio, where he knew everything was monitored, and I realized right then that something very deep was developing between us.

The question was, how far would we go?

*

My world had suddenly changed. I'd gone from a girl who was new to the country and had no direction to be an intern with a news station, who was going to Italian classes and conducting a secret relationship.

I felt like I was cracking, the layers of my soul ripening while I dove into an ocean of change and its shock wave. I felt like I was walking around in shock, unable to take it all in, but enjoying every second of it.

My agenda was booked with classes some mornings, and this internship from 2 to 6 in the evenings. Arash picked me up from class, we had our lunch date, and then he dropped me off a block from the IRIB station. A block away prevented anyone on the block from seeing me ... and anyone who saw me on the block while I was being dropped off was written off as my bad luck.

The internship was fun and awkward at the same time. I was the Sport anchor/reporter's intern. In Iran, the Sport section was primarily male dominated. The country was mostly male, and that was particularly true when it came to sports. Women weren't even allowed to go into the stadiums to *watch* sports. This included interns, reporters, and any other person with estrogen!

I couldn't believe that when I heard it. Rumor had it that some women protested and others snuck into the stadium, dressed up as guys with fake moustaches. If the game was going on, I preferred the latter, so that I didn't have to worry about getting caught. And as an intern in the Sport section, I absolutely intended to go to the games.

Brushing that aside, I got along well with my supervisor and made friends with the camera guy, microphone guy, and driver, and realized they were just regular people living an irregular lifestyle. Irregular, because their public display differed from what occurred behind closed doors. They weren't what they appeared. They were

Muslim, yes, but the kind who conversed with women and looked them in the eyes, and—of course—worked with them. For the first time, I was interacting with men other than my family, and finding out that I'd been right—not everyone believed in the system. Most people just tolerated it when they had to.

The guys were cool and we laughed with each other, but they showed respect and knew their boundaries. The two worlds of Sports and English fused for this little intern, despite some parts that made it difficult. Overall, it was an eye-opening experience as far as culture! Living as a civilian was one thing, but working alongside federal employees in a federal atmosphere was a dive into the deep end.

Even the ultra-religious people turned out to be okay. They had some of the best jokes in the bunch!

But the place had cameras, and the controlled telephones were sure to catch everything. Everyone was careful not to say anything about the government, and the men were very careful of how they interacted with the women. No dating permitted on site!

I kept to myself and interacted with my group and the Farsi Sports group, where I felt more accepted than other places. My responsibilities were lame, for the most part, and consisted of logging tapes and taking this tape from this department to the other as a delivery girl. But sometimes I tagged along with the male reporter when he wanted to get an interview outside of a stadium with a badminton player, chess wizard, or weightlifter. If they needed an English-speaking accomplice, they grabbed me for translations.

I noticed that football in Iran was a second religion, and one practiced by the entire populace. Maradona, Ronaldo, and Luis Figo were worshipped there, their faces splashed across newspapers. Local footballers had their own following, and were treated like rock stars. Girls—not me—were crazy for them, though they were forbidden to express it, and guys went out of their way to welcome the footballers into their homes.

Football was more popular than the Super Bowl, World Series, and NBA playoffs combined. FIFA and the World Cup were followed to the bone, and when word spread that Iran might be entering the Cup if they eliminated Australia, the whole country blocked out their schedule for that time-slot. They actually reserved the entire weekend for football worship.

Sometimes during the evening I saw kids playing football in back alleys or on the streets. They improvised goals and nets with round stones, and kicked around a red and white striped ball purchased for 5 cents from any grocery store. The only difference between street, no-rules football and the professional game was the amazing passion these kids had. Wearing homemade jerseys in red or blue representing favorite footballers, they mimicked whatever worked to score. In Tehran, you either had blue blood or red—colors of the national team—or you weren't part of the club. Period. Many people even bonded with their team color, perhaps leading to long-lasting relationships! Either you sang the anthem, "Blue is color of the sky" or "Red is the color of blood," and "It's the color of the flag," or you were no fun. Either you were a Pirouzi (red) or an Esteghlal (blue) fan—two archrivals.

In fact, when there was a match announcement, people left work early and—if necessary— bought black-market tickets. Some traveled from far provinces, pitched tents outside the stadium, or simply slept in their cars to wake into a dream come true. A dream pointing toward a "bloody victory" or a "sky blue victory." During these games the city appeared dead, as though it was the location for some apocalyptic science-fiction film. Considering the density of Tehran's traffic, this was a complete miracle! But some fans seemed more interested in the before and after of the game than the main dish itself. Some wagered, though betting was forbidden. These bets usually involved nothing more than food or something equally common, rather than *hoopas* of *mullah*.

In other words, I found that football was the body and soul of these people, and the people projected onto players and the game all of their will, love, passion, sadness, loss, and hope ... more and more hope, and lots of sweat and blaring horns. I'd never realized this, but my position with the station made me start to see the society—and its people—in a whole new light.

*

344

Then the day arrived, with Iran two victories away from their first World Cup qualification game, and facing Australia. The game would be held in Azadi Stadium in Tehran.

All the men were prepared to go to the stadium or climb its walls if necessary, and all the women would have their homes and meals prepared in advance of the game. Housewives put aside chores, knowing the men would not even notice. The game was more important than the Royal Wedding, or the inauguration of the first female (assuming one day there will be one!) president.

And this intern was ready to tag along with one of the reporters for support, no matter how many tapes I had to take from one building to another! I really wanted to get into the venue.

Although Azadi Stadium seated 100,000 and was considered the fourth-largest football arena in the world, it had no room for females. I still didn't understand the reason for this harsh ban. Excessive hormonal cursing? Or maybe the men lost control after seeing a goal and desperately needed to kiss someone? It seemed to me that it was a punishment for women, with no logical motivation. It was even meaner than most of the rules. I thought long and hard, and all I could come up with was to wear a hat and speak in a thick voice. If I was lucky, maybe I'd pass for a man.

A classmate had actually done this and gotten away with it.

Obviously she had no boobs, and after cutting her long braids and splashing on men's cologne, she thickened her voice, assumed a hard, tired expression, and dazzled her way in. She claimed that everyone had been fooled, but I wondered myself if the men had simply not cared enough to stop her. Perhaps they understood that it was an unfair rule, too.

"Some girls really work their mind and do the craziest stuff," I told my dad—a football fanatic who always tried to make it to the stadium with Kamran. Kamran would get the tickets and off they went in their red Piroozi jerseys.

Kamran gave me this sole piece of advice: "Stop plucking your eyebrows for a month or two, and then you won't even need to thicken your voice!"

It was true, though it was also cruel; some girls were hairy, and without the tweezers, no one would have been able to tell the difference between them and a man.

346

I really wanted to get in, but even when I went to the station with a plan, and without makeup, the reporter refused. He said there was no point—they would find out and he would get in trouble. He was right, but I wanted in. Unfortunately I didn't have a route; not even my American passport was going to get me in.

And no one was going to help me. So I decided to take matters into my own hands.

I called Arash to let him know, and he harshly opposed the idea. "What? You will be walking into a rough, tough, mean, dirty, spitting-machine of a crowd!"

"Can't be that bad. I mean, I always went to Madison Square Garden, and it was all right."

"You wouldn't last an hour. That is how rough it can get."

"I am going." I couldn't be firmer on the matter, and I wasn't going to let him talk me out of it.

I knew that he knew I wouldn't back down, though, and at last he agreed to at least pick me up and provide a higher view, a clearer perspective, before I drifted off into something I thought of as a dream.

This was how he approached it. "Can I go with you?"

"Are you trying to convince me not to go?"

"Yes, but I won't win, so let me come and drive you there. Please."

Since we both knew how stubborn we both were, I agreed. Anyway, I was a little bit scared it could be dangerous.

Soon we were on our way to west Tehran, toward Azadi Stadium.

*

The streets and entire area surrounding the stadium thrummed with crowds and vehicles. I couldn't see any women—not even the black crows—and felt weird and awkward being the only one. But I was excited to be at such a historic event, and knew that I was following my own heart.

I glanced at Arash. "How can we get in? Any ideas?"

"Umm ... you can't. This place is only for testosterones, so you, *azizam*, are a black sheep in this particular family. And by the way, you already know that."

"So this is how you were going to take me?" I asked, pretending to be upset and curious.

"I asked if I could drive you, not take you into the game," he said with a grin. He fixed me with a stern gaze. "You don't understand how heavily it is banned. Meaning not allowed, against the law, illegal!"

What more could he say? Either I was willfully ignorant, or simply *wouldn't* understand. He had driven me here so I could see the testosterones alongside *him*! Not to help me.

Buses nearing the stadium brimmed with extreme fans, horns blaring at clumsy drivers or simply because they could. Arash shuddered, imagining what would happen had I taken a bus to the game. Not only would I have suffered isolation, but a barrage of insults on the order of "I want you!" "You are mine tonight" "Hey, how much do you charge?" or "Do you accept coupons?" There would be no limit to the depth of disrespect and awkwardness. So it had been—would be—for years.

"So I'm not even allowed inside?" I asked, frustrated. "Then why do they have sport interns? What's my purpose? Why did they give the job to me when I'm not going to be allowed to do it?" My temper was getting the best of me now, particularly with Arash refusing to help me. I'd counted on him to help me bend the rules a little, and instead he was coming down on the side of the government!

"To help them out with other stuff. You are *learning*. Now you know you can't go inside a stadium!" he said, chuckling.

I glared at him. "Am I to try and understand—logically—the backwards rules you're trying to make me understand?"

"To a logical backward comprehension, check," he said, smiling broadly, and gripped my hand.

I laughed, favored him with a smile. If I wasn't going to get my way at the stadium, maybe I'd be able to get it somewhere else. "Aha ... I need a drink, but that would be banned and backward? No? Does that count?"

He absorbed the words with relish. "How about you come over to my place, we order some wine—from the illegal guy—and watch the game at home?"

I felt a rush of excitement; I wanted to be with him, though I knew the risks of going to his house on my own. The emperor knew I was at my internship and, with the game starting, was undoubtedly distracted ... although it didn't take much for me to be caught on his radar, since he'd discovered me lying.

Still, this could be my first time going to Arash's house.

"Okay," I said, not knowing what to expect. We were going to be alone. All alone ... for the first time.

No Bahareh, no Elham. The football game was the third wheel this time! No one would even think about looking for a boy and girl, alone, in a black Patrol, cruising the streets.

I wondered how it would be, how he would be ... I trusted him, of course, and knew he wouldn't hurt me. But was I really willing to lose my virginity—that highly prized and important thing—for this man?

Was I ready to take that step? It would mean choosing an entirely different life.

But this was simply another piece added to the fun jigsaw puzzle of my life.

We parked in the garage, climbed out of the Patrol, and headed up as if we were married or something, talking and teasing each other all the way up the elevator. When we arrived, I saw that Arash's apartment was well designed and decorated, telling me a lot about his likes and character.

"My humble home," he said, grinning.

I scanned the place. There was a definite sense of atmosphere and feeling, clearly arranged by an organized mind with an understanding of fine art beyond—traits usually not found in one man.

Arash noticed my interest. "I collect most of the art on business trips, and must pay a hefty tax just to bring them into the country. A crime, that tax—it should go to the artist, not the government."

I agreed completely. Some fine pieces here, which were definitely out of the reach of most people living in Iran, with its ever-worsening economy.

Arash stepped closer. "Do you want to shower?"

What in the world did *that* mean? Was he showing me his perverted side or London side?

Enough ... I trusted him. I wanted to prove that he wasn't like the other guys, who took advantage of girls and forced them to do things they didn't want. I wanted to prove that *I* was different.

"What does that mean?" I asked with attitude.

Quick and calm, he replied, "Relax. It's hot, and I thought you might want to shower after taking off that *wimple* and *manto*."

The attitude stayed. "Well, why don't you turn the AC on?"

"It is on, but will take a while to cool this place. Relax, I didn't mean anything by it!" He gave the space a noncommittal wave, as if saying 'Look how big it is ... it'll take a few minutes to cool!'

Then he shrugged. "Do you want *sharbat* instead of wine? The illegal guy is probably watching the game, too, so we'll save him the trouble of coming over during this football frenzy!"

"Yes, please ... that works better. It's so hot! And I am *not* taking a shower my first time in your place!" I said this with a laugh, to show him that I was joking, and not upset.

He laughed and handed me a cool, fruity drink. It was just the ticket, as well as a symbol of Arash's hospitality. After he prepared the drinks, we crashed on the couch to watch some action-packed football, and bask in the low hum of air conditioning.

"How are you liking the internship?" he asked.

"It has its ups and downs, but I like reporting. Maybe reporting will be my path?"

"As a career?"

"Yup!"

"It's difficult for a female to have a sports reporter career here. But we do have female reporters ... it's definitely there."

"Hmmm, I don't know. Sometimes I wish I could take off to New York again, where I didn't have to deal with all this discrimination. It really irritates me to have to live with these restrictions, and I don't say that because I am a feminist!"

"For you it's odd, but people who live here are used to it. They protest here and there, but the day I see change is the day I see you put aside your stubbornness!" he said, laughing.

"Hey! You need a slap!"

"I'm all cheeks, babe!"

I slapped him softly and kissed him with finesse to make up for it.

Just then, Iran tied with Australia, and the crowd stood roaring. "Listen," I shouted, interrupting our kiss.

We could hear scattered shouts and jeers and comments through the floor, through windows, and even from the streets below, yelling for the player who'd just scored the goal.

Arash laughed. "Everyone has magically transformed into a sports announcer and patriotic follower, because of this game. But no one can say it better than you..." He ignored the noise and pulled me into his arms.

Instead of kissing him again, though, I jumped up and started yelling myself, getting into the spirit. People could have heard me— and I thought about that for a split second—but as long as it wasn't my dad, I didn't care. I wanted to feel like I was part of the society, feel like I was one of the people, if only for a moment.

"Maybe there should be many games like this!" I said, downing my sour cherry *sharbat*. "We could hang out and make out more often!"

"*If* we could make it this far," he said softly.

I leaned back and looked into his charming but mischievous eyes, feeling safe and happy. I knew what he meant: It had taken a very specific set of circumstances for us to get here today, and we couldn't count on that happening again. But he didn't make another move toward foreplay, and I appreciated that.

He looked back and said, "I know what's in your head, but it's all good. I enjoy our time together, but want to be with you when the time is right."

What did he mean? Marriage? I wasn't even thinking about marriage! "You mean having sex?"

Did I say that cautiously enough?

He narrowed his eyes, trying to figure this tangled web. "Yes. It's taboo in Iran to have sex before you get married ... but I think you should have sex when you are ready. All this is bullshit regarding the girl being a virgin until she says 'yes!'" He took a long drink. "It's a nice border where love and sex meet ... that's where I want to meet you." His direct gaze pierced my defenses.

I felt he really had feelings for me, although at that point I wouldn't call it love ... yet. I didn't know how he felt about me, and realized suddenly that he was as much of a mystery as the rest of the country. And I chose—for the time being—to be in this mystery with him.

"I don't know," I said, voice trembling, "when, or if, I can meet you there..."

"Don't worry. Whatever will happen will happen. I just want you to be comfortable and know that, whenever the time comes, *we* will know. It's a bit weird how they think about this in Iran, because everyone tries to be someone they are not, or act one way in front of their families and another with friends. You are lucky to have Elham and Bahareh, who you can be honest with. But about us ... let's just be, and..." He hesitated. "You don't have to be afraid about this—" He pointed at his penis. "It is well behaved," he joked.

My mind swirled with thoughts. I looked at him with deep regard. "I have so many questions about this, and don't know how to discover the answer without being judged by everyone else." My mouth twisted with frustration.

"Yup. But let's make it simple. If you are ready and when you are ready you will know, right?"

"I have no idea. I hope so," I said, giggling.

"You will, beautiful. Just buzz me when you do, and I'll take the next jet out!"

I laughed, and that ended the sex conversation. There was so much I didn't understand, and I'd told him the truth—there was no way for me to get any education about it in this country, where it was against the law. So I really didn't know what I wanted, or how to make that decision.

For the moment, it was enough to know that he understood, and that he'd be patient with me while I tried to figure out my place in this new world.

*

Iran ended up in a draw with Australia—a big thing, because Iran was now only one win away from the FIFA World Cup in France.

This also meant smiles, free pastries in the streets, and even free cab rides! The whole country partied like rock stars. They had yet to be *in* the World Cup games, but a party at this stage of the competition was inevitable. Thousands of people filled the streets with music and dance. The girls wore colorful scarves, and looked hot even without makeup! It was a movie screening for me from the window.

"Can we go out?" I asked in a begging tone.

"They get too crazy," Arash said. "And the police will eventually break it up. The black crows might be bussed in to crow them away." He laughed harshly.

We stood together, agreeing that some of the dances were good enough to be made into music videos. A few brave girls danced in their own risqué styles, some as it entranced, waving flags and scarves. Horns blared and beeped from an army of various vehicles, most creeping along to avoid pedestrians and shouting along with them, "Iran! Iran!"

"It's like they all died and went to heaven! It's samba time!"

The yeasty, hot aroma of pastries drifted into the window. A cluster of people cried: "Here we come France, watch out Iran is coming. Iran is flying. The Aladdin carpet is moving!"

Here was a powerful national unity ... here was hope. All through the streets and in every home...

The naked reality of this, its very sound and smell, had my eyes brimming with tears. I felt full of life, and as if I actually belonged there. I'd never seen this sort of emotion because of a simple win in a sport, and realized that I was feeling the national spirit—the one thing that everyone could publicly cheer for. These people pulsed and shouted and danced with life itself, and the game gifted them with an outlet for its expression.

I faced Arash, proud to be an Iranian, and he bent down and pressed his warm lips to mine.

One moment in all of time ... one I would never forget, with my people, my first boyfriend, and the passion bonding us together.

Chapter 15: *Nazri*

Days passed and I was having fun with the internship, Elham, Arash, the cousins, and the little get-togethers at my house with Neda and Saloomeh from Tatbighi. I missed Mina, Azin, and Nooshin because they were primarily traveling. Mina was mostly in Canada, where her father was finishing up their immigration work to eventually move there. Azin was in California visiting relatives before her college in Iran started, and Nooshin was in DC visiting her own relatives.

One day I woke up to loud, religious-type music coming from the street. What in the world was this? Another football scene? Couldn't be another revolution, or bombs would be coming in from the window! I knew it was a national holiday because I didn't have classes, and hadn't had to go to my internship.

Climbing out of bed, I padded to the window. What was that?

Below me, the wide street hosted a sea of black. Men wearing black-collared or simple shirts, struggling with some heavy iron object on their shoulders. A water guy stood on a corner, dispensing water in plastic cups (apparently for free) for the sweating participants, who were getting a cardio workout.

I could see more water stations spread along the street, and the music grew louder. It was like a parade, but religious. I could see Arabic script on the cloth covering the metal object that the men carried, and behind it marched many other men, stretching back at least five or six blocks.

These men behind would run up to the metal object when they were needed, to take it from one of the carriers. These carriers seemed to run out of steam abruptly, as if they just couldn't handle it anymore, and another would come in to take their place.

The men closest to the front line—but still not carrying the metal object—were flogging themselves to the point that some of them had bloody backs.

Of course there were no women involved in the parade. Not that a woman would have been able to carry whatever it was they were carrying. But there were some pretty hot girls pacing the men in their struggling shuffle. They wore full-blown makeup and what appeared to be new *mantos* and scarves, as if ready for a nice dinner party or simply lounging somewhere.

I had no idea what this all meant, but was anxious to find out. They had camels and sheep down there, and more water-guys taking care of them. Nothing made sense!

I wanted to go out, but what should I wear? Regular clothing? Or should I get dressed up like the women in the parade?

Easter and Rosh Hashanah weren't this extreme ... or maybe I wasn't used to this. The only religious Muslim holiday I knew of was *Ramadan-finoto*, the holy month of fasting, but I doubted they marched in the streets for that!

The emperor told me we were going over to my Aunt Elahe's for lunch, to meet all the cousins and get lunch from outside. I quickly got dressed in regular Delkash clothes, ignoring what was going on outside, and headed for the car, where my parents were waiting for me.

Some of the main streets were blocked off for the march, but I wanted to observe and absorb it more before I asked anyone what it was. I could see my dad looking at me through his mirror, waiting for me to bombard him with questions, and my mom gave me a look or two to make sure I was still alive. She must have been shocked that I wasn't already exploding with ideas and thoughts.

They didn't realize that I'd grown up enough to try to come to my own conclusions first, and ask questions second.

"This event should be respected," my dad said suddenly, turning the music low.

Respect, I agreed with. But I struggled against the contradiction of people living in two worlds. I would travel a long road before fully understanding this country I was born into, despite its differences.

"But what is it?" I asked, confused. "Why are the women dressed that way? Why are the men whipping themselves?"

"This is called *Ashura*, and the day after is called *Tasua*. The Muslims are mourning a tragedy by holding special ceremonies in different cities, and public venues like mosques offer food to the people," he said, looking at me like he expected me to freak out, though I couldn't understand why.

"What's up with all the chicks? And those guys?"

"That's trouble! They want to find a hot date, but that is nothing relevant to the mourning!" my mom snapped.

"They mourn the martyrdom of Imam Hussein, the third Imam," continued my dad.

"Okay, got it. But this is a brutal way of doing it, isn't it?" I asked. I decided to skip the idea that those girls were just looking for dates—asking about that was just going to get me in trouble.

"Everyone has a way ... this is Iran's way, as we are primarily Muslim Shiites," he replied.

"So this is all to remember him and commemorate him?"

"Yup..."

"So they are suffering because he suffered ... reenacting his pain?"

"Yup ... you are getting there!" he said, chuckling.

Personally, I felt no connection with Islam and this whole commemoration. It didn't make me feel good. Christmas made me feel good, but that was like comparing apples and oranges, and it was a complete different faith. But the cool thing was that they were so passionate about doing this, and even the girls were into it, in their own way.

I came back to reality to hear the brakes and find the car parked in front of my aunt's.

"We are here already?"

We got out of the car, and walked up the front door. Inside, I saw Bahareh, Ghazaleh, and Kamran. The girls were fully dressed in *mantos* and scarves and ready to walk out the door, carrying big pots. They weren't wearing their everyday stuff, but short, stylish, fancy *mantos* and scarves. The house held an aroma of mouth-watering food, but only a large bowl of salad was on the table. Nothing was cooking. Why did we have pots if we were getting lunch from outside?

Makeup-free, I stood outside, the pure sunshine beaming through the window and illuminating the exotic, natural beauty of my cousins. Then I realized that the 'trouble' my mother had talked about was going to include my cousins, and me, by association!

Bahareh said, "C'mon Delkash. We are going to get the *Nazris.*"

"*Nazris?*"

"Yes, c'mon. We'll explain in the car."

"Is that a Farsi word?"

"Just get in, we'll do the explaining in the car. Want to get rid of the folks so we have lots of time for ourselves!"

She wasn't going to wait, so I started walking. There was no need to explain to our parents where we were headed or what time we would be home, evidently, so they got a simple "*Khoda hafez*"—goodbye—and we vanished.

I jumped into the car, where my cousins sat applying makeup before turning on the engine.

Still confused, I asked, "Okay, where are we going?"

"We are going to a *Hossein* Party!" said Bahareh.

"Is that where Kamran went?" I asked, noticing that my cousin had already departed.

"Girl, I have no idea where he went. Probably to meet his girlfriend and pick up *Nazri* on the way. We are getting *Nazri* too, but in the *Hossein* Party," said Ghazaleh, gently applying her eye shadow.

"Soooo … what do *Nazri* and *Hossein* Party mean? I thought this was mourning, for crying out loud!"

Ghazaleh couldn't have been more animated. "Today is *Ashura* and tomorrow is *Tasua*. All the hot guys are out and we—the hot girls—are going to check them out, and the rest … *khoda midoone!*" Only God knows. "It doesn't matter that the hotties in the march aren't aware of it ... even they are sizzling."

"That is sick! Sizzling while bleeding. You guys have issues!" I replied.

"Chill out, Del, let me give you the low down. One, this is a religious ceremony to remember the third Shia Imam. Two, all the *sharbats*, chains, and music you hear are part of *Ashura* and how the memory of the Imam is mourned. Three, *Nazri* is free food the mosques and some people give out," said Ghazaleh. "You got that part?"

I nodded, but was interrupted before I could answer.

"Next is what people do because we live in a restricted country. The girls and guys looking hot is not in any way related to this event, but since we don't have public clubs or bars, we find ways to have fun. We use these events for that. And we know it might seem irrelevant and rude, but whatever. The whole girls and guys gathering makes it a *Hossein* Party. Hossein was the name of the third Imam. Got it? That's the whole scoop!" she said.

Bahareh cut in at that point. "Oh, she forgot, *Nazri* is the most delicious food you can eat. It's the same dish your mom might make or the restaurants might serve, but it tastes soooo good on this day!"

I frowned. "Alright now you are superstitious! Because it is cooked on this day, suddenly it has just the right amount of salt and pepper?"

"No seriously woman, I don't know what it is, but it's better. They are called *Hossein gheymehs,*" she said. "And the places you get the food are also the places to make contact with the eye candy!"

"Oh my," I replied, trying to take this all in. "Why do people give away food?"

"A backdrop to the Nazri story is that some people—the religious ones—make wishes or prayers, and as an offering, they make *gheyme* stew or do some other charitable giveaway in the form of food or money during *Ashura*. You can look at it as donating, or feeding the hungry."

"Or not so hungry! You consider yourself 'hungry'?"

"No, but it's tradition. Don't look into this too deeply! Those who eat it pray that the person gets their wish—it's basically holy food," said Bahareh.

"What's up with all the marches on every main street?" I asked.

"This is how they commemorate the event!" said Bahareh. "Listen woman, it'll sink in. We know it's a new chapter in your life, and can be overwhelming," she continued.

"And to further confuse you," Ghazaleh continued, "the mosques have some poetic recitations in memory of Imam Hossein in the battle where he was martyred. Several parks, which we will check later on today, perform plays dramatizing the Battle of Karbala. It shows the suffering he and his family went through."

"Wow," I said. "That's intense."

Now the car approached a house with a flock of people in front. Everyone was shouting so loudly for food that you could hardly make out what they were saying.

I was taking it all in. This should be interesting. "How do we even get the pot to the front door?"

"We don't. The pot has imaginary wheels!" said Bahareh.

She made me smile. Unloading the car was no treat, but together we accomplished it and got out. Bahareh carefully pushed her wheeled pot toward the house, halting before a short stocky man with amazingly white teeth. Immediately, he passed the pot to another man, and the pot magically moved out of view.

Over the twenty minutes it took to reacquire the pot, Ghazaleh, Bahareh, and I checked out the flock, chatting and watching the passing row of *dastes*, or marchers.

I noticed a few people exchanging what could only be telephone numbers, and it became clear this event was also unifying different people. Some bore expressions of displeasure, but participated anyway for the greater good or simply to hang and eat a hearty meal!

I sipped on one of the berry *sharbats* they were handing out, and it was fresh and icy cold. The story of the *sharbat* distribution was that since Imam Hossein and his family were starved of water in the Karbala desert before he was martyred, they were now serving cold drinks.

"Ladies, here it comes!" Bahareh said, and grabbed her pot from the same man who took it earlier. He favored her with his bright smile.

By the time we returned home, we had three pots filled with rice and *gheyme*, rice and *kebabs*, and *zereshk* (*barberry*) rice with chicken, *and* Ghazaleh had received three phone numbers. She was contemplating who she wanted to call! The heavy load perfumed the car, and required two back-and-forth trips to get it in the house!

After lunch, I knew why Bahareh craved *gheyme*—it was absolutely delicious! Possibly its ingredients were no different than any other *gheyme* on any other day, but this batch was connected to a special event, and charged with the magic present in all holidays.

Although I was touchy about eating too much rice, I devoured the entire dish.

I wondered what Arash might be doing on that day. We hadn't talked, and I missed him. Using the secret phone in Bahareh's room, I quickly called him, and learned that his father had a big *Nazri* event in progress. He had his hands full, but wanted to bring me some *Nazri* as an excuse to see me—two offers I just couldn't refuse!

We planned to meet at a park hosting a play for *Ashura*. I wondered whether it might be safe to be with a guy on such a religious day when all the *Komiteh* people were out watching. But I'd seen people exchanging numbers, calling the whole thing a *Hossein* Party, so why shouldn't I see my boyfriend?

I hung up the phone and stuck it back in its secret place, thinking that it would all work out, and we'd get to see each other.

After a few minutes of planning, Bahareh agreed to drop me off at the play, then head for another round of *Hossein* partying. "Wish you could join, Del, but Arash would kill us if we took you!"

"I know Arash would never say no. Anyway why do you always say that? He doesn't own me. I have an opinion of my own. You guys need to know you have a life of your own."

It was annoying how she made it seem like Arash determined where I went. He was my equal, not my supervisor. Maybe that was a Brooklyn mindset. I wondered how deep this type of thinking was embedded in this country. Arash and I didn't feel that way, but that was probably due to the fact that we'd both been out of the country.

"We do, but some men just like control. Especially Iranian men," added Ghazaleh.

"Yeah, but that's the more traditional version. These days it's half-and-half," Bahareh butted in.

"Anyway, back to the *Hossein* Party, ladies ... I want to see guys showing off their muscles!" she said, laughing.

"They might not have six-packs, but they're all sizzling," joked Ghazaleh. "We support them by following behind them!"

I chuckled. "You mean you guys are cheerleaders?"

"Yup, and once we know their names, we'll shout for them!"

This is better than bar hopping! I thought. On this one day, the girls were allowed to do what they wanted, and express themselves. And maybe—if they were lucky—they'd meet someone who actually meant something to them.

They dropped me off at the park to meet Arash, and drove off to meet their own soul mates.

I stepped across the park and its lush green space, its clusters of animated conversations.

"Your first *Hossein* Party?" Arash asked, stepping out of the concealing bulk of a tree.

"A blast to say the least!" I said, smiling broadly and happy to see him. "It definitely has a beat to it."

"Yup…"

We stood in the shade, talking and stealing a kiss or two. I thought about how much I had missed him, even though we had been apart for fewer than twelve hours. I wanted him more ... I wanted his touch, his cologne on my body....

I was growing more curious about him, and thought it was only a matter of time until I decided I was ready to take the next step. The only question was ... could I deal with the consequences I'd inevitably face?

*

Arash needed to stop at a gas station before taking me back, so pulled into the one that was least crowded.

"I won't be long," he said, getting out of the car.

I heard him clunk the fuel nozzle into the tank, and caught a potent whiff of gasoline.

Abruptly a guy approached my window. I sank back into my chair wondering what he wanted. He brazenly stuck his smelly head up to me and whispered a speedy string of words. Alarmed, I jerked away.

The man backed off, and shifted his attention elsewhere, but repeated his nonsense even faster.

Something about CDs ... but it was muttered so quickly that I felt certain he must be selling drugs. The ratty bag he carried wasn't completely closed, and I could see brightly labeled CDs poking out. I glared at him, wishing he'd just go away.

He repeated his mumbled mantra, and after five or six times I understood. My brain had quality translation software.

"*Navar, disc, pasoor ... navar, disc, pasoor ... navar, disc—*"
And on and on it went, repeating these three words.

Do you want any illegal tapes, CDs, or playing cards?

So he was peddling illegal stuff, trying to make a buck or two. Another one like the movie guy, murmuring away so he wouldn't get caught with stuff that would get him in trouble. I realized that he wouldn't approach anyone unless he thought they had money—or inclination—for that sort of thing, and didn't bother answering. I just rolled up the widow, signaling for him to get lost.

The scruffy stranger grinned, revealing the blackest, most decayed teeth I had ever seen, and shuffled off to find another victim.

Arash got back into the car laughing. "Babe, you figured that one faster than ever!"

"Lucky for me! You seemed to linger a little longer than necessary out there…"

"Haha! He was just trying to sell some entertainment stuff and cards."

"I know! He and his odor were close enough for me to get a look into that dirty, rusty bag of his!"

"Were you able to make out what he was saying? They say it so fast."

"Yes, after six times of repeating it! Does anyone really buy this stuff?"

He turned the key and the engine purred to life. "You would be surprised. This is another way things circle around—these guys are like mobile entertainment stores and, believe it or not, really useful in spreading the latest in the world of the arts!"

"You didn't have him in your face. He was kinda scary, the way he said his sales pitch! You'd think he was dealing opium or heroin."

Arash nodded. "I know—another way of making a living ... tough times!"

He shifted the car into gear and drove off to Bahareh's house. We had planned to meet at the same time, so we could walk in together.

Before he let me go, though, Arash turned to face me and looked at me with one of those flirtatious looks that lasted forever. "Call me tonight?"

It sounded more like a statement than a question. I accepted by looking back at him saying that I'd think about it.

In truth, I couldn't wait to call him.

Chapter 16: Anticipating *Eid*

After the mourning, it was back to work, internship, more Arash enjoyment, and prepping for anything else coming my way. University classes were to begin early the next year, so I was trying to get as much pleasure in as I could, while I had the time. I had grown familiar with my regimen, and as each day passed, I felt closer to my classmates and the people I dealt with. They were kind and real, and it invested me with a sense of security and protection. I was really starting to understand my place there. At the internship, we worked hard, then had fun in the late hours when the *Herasat* was mostly asleep, and the studio was more relaxed.

Then suddenly the year's end beckoned, the aroma of spring fresh in the air—green grass mingled with jasmine, cypress trees, and freshly watered soil. People were having a change of mood, anticipating *Eid*, the New Year.

I recalled watching my mother prepare for *Eid* back home in Brooklyn. Now, I observed it as the whole country did the same, and found this cleansing, even touching.

It was the same rich feeling, but now that I was near the source, everything was different! It was like having bread while it was fresh at the bakery ... or having a kiss at midnight near the water, where you could feel the sensuality. Before, *Eid* had been something that happened only on one night, and was then finished. Here it was for two weeks total, and was a much bigger deal. It wasn't about religion or Islam, but flipping the pages of time to begin a new chapter.

Even the taxi drivers were in a better mood and playing happier illegal music in their cabs.

*

I soon realized even the *Herasat* members in the TV studio were in the spirit, and prepping for the holidays. It was a full two weeks, which meant all the hotshot wealthier Iranians would travel abroad or get off to their fancy villas near the Caspian Sea in Shomal. My uncle kept a big villa there, in Darya Kenar (Seaside), and invited the entire family for the holidays. Each gated community bore its own name and employed full-blown doormen and professional security officers, many of them former military police.

Money went a long way in Iran, and the wealthy surely stood out with their luxury, high-end, homes, cars, and even high-end *mantos* and scarves.

The emperor had told me to request a two-week vacation for the *Nowruz* holiday, and it was granted immediately. No one had any trouble taking time off there, as the supervisors were happy to allow it, and even made casual chit chat while going through the calendar.

At home, my mom was doing the end of year cleaning, dusting and polishing every hole in the house with the assistance of hired help—a tall, mid-fortyish man sporting a moustache worthy of Hercules Poirot. Occasionally he brought along his little son, because he couldn't afford a sitter, a widower, and didn't want the kid wandering the streets of the down-est part of downtown Tehran.

The strangest part was that he always showed up impeccably dressed. Probably wanted to leave an impression!

My mom warned me not to run around wearing skinny shorts and a tank top when he was working.

"Why?" I objected strongly. After all, this was my house! "It is *our* house and we have authority inside our own house! I'm going to wear shorts!"

I was sent to talk to my father about how to be appropriate, even inside my own house.

"Are you saying that I dress sexy with these shorts, and I am trying to grab attention?" I asked. "I don't care about this maid-guy, and don't care what he thinks!" I continued, now more confused than ever. Why was it always the girl's fault? Why did we have to be so careful, when we really couldn't control what a guy was thinking? And why did it matter, when what the guy was thinking probably had nothing to do with what we actually intended or wanted?

"I get you, beautiful, but he is a man and from a different place in Tehran. You are too westernized with your thoughts. I just need you to keep on your jeans when you're around him," my dad said patiently, as if he was saying the most reasonable thing in the world.

"So, if I have too many 'Western' thoughts, why the hell am I in a country that is too traditional for me?" I blurted back. "I belong in the Western world! Why the hell did you bring me here when I so obviously can't fit in?" I shouldn't have said it, perhaps, but I was so tired of trying to fit in and figure out the rules that I couldn't help it.

"It's a culture clash, that's all. And don't question why I brought you here. Aren't you having fun, getting to know your cousins and your culture more?"

"Dad, at this time I am so disgusted with this culture that my answer is *no!*" I shouted. I ran out of his office and into my room, where I could be as Westernized as I wanted to be.

Frankly, I wanted to smack the living daylights out of the maid, but afterwards I realized that my folks were right. On my way upstairs, the guy looked at me as if he had been released from prison and, with no porn magazines available, was using whatever he could get. He was a good maid, and the ladies in the neighborhood liked his cleanliness, so they had him completely booked. My mom was happy with him, and he was heading to my aunt's as well, which meant there was no getting around it.

Evidently girls had to follow those types of rules even when they were in their own house, depending on whether a guy was around. And I was getting very tired of it.

*

Prior to the New Year, the streets bustled with people from smaller cities outside Tehran, and many Iranians flying in from Germany, France, and the US to spend the holiday with their families. Others were out in the streets, shopping for new clothes. It wasn't about buying a Christmas tree or ornaments, but crowds poured into the streets to replace the old with the new. That included furniture, clothes, curtains, and anything that was smelly, rusting, or deteriorating.

The markets were abuzz, selling small goldfish, hyacinth (*Sonbol*), and wheat and barley sprouts (*Sabzeh*) for the table. It was all for setting up the *Haft Sin* table. This involved placing the pieces representing the seven angelic heralds of Life, Health, Happiness, Prosperity, Joy, Patience, and Beauty on the table, each beginning with the Persian letter *Seen*, or S: *Seeb* (apple), *Seer* (garlic—my favorite!), *Senjed* (dried fruit from the lotus tree), *Sonbol* (hyacinth), *Sekkeh* (coins), *Samanoo* (sweet pudding), and *Somagh* (powered sumac berry).

Among these seven, we had the other 'happy that I'm here' items on the table, including candles in fine holders, a mirror, painted eggs, and goldfish, while some Iranians displayed the Quran as well. I wondered if everyone used the Quran, because this was purely a cultural holiday marking the first day of spring or Equinox—nothing Islamic based. My aunt didn't use the Quran, so it was probably optional.

Bahareh came over one night and told me, "It's *Eid*, so I've got to buy some new clothes. Do you want to come?"

"Yeah, but I don't like any of the lame designs in these boutiques. They're so old school, woman!"

"You think? I am going to take you to a fashion show—forget the boutiques. They are overpriced, though they all have sales going on for *Eid*."

My eyes widened. "A fashion show? You mean a real show where they strut down a catwalk and turn and blow kisses to the crowd with Vanilla Ice in the background?"

"Um, yeah. Vanilla Ice doesn't have concerts here, though. His only tour was cut short for food poisoning!" she said, laughing.

"Are you playing?"

"Not about the fashion show, you geek! This country has more fuel and imagination than anything you've seen! Let's have some chai and hop into the car. The show starts in an hour, and the traffic is brutal, this being the week before Eid."

Teatime was anytime in Iran. Everything started and ended, slowed and sped up with tea. You couldn't do anything without tea being in the picture.

"You want some Jack Daniels?"

"Sure, let's have some tea first!"

The above was always on the agenda!

"So who are the models in the show, anyone famous?" I joked, though I was really curious.

"*Baleh Baleh—shak nakon!*" *Yes, of course—no doubt!*

I could hardly contain my excitement. Another facet to this country ... one I never dreamed existed!

*

After chai, Bahareh, Ghazaleh—who had joined us a bit afterward—and I put on our scarves and drove off.

It didn't take long until we arrived at a regular, nondescript building.

"Impressive, eh?" Ghazaleh said. "Looks like a warehouse built in 1941..."

"You've got to go more ancient!" I said. "Like, maybe the medieval times."

We got out of the car, walked toward the building, and stopped at the dented basement door. I squinted, leaning toward the entrance. "Listen..."

Muffled music could be heard—the type without vocals, maybe techno or European house-style, layered with traditional instruments that sounded like the *setar* and *santoor*.

Bahareh poked a red-glowing button beside the door, and a bell rang. The door ground open, and we stepped into another world.

Right away, we could see that the place was much larger than could be presumed from a glance at the exterior, with two big rooms separated by a long, improvised catwalk. The models displayed themselves in one, while the other displayed racks and racks of clothes for sale from Turkey, Sweden, and Italy.

Other women milled about, checking out the models, clothes racks, and each other.

"Look at those colors," I said.

Lithe models stepped with fluid grace up and down the catwalk, their designer *mantos* and scarves mixing contemporary style with old Persian calligraphy—the nicest I had ever seen! I had entered the land of creativity, and as far as I could see, only women were present.

Bahareh tapped my arm. "C'mon, let's go." She took my hand and led me into the *mantos* room. Brunette woman, each with a unique, exotic, and aloof Middle Eastern facial structure, dominated the huge space. *Any man's paradise*, I thought. A harmony of fragrance haunted the air like invisible music, wild, fruity, and herbal, composed by the mélange of perfumes anointing the models and guests.

I recognized some of the scents as popular brands, but later realized these girls created their own, mixing and matching in awesome alchemy, conjuring a brand new fragrance. It was another way to express themselves and their artistry.

Bahareh had opened her own little space, shakin' it with mini dance moves, as the models strutted one by one along the catwalk, showing off cutting-edge *mantos* and cutely-wrapped scarves. Ghazaleh and I stood transfixed, watching the color-splashed show. Some of the models actually smiled. A few narrowed their kohl-lined eyes, lips firm with attitude, and sharp as their feline cheekbones. All of them were, of course, sexy, while a few gave off an icy aura of stunning elegance.

Sharbats were being served to all guests, and everyone stood around chatting, making new friends, and sharing ideas. Bahareh noticed some of her friends, and we joined their group. Within thirty minutes, I was standing amongst mostly strangers, but feeling a sense of kinship with them, in that we were all there to step out of the box and express our creativity. Or just appreciate the creativity of others.

Afterward, we all made our way through the noisy crowd and into the clothes-filled room on the other side. Here the chaos was muffled, the women paying rapt attention to the racked merchandise.

"What is the story with this?" I asked Ghazaleh, who was picking busily through a pile trying to find items her size before other chicks could lay their hands on them.

Without glancing up, she said, "Well, there are a couple of ladies who travel to Sweden, Turkey, and Italy before the holidays, buy up and bring back the *jens* (products). This stuff is European— fancy shamcy!—and some of it is real nice and sexy, but pricey. There are even designer clothes ... take a look," she said, pointing to all the clothes.

"Get outta here!"

"Seriously, Del, look for yourself. These are all American or European brands. Some might be fake, or Asian knock-offs, but whatever. They are as close as it gets, and they are nice! Better than your Canal Street! Haha!!"

"My Canal Street vendors are rock stars!" I said, giggling and moving toward the *jens*.

I probed the piles before her, and found several of my favorite brands. A few were as new as the early-bird spring collections from the designers, which was amazing, and absolute heaven for me.

"You know," she continued, "sometimes the new fashion trends get here earlier than in the US. Weird, I know, but we are fashion-hungry and central and eat this stuff alive!"

I remembered the clothing hanging in her closet, and the fact that it was all designer labels. I'd wondered where they got it, since there weren't any shopping malls in the area. Now I had my answer.

If I'd known this show was going to be like this, I would have taken my checkbook!

There were piles of denim jeans in a spectrum of colors and styles, shirts, blouses, skirts, dresses, jewelry, makeup, and shoes. The mall had been imported to this big room tucked beneath an anonymous building and advertised by word of mouth.

Toward the show's end, I found I had gathered much more than anticipated, and didn't have enough cash on me. The lady in charge approached and told me I had made a nice selection, giving me the impression that I was looking at a big price tag. This was the time I wished I was in the mall shopping with the emperor's credit card!

Bahareh, barely visible behind her own heaped selections, said, "You are doing some major shopping, lady!"

"You noticed?" I said sarcastically.

"Their stuff is good. It lasts, and suits your style. This lady goes abroad once or twice a year and brings back top-notch stuff."

"I don't think I have enough dough on me," I said with a sad tone. "But I don't want to miss out since the sizes are limited."

"What? Oh, how much do you need?"

"I'm not sure. Haven't looked at the prices yet!"

She laughed. "You spoiled brat! Given that this mountain beats Kilimanjaro's size, I would estimate one million *tomans*! That's roughly one grand in your language. But don't worry, I can write a check. We are good customers with this lady, she will accept it."

"Really? She would just trust like that? I mean it's not like using a credit card, is it?"

"Yup. She is a cool cat and been doing this for years," she answered, like this was a normal process between them.

I wondered if everyone had this kind of trust here. Could everyone have a relationship like that with the vendors? It was certainly different than things were back home!

Bahareh moved off to talk with the lady, who looked to be in her early forties, and whose wardrobe—from head to heels—was certainly European. Later, the elegant proprietress sidled up to greet me, telling me today's bill could be paid after the holidays, or whenever I had time to come by and drop it off.

After a few minutes of conversation, I learned that her name was Atoosa. She was a fascinating woman, whose husband was a prominent engineer in Tehran and conceived of this business years ago, while traveling between various countries. So it started taking off, paving the way for other women in the fashion world. In fact, she owned this very basement, and rented it out to women looking to display their products—whether they were their own designs or designs from other countries. Some girls were even starting to design new lingerie lines, and new *manto* fashion wear, with funky head scarves. The scarves were good stuff, I thought, on my head in Tehran and maybe someday around my neck back in the Big Apple ... whenever that time would come. I missed it.

Without realizing it, I'd already started planning how I was going to get back there.

Atoosa was a true entrepreneur, and I admired her courage. She inspired many women to pursue their passions; one of those females being my cousin, who wanted to create her own line but didn't have the guts to take a solid step forward. Such a success was a home run, in my book! And I'd taken it to heart; if this woman could do something like that, surely I could as well.

We exchanged numbers and I promised to drop off the money before Eid. Bahareh's good reputation extended to cover me, and I didn't let her down.

With bulging bags, lipsticked smiles, and a few new relationships, we headed home. Along the way I daydreamed about wearing some of my new clothes for Arash, and knew he would like it.

Once we were home, the emperor said we would be driving to Shomal (North of Iran) early in the morning.

In other words ... giddy up and start packing!

Chapter 17: Road Trip

"We will be heading out the night before *Eid*," he said, "to bypass traffic and have breakfast in the middle of the road. *Chaloos*, that is," he finished, referring to the twisty, scenic route toward North Iran, which was also called Shomal. It was a beautiful road filled with nature, kind of like the highway in New Jersey.

"Your grandmother, cousins, and Aunt Elahe will be gathering here at 6 in the morning, with some other distant cousins, and off we go. So prep up, *dokhtaram*." Dear daughter … I loved it when my dad used that term. I felt I belonged to a family that loved me unconditionally, and who better for that than a Persian dad? A dad that was strict in his very own unique but diplomatic way.

This would be my first *Eid*, first driving up *Chaloos* experience, first Shomal visit, and first time spending the holiday with all the family in one house for a week. It was also my first vacation, my first breakfast on the road ... I didn't even get what was so special about eating breakfast with all your folks in the middle of a dusty road. Maybe the road was so beautiful that they hitched a good spot there just to have bread or cheese or something like that. I didn't get it, but I went with the flow on this one.

I packed a bag with my new clothes, trendy scarves, and new shoes, excited to visit this place called Shomal.

Once everyone was asleep, I called Arash from my secret phone to tell him we would be gone for a week. To my absolute surprise, he told me he would be there too!

"Are you following me?"

He chuckled warmly. "No! We have a villa there in Izad Shahr. That's the thing to do for *Eid* for lots of Tehranians. Everyone drives up to Shomal to chill, hang with family, have barbecues, and be together for the New Year. It's where all the cool people go!"

"Hm, so it's happening?"

"Let me make it a bit more clear for the New Yorker. It's like when city people go to the Hamptons."

"Crystal clear and glittering, and now I am even more hyped!" I said. "Where is whatever it was you just said?"

"It's on the other side of where you guys are at ... a forty-minute drive. Don't worry. I will ride up to your neck of the woods with my buddies, to see you."

"Really?" My heart quickened. "Listen, I am going to be with the family in one house, so I don't know if I can call you, even with a secret phone," I noted.

"Gotcha, but don't worry. I'll come to the seaside in Darya Kenar, where everyone goes for coffee or French fries most evenings. Maybe we'll see each other there."

"French fries?" I knew I'd heard correctly, but this still surprised me.

"Yup. Smothered with ketchup, and even a *hookah* to accompany that!"

"So, that's the *it* thing to get?" I asked rhetorically.

"Well ... the menu has lots of stuff you would eat with your fingers, but that's the *it*!"

"Fattening, high-calorie, lots of trans fat … but it's *Eid*, and you are supposed to be happy and free spirited!" I threw that in with a wink, like he'd catch it on the other side of the phone.

"By the way, there are a lot of 'Jordan'-type activities there, so be careful," he joked, but under that he sounded serious.

Jordan-type activities … I knew exactly what *that* meant. There were guys and girls hooking up, and he wanted me to stay away from it!

"Are you jealous, telling me not to flirt with other guys?"

There was a pause. "Something like that ... but you are on the right track!"

I suddenly wished he was right there next to me, admitting such a thing. It was the closest we'd come to talking about our relationship, and I had a feeling it could have led to more. After all, I thought we were both getting tired of the whole virginity issue.

"I'll leave our potential Shomal meeting in the hands of fate herself!" I said, having no idea what it was like up there.

"*Ye boos bedeh zood,*" he joked. *Give me a kiss, quickly.*

"Nope, I can't. Have to keep my lips virginal!"

"I've kissed you before, though!" he teased

I giggled, blew him a muted kiss without getting the phone filled with saliva, and dreamt that one day I could be with him without hiding it from my parents, and using a secret phone, and kissing him in the darkness of the movie theatre. One day I'd be able to express myself without fear of my surroundings.

*

The next morning, four cars with lots of baggage cruised back to back. The men were driving, some with frowns, because they refused to wear eyeglasses or sunglasses. The emperor appeared most up-to-date in his new Porsche sunglasses and brightly colored polo shirt, as if he was fresh off the golf course.

My mom, who I considered the most beautiful (inside and outside) woman existing, was happy about returning to the Shomal of her childhood, and reliving memories on the road again. My mom loved Iran, and had sacrificed lots to detach from the family here in order to move to the United States with my dad. She never regretted the move because she adored my dad, but there was no doubt she missed her family when we were in the Big Apple. Aziz Joon was at the top of her list and Agha Joon—my grandfather—who had passed away. Her family was very close, and shared everything with each other. So it was no surprise that they followed each other on this road, constantly talking on their phones and remembering this or that experience, or checking in to see when we would be stopping for lunch.

Of course there were many different opinions about *when* to stop for lunch, and where, and they were getting nowhere fast until my father, who was the eldest of the crew, suggested stopping at a place shortly after halfway. Everyone went mute, signaling *chashm* (to obey the elder without question), and then quietly commented: "Can't believe I have to wait that long." But no one really complained—the decision had been made by the eldest, and that was just the way it was.

Chaloos was by far Iran's most beautiful road. At one point, the Kandovan Tunnel connected the dry part of Iran with the green region north of the Alborz mountains, which led eventually to the town of Nowshahr in the province of Mazandaran, which was considered Shomal and lay at sea level. The road was breathtaking, comprised of twists and turns, which, depending on the season, opened onto a variety of artist's vistas stretching toward the horizon. Spring was the best time, and I took pictures left and right!

We stopped at a restaurant in the heart of the mountains. Knee-high tables covered with Persian rugs functioned as customer seating, with big pillows—*poshtis*—used as backrests. The yeasty, hot aroma of fresh-baked bread ghosted from the kitchen, turning up the volume of everyone's hunger. Near one corner rushed a miniature waterfall, clearly natural, spilling down into a stream and snaking through the restaurant's center. Chickens could be heard clucking and scratching in the background, and the rest was silence and fresh air.

Fortunately, it took less than five minutes to seat ten people comprising some immediate family, extending cousins, and Kamran's friend Hessam.

I looked at the menu and had no idea what to make of it, so I just told my mom I wanted *noon o panir*—bread, cheese, and fresh walnuts with watermelon. I had no idea what breakfast buffet I was in for! First out was freshly baked Barbari bread, crisp, salty, and latticed. Then they brought out my favorite—*sanghak*, a stone-baked oval of sourdough, dimpled and hot. My mom used to buy it from this little Iranian grocery store in Long Island, but this was much tastier than any we'd had in the US.

The bread was the centerpiece of breakfast. Then came butter, and a certain cream (*sar shir*). Initially, I thought the cream was like cream cheese, but when I tasted it, it was a sour cream consistency with ricotta flavor. Everyone attacked it once it landed on the table. Then we had the Shomal jams, which was what local, organic jam was to New York's Hudson Valley.

Eggs followed, and then breakfast was wrapped up with chai. Tea was very special to the Iranians, and we even had a special way of brewing and pouring it. No one would be caught dead using tea bags! In fact, I'd learned that an Iranian was evaluated by their skills at brewing tea and making rice. Both were a process, and if you thought you could make either within two minutes, think again!

If you were a skilled tea server, it even meant that you were ready for marriage.

After we were finished with breakfast, we went souvenir shopping. This confused me, since we hadn't even reached our destination yet, but I went along for the ride. There was a shop connected to this breakfast joint selling jams, pickled garlic, sour fruit roll-ups, and big round cookies, stuffed with walnuts and cinnamon, in a special type of roll.

The pastries were known as *Kooloochehs*, and everyone picked up a box. My dad took four jars of garlic.

"Dad, we are all in one house for a week, and look at the amount of garlic you're getting. You will murder my sense of smell and nostrils! *Have mercy!*"

"Everyone has to have garlic when they are eating their first meal of the New Year with the *sabzi polo mahi with koukou sabzi*! And besides, they say no matter how much garlic you eat, the humidity in Shomal won't let you smell it. And Del, everyone brushes!" he said, laughing.

"With what kind of toothpaste?" I said, but was just ignored.

This would be interesting. The whole villa had three bathrooms for the entire clan, so waiting in the mornings and nights to use the toilet, shower, or brush your teeth would be like waiting in a long grocery check-out line.

After filling the cars with more than the necessary jams, garlic, and *Kooloocheh*, we hit the road again. A couple hours more and we would be in Shomal.

Each car carried an individual Coleman, into which someone would pour tea, so that everyone could have a cup while we were driving. Out came the *Kooloochehs*, marking my first taste of one, and I swooned with delight. They were heavy, but I could care less.

Watching the views on the road in my *Kooloocheh* and tea solace filled me with peace. The cars were still back to back and communicated so intensively that sometimes we would pull over and people would switch seats, to go in the car with the better music or better conversations.

The girl cousins were all in the emperor's car, because he had agreed to put on NSYNC as opposed to his boring *Sonnati* (traditional) music. When I listened to the *Sonnati* stuff, it only depressed me.

Anything pop soothed my mood, Backstreet Boys included!

406

The entourage approached the Caspian coast of Shomal, a scenic green blanket stretching to the hazed blue sea. Traffic picked up, cars and other vehicles whisking along like bees swarming to honey as we all ran to escape the harsh realities of the city life.

It was beautiful, with rice stalks in the distance, and locals dressed in vibrant colors with red cheeks in contrast to the black *mantos* you might see in Tehran. They appeared to be so carefree and happy. Bright-eyed children waved, selling corn from improvised wooden stands, and the warm air carried a whiff of jasmine.

When we arrived at the gate, the doorman heard the name of the villa we were going to and immediately let us in.

So we were finally there! The villa was my father's friend's, who had opted to go to Los Angeles to visit his family there, and was letting us use his place. It had a couple of bedrooms and three baths. No one family was given a single bedroom, so we were divided: one for the females, meaning all the "girls," another for the kids, and the last reserved for the men.

The living and dining rooms and backyard were considered public places, and all the family had access to those places. But the bathrooms were another story.

These had to be shared in various ways. Someone might be taking a shower, another applying makeup, while a third washed her feet … all this while engaged in very serious conversation regarding an important subject like Aziz Joon's neighbor's daughter getting a divorce! Oh, and by the way, this was by the women's section!

In the other—situated in a remote corner of the house—the men did whatever men do.

The day of the New Year, *Sah Tahvil* as they called it, the entire family stood together in front of the TV. The moment *Sal Tahvil* was announced was like the ball dropping in Times Square! Everybody started kissing, one from the left, one from the right, and hugging, sometimes double hugging! This was March 21st, the famous worldly equinox, when the sun crosses the celestial equator dividing day and night. It was my first *Nowruz* celebrated in my country, and even though I had so many divides in my head, it felt like home.

Once this love and affection died down a bit, it was time to eat!

On the long table was *sabzi polo mahi*—steamed rice with chopped parsley, dill, and chives served with fresh white fish. The traditional meal, with mountains of garlic on the table! They were a hit!

The entire family stayed indoors that day, basking in the well-earned or not-so-well-earned vacation.

Chapter 18: Calling "The Man"

The days that followed were spent mostly in a state of languid quiet—the way a vacation should be spent. Everyone ate together, shared stories, and had the occasional Iranian siesta. The men played poker on the dining-room table, having figured out one another's infinite variety of poker faces. They were extremely advanced players, and took a lot of pleasure in beating each other regularly.

One night, Kamran, Bahareh, and Ghazaleh decided to throw a party. Kamran invited some of the people he knew in Darya Kenar and the surrounding gated communities. Our parents were OK with that, just because they were also involved, and drank while on holiday. Even my dad said that we were on holiday, and should have fun. I was shocked; was this a new part of my dad? I felt in Shomal, especially in these gated, wealthy communities, the Islamic rules were a bit less strict. I mean, the guys were playing poker for one, and now we were ordering drinks and the emperor was cool with it. It was almost like the entire family was happy to be getting a break from the constant restrictions.

I wondered if the emperor was okay with everything while it was the New Year, and if I could turn that to my advantage, to see Arash. Then I realized that if I even mentioned a guy, Dad would probably turn into the uber-protective parent again. So I kept my mouth shut.

We didn't have any drinks, so we needed to call "the man"— the Shomal equivalent of the Ray-Ban-wearing movie guy—to bring us a couple of bottles of vodka.

Forgetting that in this country lots of stuff including the black market is male dominated, I stepped up to the plate to call him. No one had any problem with that, but that was because I was talking to my family, who were very liberal. And we were on vacation. It never occurred to me that it might be odd for a girl to call someone from the black market. It didn't occur to my family, either.

I got his digits from Kamran and dialed away. "Hello?" I said.

"Yes ma'am," said a gravelly voice. "What would you like?"

Right to the point—all business! "Can we have a couple of bottles of vodka—"

Abruptly another voice cut in: "*Khanoom en karha chie, chi darid sefaresh midid?*" Since that meant "What are you doing ma'am? What do you think you are ordering?" I felt a rush of anger, wondering if I'd been given the number for the *Komiteh*, or maybe a higher authority!

"*Khanoom yani chi!*" I fired back with a New York attitude, frustrated about why the operator had come on the line, interrupting my call.

"*Hamin alan ghat konid!*" said the operator, with such rage I thought he might fly through the line and strangle me.

I hadn't connected the dots, and was still trying to win my debate.

"Who is this?" I demanded.

"Be shoma hich rabti nadare, hamin alan ghat konid!" he repeated again.

This was getting annoying!

Kamran, who had grasped what happened, jumped up, hooked the phone away, and hung up.

"What in the world was that all about?" I said. "Oh my Lord, was that who I think it was?"

"Yes, and I forgot to tell you that you can't talk to them like you would in the US. It's a no-win situation for you here," he said, laughing. "They have nothing better to do, and will fight with you until you give up! They were probably listening to his phone calls."

"Don't worry," said Bahareh, who had overheard from the kitchen. "I will get some alcohol from the neighbor two villas down, no biggie."

I shook my head, still too surprised by what had happened. They were actually bugging the black market guy's phone? And why had the officer insisted on lecturing me? Why couldn't he just have disconnected the call? But that was the point, I thought: They wanted us to know that they were tracking us, and tracking anything that

413

happened on the black market. They wanted us to be paranoid about that sort of thing, so we wouldn't do it anymore.

Initially I got a bit freaked out, but then I saw how nonchalant the others behaved. Good thing for us the neighbors had vodka and also joined the party, which went on until 3 in the morning.

*

One day, my mom, aunt, and cousins decided to head out to the beach. Excited, I put on my new two-piece fire-red bikini and off we went. I wanted to show off with them in front of Arash, but I had no idea where he was, or how to reach him.

Once there, I could see how the beach was set up to keep the women separated from the men. A wall of canvas had been erected, concealing the women and providing a private space where they could swap their *mantos* or *chadors* for bikinis. Simple rules: no men, no boys, no cell phones or cameras. It was like nothing I'd ever experienced, particularly on a beach.

Some women wore the latest, most contemporary bathing suits, as if they were models straight from that month's *Sport*

414

Illustrated cover! Gorgeous, their shades and glossy lipstick irresistible eye-candy, they mostly relaxed and worked on their coffee-colored tans. Other women wore bras and underwear, and that was just disgusting! Opposite the cover girls, a few were so religious they didn't even rely on the canvas barrier and chilled wearing their *mantos* and *wimples* in the hot sun!

"These are our Olympic swimmers, Del," said Bahareh, giggling. "They are also highly *khosh teep* (stylish)."

I turned toward her. "Where are the guys?"

"Oh, well there is a way to check them out." Her mischievous smile said it all.

"How?"

"Take off your clothes, and swim far out beyond the canvas. The guys usually swim out there, too, and then you can talk!"

"What's the point of that? Are we skinny dipping, by the way?"

"No, you dork ... but I love it when we someway, somehow fight the system," she said, rubbing oil on her legs.

"Can you be arrested if you're seen that far out? You know, checking out some guy?"

"Yup, we have the 'sea *Komiteh*' on the water too. They are everywhere!" she joked, but her eyes were serious. "Just have a little bit of fun ... don't get too crazy. Or just check out the latest mode in fashion from the girls on the beach. They're wearing it, *and they're wearing it before anyone in America.*"

I looked around and saw my mom and aunt gossiping away in their two-piece bikinis, Ghazaleh reading her book, and as my view expanded I noticed some of the ladies were even topless! Man, who said this was an Islamic country! But no... there were no men on the beach, and I assumed no one was a lesbian here. Which meant that no one could get turned on by seeing women like this. So it all fell within the boundaries of the law.

I really wanted to spend a day on the beach with Arash, but seeing this one and its set up, I knew it would have to be at a private pool, or maybe sneaking onto a public beach late at night. I chose not to obsess over this, and work on my tan. After applying Bahareh and Ghazaleh's mix of coffee beans and oil, which supposedly gave a good tan, I laid next to everyone else, chilling.

Before I went into hibernation, I noticed something that might just be a new wave of fashion.

"Are those the stretch *mantos*?" I shouted so loud that my mom, aunt, and cousins jumped to their feet and scanned a cluster of ladies wearing sticky, stretched swimwear—the couture, super-trendy Muslim looks.

A lady overheard me, and stepped over to describe this phenomenon. "*Dokhtar khanoom* (*missy*), these are *burkinis*, the new revolution of bikinis—a *burka* plus a bikini." Her smile said it all—that Muslims could even wear a *burka* when they were swimming. I didn't know whether this was depressing or hilarious.

"Really?"

"These new swimsuits," she continued, "are *kheili sheek* (*fashionable*) and super comfy. Finally, someone had come up with a solution!"

I paid polite attention, but this was really ridiculous. It was respectable, but if these ladies participated in the Olympics, wouldn't this attire slow them down? How was it rational to wear something like that?

But if we did, would we be allowed on the men's beach?

"It comes with a head-piece and a long-sleeve top down to the knees, with the skinny pants ... the best thing is that some of them have ties to keep the top in place while you are doing the breast stroke. The material is exquisite. *Enshallah (if God wills) shoma ham az enha beghirid (you guys will get the same).*"

"So how would you get a tan?" I asked curiously.

"*Madar en harfha chie ... Bronze mikham nasham!*" (*I'd rather not get a tan!*)

The tone in which the woman answered was so funny that I squeezed Ghazaleh's hand, trying not to make it too apparent that I was laughing. I felt a deeper bond forming with my cousins, and loved it. The only element missing was Arash. Why was I thinking about him so much?

I was not in love with him, but he was constantly on my mind.

I wondered whether it was the same for him.

*

That night, the family decided to grab a bite to eat, so everyone prepped up and we decided to walk to the seaside restaurant. It got packed at night, and I crossed my fingers that because it was Thursday night—equivalent to NYC's Saturday nights—Arash would be there too.

Not only were my fingers crossed, but I had my toes wrapped around one another as well.

Chapter 19: A Lamb Among Wolves

My mom had convinced the emperor to allow us to go out for dinner alone. He first said we should all go, but then my mom reminded him that we wanted girl time, and it was a gated community after all … what was the worry? Then Kamran chimed in and said he would meet us afterward with his friend Hessam. Finally, my dad gave his approval. But we had a curfew and that was 9 sharp; by car, taxi, or by foot, we had to be at the villa at 9 sharp. He smiled while saying it, but I sensed he was dead serious.

And since it was my dad, and the oldest man in the group, it meant everyone had to obey.

While I sat waiting for my cousins to finish getting ready, I started asking questions to keep myself busy. Of course the only thing they could think of was how we were going to meet guys while we were out, while the only thing I could think of was Arash.

Bahareh wasn't really seeing anyone, and Ghazaleh wasn't into anything serious, either. It seemed they didn't have boyfriends … but then again, no girl in Iran "looked like" they had a boyfriend. And then you would suddenly find out that the black crows—smelly and mustached—in class had boyfriends after all.

When we finally got out, I could see that Darya Kenar's main street was the same as Jordan in Tehran. No wonder Arash had gotten nervous! Cars cruised up and down the streets, as the people looking for the right person to exchange numbers with.

"Here we go," I said. "Check it out…"

A shiny silver Mercedes slowed up, obviously interested in us. I had to say we were hotter than most girls walking the street.

The Mercedes pulled up to the curb, and a man leaned out of the window. "What's your name, beautiful?"

He was gazing at me, as if I was walking alone.

"*Torobche,*" said Bahareh (literally meaning *radish*, but slangishly meaning *none of your beeswax*), grabbing me as if to protect me. "*Ba oon ghiyafash tike ham mindaze* (with that face he is teasing, too)."

"What's wrong with the face?" I mumbled.

Bahareh went on: "*Dokhi joon* (*dear girl*) *en chi bood, to ba behtar az enha mitooni bepari* (slangishly meaning *what was that, you could score much better*). And by the way, might I remind you ... you've already got a man!" she said, as if protecting me rather than being jealous. I felt the same toward Ghazaleh. None of us felt jealous of the other; they were funny, progressive, and accomplished, and I loved them.

"So you answer with *torobche?*"

"Yup, and if he is super *poroo* (*the type that teases more*) he will ask, '*khonat kojast?*' (*where is this radish's house?*) and you will answer '*to baghche*' (*in the garden*)."

"Or," I joked, "you can say *be to che* (*none of your biz boy*)."

Bahareh regarded me with her dark, gentle eyes, and Ghazaleh giggled.

"We pick and choose as we please!" And we all put our arms around one another for a big cousin sandwich hug.

"It's a long way to the restaurant, *mikhai auto bezanim* (*do you want to catch a ride*)?" Ghazaleh asked.

"I do," I said. "But I don't see any taxis here!"

"No, silly ... auto means you catch a ride with a hot guy!"

"You mean just randomly get in some guy's car?"

"Yup, and if you like them a lot, you can get their number. You may or may not buzz them up, but at least you get a free ride!"

I narrowed my eyes, taking this in. "So, how do you choose which car to jump into?"

"It doesn't matter; as long as the car has wheels, and the guy doesn't look like a weirdo, it's all good!"

"Whatever you say…" I couldn't believe that was a *thing* girls did here. But in this gated community, I felt like they paid off a lot of the black crow people and their *Komiteh* mates!

Before I knew it, Ghazaleh had taken the initiative and was flirting with an upscale car, as opposed to one of the falling-apart-looking Peykans. And we were soon riding in some random stranger's vehicle, heading to the seaside restaurant.

This was so weird. A free ride from some stranger who could suddenly turn away from the agreed-upon route … and then what? It wasn't like we could jump out! What if they captured us and decided to trade us?

I was a bundle of nerves. What if Arash saw me? What if the emperor saw me? It seemed so natural to the girls and even the guys, but to me it was epidemic! Lots of girls were doing the same!

I could see Ghazaleh had the hots for the driver and sensed butterflies in her stomach. We eventually arrived at the restaurant and Ghazaleh exchanged numbers, but I could feel that these guys had girlfriends. The cell kept ringing every two minutes, and he kept declining the call. Besides, who in Iran *didn't* have a relationship? *Everything was such a show!* Everyone was just scared of the other person knowing!

All at once I was shocked to see a face so familiar I jumped. That handsome faced glared at me, the eyes judging and fierce.

Arash...

He looked so angry, and I gasped. I had never seen him look that way…

Bahareh noticed this immediately, and also saw the *Komitehs* in the background.

"Just be chill," she said.

Ghazaleh, who saw us both looking at the same guy, knew that guy must be Arash. Seeing him for the first time, she said, "He is such a *tikeh* (literally meaning *piece* but slangishly meaning *hottie*). It looks like *gare be khodesh* (*he has problems with himself*)!"

I stepped between my cousins, whispering, "Guys, I think he just saw us jumping out of the guy's car and is having a cow."

"Girl, that is what's called *gheyrat*, and all Iranian men have it. Kind of like jealousy, but a bit more extreme. Actually *way more* extreme," said Ghazaleh.

"Yeah, to the point that a fight might break out," added Bahareh.

"'Did you look at my girlfriend?' And the other replies, 'Yes, who are you to tell me who I can and cannot look at?' That's the pride talking. Then the whole thing goes back and forth, until one either lands a punch or one of the girls jumps between them, sparking up the drama!" Ghazaleh said, giggling.

I was taking in this movie plot, but was also becoming angry about Arash getting so angry. Who was he to tell me what I could or could not do?

"They get a bit too jealous, to the point that they get offended. But it looks like Arash is keeping his cool rather than picking a fight."

"Is this true for all Iranian men?"

"Well, let's just say it runs in the blood, especially in Iranian fathers! Like the emperor! In his blood it doesn't run ... it sprints!"

Arash watched as if lip-reading the conversation, and then began to approach us, looking like he was calming down a bit. He said his *Salam* to all of us and introduced his two buddies. His posture was tense, but he got a table and we all sat down together.

The *Komiteh* were nowhere to be seen, but I wasn't worried about that; Arash had ways of dealing with them if they showed up.

Then he stood to go order some food, and I followed him to interrogate him.

I stepped toward the line after him. "Why so upset? I've never seen you like this before…" I spoke English so no one around would understand.

"Delkash, this is not the right time to talk…" he said softly, not even looking at me. He said my full name, which meant that he was really upset.

"It was the auto, wasn't it?"

He glanced at the ground. "What do you think? You went into a complete stranger's car. Forget the fact that you already *have* a boyfriend, do you know these guys can actually *hurt* you? They can rape, they can beat the shit out of you … rob you!" He was speaking with a flat-out British accent, which I found very hot, but his gaze was serious, as if he was not only jealous but also hurt that I could be so careless.

I wanted to sleep with him right now, but firmed my voice and answered. "We were just catching a ride. And for your information, I wasn't flirting! Hell, I don't even know how to flirt in Farsi!"

It was our first back-and-forth English-speaking conversation, and we were attracting more attention than if we were speaking Farsi—the American with a slight Brooklyn accent versus the classy London guy.

Everyone from our table knew the noise was from us, and let us be.

"And you didn't feel that one might be interested in you?" he snapped.

"What? And if they were, what would happen next?" I sensed this verbal assault had to be the *gheyrat* the girls were talking about, and pushed at it. Arash knew I had no intention of exchanging numbers and calling a guy, so he was simply venting, and managing it well. This was a completely different side of him ... and I loved it! He was fighting for me! He genuinely cared! He wanted me, and it was for real. Yup ... that was when I found out it was the *real deal.*

Abruptly he quit talking, maybe realizing he was overreacting to someone he cared for and who cared for him back. He was right, and I hadn't wanted to get into that car, but that didn't mean I wasn't going to stand up for my rights.

We went back to our table once we had emptied some of the negative energy. My cousins were making obvious efforts to avoid eye contact, and changed the subject of the conversation into 'the weather' and 'how was Eid for you?' to the other guys at the table. I was still upset about how Arash had jumped at me, but there was no use dwelling on it. After all, I was a lamb among the wolves in this country, and he was acting like I'd done it on purpose. He needed to calm down.

Secretly, though, I was impressed and touched that he'd been ready to fight for me.

While in my own bag of thoughts, I sensed a hand grabbing mine under the table and clasping it.

It was Arash ... and I knew he felt genuinely sorry. He didn't look at me, as if he didn't want to attract attention, but massaged my hand underneath the table. At the table, he started making conversation with everyone else.

He was getting over it ... and the massage was definitely helping me get over it too!

It was an interesting night, to say the least, and now our early curfew was approaching. Arash got the car ready to drop us off two blocks from our villa, down an alley, and we took off for the villa. Before I got out, Arash signaled for me to wait. Bahareh and Ghazaleh got the drift, and took baby steps down the alley, slowing their pace.

"Sorry, I got a little carried away," he teasingly said. "But it's for your own good! And so is this…"

He cupped my face in his hands, leaned, and touched my lips so softly that I only felt the moist warmth of his. I felt he wanted me right now, right there … to make out or something more … but decided to continue the kiss to substitute for the days we would be apart. He had to go back to Tehran, he said, to take care of his father's business. And I was staying for the rest of Eid without him…

From the distance, my cousins watched our steamy encounter.

After a long minute, I emerged, lipstick worn off my mouth, and bearing a small bruise-colored hickey on my throat.

Bahareh suddenly shouted out, "Del, look at your neck!"

"What about it?" I said with a surprised tone.

"Looks like Arash did the works." She smiled sarcastically and reached for a mirror in her bag so I could see myself.

I checked it out and said, "No worries! This is where *wimple-and-scarf* fashion comes in handy. It will cover nicely. You know, this Islamic wardrobe does have alternative saving functions!"

I felt my lamb was turning into a wolf ... or maybe the wolf was coming out of its hiding place.

I knew cleverness ran in the family and noticed it running through my veins, too. It was a discovery mode for me, and I felt I was surfing the wave of change like a champion. There were times I did feel lost and confused, but I was living to the fullest in a new country, and trying to make the best of it.

We started walking toward the villa when I noticed some familiar faces walking up from the beach behind us. It was my dad, Kamran, and Kamran's buddy, Hessam. Arash was already gone, but I suddenly got freaked out. Had they seen anything? It was too dark

Chapter 20: Feast Before Sorrow

I felt a heavy silence from my dad, but Kamran and Hessam were cracking jokes and telling stories, so they managed to lift the mood. The emperor wasn't speaking much, and didn't even look at me. He didn't look at Bahareh and Ghazaleh that much either, to be honest, so I didn't know if he was ignoring us all or if he'd seen what I did.

Oh God, I thought, he was going to have a heart attack. And then kill me.

Once we were back in the villa, I put some foundation on my neck to color the hickey and tried to call Arash to tell him that I was worried about what my dad might have seen. But whenever I neared a phone, some family member would pop up out of nowhere. No phone calls were happening, that was for sure.

During teatime, I sensed my mom was a bit shaken up too. I didn't know what to make of this all, or whether it had anything to do with me. My mom was a bit on the lighter side, but they were both upset about something, and trying to keep their poker faces on.

"Keep it cool, Del. I don't think they saw anything…" Bahareh whispered in my ear.

"How can I? I feel horrible for lying, but then again it's my life!" I said back.

"We hear you, but I've got to tell you one thing. If the emperor saw something, he is really respecting you and keeping on the down low in front of these people. Remember, the *gheyrat* runs strong here!" she said.

Gheyrat I got, but too much of it I didn't accept. Who was the emperor, to make the calls on my life? First I was born in Iran, then he decided a better life awaited me in New York, then he decided I'd better get her in touch with my Iranian roots before I turned white, and now I had to deal with all of these stupid rules! I'd had enough, and was ready to burst.

I missed my freedom in Brooklyn and I missed talking to my girls and not making such a big deal about dates and even kissing guys. Lord, I wasn't even having sex! But if the moment was right with the right person, I didn't get what was so wrong with that!

All the girls I knew here, including Bahareh, Ghazaleh, Neda, Saloomeh, Mina, Azin, and Nooshin, were awesome, but they all strategized about how to manage their love lives in accordance with their parents. Even making sure their education was aligned with *their* plans.

It wasn't like that in New York. We didn't even talk about this stuff; we just let life take its course! But in Iran we didn't get to let life run its course. We didn't even get to make our own rules, because the religion and government were making all our rules for us! Maybe that was why Iran had so much trouble finding a leader: Who was going to be allowed to lead, when the religion was already telling us what to do all the time?

I went out to the backyard to get some fresh air and look at the stars. Bahareh noticed and came to follow me, but I told her I needed to be alone before I killed someone. Literally!

After about fifteen minutes, I heard the backyard door open, and out walked the emperor. I didn't have the patience to talk to him right then, but also knew that I didn't have much choice.

"What's up?" he asked in his New York accent.

"Nothing, could you please leave me alone?" I asked him politely.

"I want to just ask you a question. Remember that we don't lie to one another in this family …" he said, pretending to have a friendly tone.

I didn't answer, and wanted to shout at the top of my lungs about how fed up I was with this country and all the different ways of thinking here!

"Did you lie to me about who you were with tonight?"

"No. Why would you think that?"

"I went out to buy groceries and saw you at the seaside, with your cousins…"

"Are you sure it was us? We left pretty early. Remember our curfew!"

"I will ask you only once," he said firmly. "Were you with some guys? One of them looked like he was very close to you..." he continued, looking at me.

"What?" I said. My mind was running ... he had seen us together and probably seen Arash holding my hand underneath the table! Out of all the places an Iranian father could catch us, it had to be the time when I was holding hands with someone! Well, at least that was better than him seeing Arash and me making out in his car.

There was no way to deny it, because he had seen not only me, but Bahareh and Ghazaleh as well. But still I decided to deny it. Maybe he was so far away that he had just caught a glimpse and the rest was a bluff. He played poker very well, and I knew he was pro at this.

"You heard me, Delkash. Did you lie to me? Are you seeing anyone? You better tell me the truth!" he demanded.

The truth! The truth was that you brought me to this bullshit country expecting me to understand everything, even when I didn't know the culture! You brought me here and threw me into a culture that would keep me from living my life or making any of my own

437

decisions! That was the real truth ... the rest was playing with my head!

If I did tell him the truth I would be screwed, because then he would know for a fact that I had done what I'd done. So I opted for the other way, which was telling him he needed to get glasses!

"No, it wasn't us. You probably saw someone else," I snapped back firmly.

I felt like I was being interrogated by the CIA for my life and decisions! If he'd approached me as a friend—as someone who actually cared, and who I could trust—maybe I would have told him the truth. But he was treating me like a child, and my only response was to rebel against him. I didn't care what he thought about it, because I was furious that he would treat me this way, and put me in this position.

To be honest, I wished I could take my passport at that moment, and run from him and that country. From the ugliness that kept me lying and hiding from my own parents.

"Delkash, I will ask you one more time ... who were you with tonight?"

"Why do you care? What does it matter? It's my life! You already ruined it by bringing me to this messed up country!"

He stood back when he saw my defensive side, and heard my voice going up.

"What are you talking about?" he asked, shocked.

"I *hate* this country! I *hate* having to pretend! Everyone takes their kids to get a better education in the US, and here we are moving *backwards* into a *backwards* country!" I said, letting out my anger. "Don't sound like you brought me here to get in touch with my roots. I could have done that in Brooklyn by going to a school or something but no … nooo! You missed Iran and you guys *love* Iran, and now I am supposed to love it too!"

I had completely turned the tables from him accusing me to me accusing him! But it was the truth, and I couldn't keep it to myself anymore.

"So because I caught you red-handed, now you are blaming Iran for your lie?" he snarled, mad.

"You caught me, but not red-handed! I can make my own decisions and go out with who I want. The only messed up part is that in this country, people my age aren't allowed to make their own decisions! Well, Dad, I have got news for you: I was raised somewhere else, and bringing me here can't change my mentality, even if I *do* have to wear that stupid scarf and put on that ugly *manto*!" I was shouting, now, and about to start crying when my mother walked out.

"What the hell is going on here? Kaveh? Is this how you handle stuff? Del, what's wrong, sweetheart?"

"Ask your controlling Iranian husband!" I screamed, and whirled around, walking away before I started crying in front of them both.

"You have so much in front of you ... why are you crushing it with these loser guys?" my dad shouted.

At that point, I knew he had seen us, and knew that my mother knew. But I also knew that I had made my point. If I wanted to see a loser, I would see a loser. Not that Arash was; my dad was just upset that I'd lied to him. Not that he'd given me a choice; he was so attached to the social rules and what others might think that he'd let that become more important than his own daughter.

And so the girl had to be put in a cage until the prince, without any lies, came and picked her up from the castle through the front door. They couldn't date to get to know one another ... no ... because they might kiss, and through that kiss she would lose her virginity and reputation!

Screw that, I said to myself. I got into the stairway of the villa, put my face in my lap, and cried.

*

I had fallen asleep when I felt someone trying to fit on the staircase and squash next to me.

"*Mom!*" I said, almost falling off.

"C'mon, make room for me!" she said, laughing.

"There is none!"

"Yes, there is!" And she started tickling me, leading me to sit on the lower stairs in front of her.

"*Azizam*, you okay?"

"Depends on how you define okay."

"Don't get smart with me. Your father is just trying to protect you," she said.

"From what? What is this dangerous thing that is happening, that I need to be protected from? Why doesn't he hire a bodyguard for me if he's that protective!" I said defensively.

"Del, you know I have never talked to you about sex, but I think it's time. Especially since you are growing into such a doll!"

"Flattering, Mom, but I am all ears. Why is this stuff so taboo here?"

"Well, for one thing, this isn't a subject that is discussed. It's the culture, primarily, and mixed up with all these Islamic thoughts that a girl should be untouched before marriage. You know, like a virgin," she explained.

"I prefer Madonna's 'Like a Virgin' to the Islamic like a virgin!" I said, laughing.

She giggled too, and continued, "So it's really shameful if someone has a boyfriend, kisses, and has more intimacy with him. Now, that said, I know you are growing, and I am not going to mandate anything to you. But I want you to know that you should be private in this area. I am *not* saying to go and have sex, but respect yourself enough that you have sex with someone that you emotionally connect with. I am still not saying to have sex … *again*! But I want you to see the bigger picture," she said, looking away.

"I know it's complicated here, and your father is a very Iranian man, set in his ways, but you do make your own decisions and both of us are here to share our wisdom with you," she continued.

Wow! Now, that was touchdown! It was the first time my mom had opened up like this, and I treasured them as words coming from someone who had seen both sides. She had grown up here and married the emperor to go live in the US. She had seen both worlds, and I could feel that her words were golden.

"Let's go back inside. We are leaving for Tehran in a couple of days, and you should enjoy Shomal to the max."

I gave her a kiss and she wiped my tears, just as a good mother does! That night, she'd become my hero. I just hoped she could maintain the role.

Chapter 21: The Pretentious Flow

We left Shomal a couple of days afterward, and I refused to speak with the emperor the entire time. I preferred all of our communication to be made through my mom. I was still furious with him for acting so selfish, and though he kept trying to make conversation with me, he was out of luck. The issue hadn't been resolved, but I think he missed me and wanted to break the ice. His thoughts were his thoughts, and for a guy his age it was impossible to change. Well, for an *Iranian* guy his age.

I needed a break and wanted to be alone, so I was happy we were going to Tehran so I could go back to my room and watch *Tango and Cash*, followed by *Home Alone* for the millionth time. It was my only return to New York! Or should I say, the States.

We arrived to see an empty Tehran.

This looks eerie, I thought. I had never seen the city so vacant and traffic-free. A few stores were open, but most supermarkets and *baghalis* (small local grocers) were closed. I really wanted the streets to be normal, to hear kids playing football, causing cars to honk horns. And to hear the sound of melon trucks passing, laden with fresh cantaloupe for sale. I wanted things to go back to the way they were supposed to be.

At the same time, I wanted everything to change.

Back home, we quickly unloaded the car.

My mom told me that we would be going Eid Didani— to my mom's eldest cousin's home. He was the oldest in the family, and the younger members of the family had to visit him for respect purposes.

"So ... he sits there and waits for people to come and visit?"

"Yup. Well, he is a bit older than old, and your cousins will be visiting him, too. They might even be there tonight."

"Mom, we just got back from vacation! Do we have to go? Or do I have to come? I barely know him." I threw in the last part to make her feel guilty.

445

"Oh Del, he gives good *Eidis* (the gift an elder gives a younger during *Eid*)," she added, knowing my eyes would pop.

I had no real objection to the visit, but wanted to rest so I could speak with Arash that night. I missed speaking with him and joking around with someone who understood me and was from the other side. I knew going to this *mehmooni* (little visit, or party) would drag on until dinner. All the ladies would start talking, most likely gossip, and the men would start playing backgammon, and next thing you knew it was 2 in the morning!

But I knew that arguing would get me nowhere, so I prepped myself up to eat good food and have an extremely boring night...

Our arrival at the cousin's house was a barrage of smiling greetings, warm kisses, and repeated voicings of *Be farmaiid* (*welcome*), perhaps five or six times.

I knew the remaining seven days of Eid were probably going to be spent this way.

Inside (finally!), we found the table brimming with nuts, fresh pastries, a variety of fruit, watermelon, candies, and, of course, fresh tea. The hosts insisted that everyone keep eating, so in order to avoid repeated commands to "Please eat something," I made sure to keep a piece of pastry or apple near my mouth. Every time the room hit one of those rare pockets of silence, someone broke it with a hearty *Befarmaiid-yek chizi bekhorid*, again repeating the same slogan to have a bite to eat. It was so annoying that I strategized to keep my hand on my fruit plate so they would look away from me.

As assumed, we stayed for dinner, and it was a grand five- to six-hour Eid Didani before they called it quits. I listened to scattered conversations, but all of them were boring and really didn't interest me at all. All I could think about was Arash.

Once we were home, and everyone went to bed, I called him.

He, of course, was expecting my call.

I could feel the intensity of our chat as we talked about everything that had happened over the past week, and new stuff that had occurred. Obviously, he got upset over my fight with the emperor, but I felt it was only him that knew where I was coming from. I didn't like fighting with my dad, but I was having more and more trouble understanding Iran and working to fit in here. Either my dad didn't care or was choosing to ignore how unhappy I was. If

447

it was the latter, then that was really hurtful. If the former was true, that would also be devastating, because he was supposed to be my support factor and know the consequences of bringing someone to a country with all these heavy rules and cultural angles. But if he didn't see what he'd done to me, then he wasn't taking very good care of his daughter.

I couldn't say these things to my parents, but I could say them to Arash, and expect him to understand. Or at least listen.

He told me to brush it off, and that he was my dad, after all. I told him I would, but that it bothered me and I was only putting it on standby temporarily.

"At some point, I'm going to have to say something to him about it."

"Stubborn, aren't we?" he joked.

We chatted for quite a while, until I passed out on the phone, exhausted by emotion and stress.

The remaining days were spent in the same format, and I ended up going back to my internship, which was ending on the tenth day of *Nowruz*. On the thirteenth day, another Iranian tradition kicked in and had everyone running off for picnics and outdoor activities in the park.

I wondered if these people ever worked, since they always seemed to be on some kind of cultural or religious holiday!

The last day was called *Sizdeh Bedar*, and with it came the end of the *Nowruz* holiday.

Afterwards, everyone hopefully and reluctantly returned to regular life.

On this occasion, in addition to the four-car train, some friends joined in for the twenty-kilometer trek to Karaj, where it was mostly green. So again we had the family, including Bahareh and Ghazaleh, Aunt Elahe, Kamran, Aziz Joon, and another flock of second cousins. Now I really couldn't keep up with the distant relations!

Another round of excessive traffic, and this time you could see a strand of green grass (*sabze*)—taken from the *Nowruz* table— displayed in the rear windshield of the car ahead of you as they drove to the park.

In the car, Ghazaleh said, "You also have to knot two pieces of grass together, Del. It's tradition."

"Why? Am I maintaining the lawn, too?"

"No, you dork!" exclaimed Bahareh. "They say it's the knot of *love*! It's actually rooted in our psyche that stuff like goodwill and love exists in everything! Lots of girls do it with hopes of meeting *the one*!"

"But it's nothin' like Woodstock in America!" Ghazaleh said, giggling.

I scowled with sarcasm. "Um, nice comparison, woman!"

"Ohhh, just keep the tradition going. It's fun, and I try to make my knot with Crazy Glue so no one can open it!"

"Stop being so cheesy," said Bahareh.

"Whatever!" Ghazaleh said in return, with her upper lip a bit slanted, conveying she was annoyed.

"Oh, and this green *sabzeh* has to be thrown in a stream or river toward the end, to erase all negativity from our homes," said Bahareh.

"So in other words, you are polluting the water?"

"*Aroom* (*relax*); it's grass, so it goes back to nature, Ms. IQ."

I laughed. I looked forward to spending time in nature, especially when Tehran was the city known for smoke and dust.

In the park we made fresh *kebabs*, had as much tea as you can imagine—after marking the nearest bathrooms—and played dodge ball, with the girls wrapping their *mantos* around their waists so we could move freely. Finally, we tossed the knotted *sabze* in the pond, where it basically stood upside-down in the water in front of us. Then we started knotting the grass we were standing on until we were sure we would get married!

After sunset, we drank another cup of tea, and got back on the road again.

*

I had learned quite a bit about myself in Iran, and I appreciated learning more about my roots and where I'd come from, but I was growing more and more miserable in this rule-infested country. I wasn't allowed to do the things I wanted to do, and was told again and again that I wasn't good enough to do things. Worse, I was expected to be okay with all of that. I'd seen how the rest of the world lived, and I wasn't falling for it. It was a beautiful place, but I knew I couldn't stay there. Not for much longer.

Then there was Arash. My first boyfriend, my first guy friend, who really helped me see everything in Iran, from football stadiums, to explaining every incomprehensible subject, to a romantic love experience…

True, I hadn't yet slept with him, but knew that I wanted to, even when it was considered taboo in that country. I didn't have any problem exploring my sexuality with someone I cared for. Who could predict the future? Why would I have to agree to keep a part of myself in the dark, for something that might never happen?

The bigger question had become why he was waiting for me. I was certain that he could have been sleeping with many other girls. So why was he waiting for me? Because I was forbidden fruit? I thought—and hoped—that he really liked and respected me. Maybe even loved me.

Chapter 22: The First Time

My internship had finally come to an end, and I actually felt sad leaving. I had developed a friendship with everyone, and gotten to know how sympathetic they were and how much happiness and love they carried. I knew I would miss the dirty, bearded guard at the door, the black crows, and the reporter I was constantly helping. They had work ethic, even though they took every other day off, and they'd taught me so much.

Their energy, honesty, and easy-going ways were things I would never forget. Who knew, maybe I would go back for a job there one day. I didn't know if that was possible, since all employees had to pass a strict test about their religious beliefs. I was a Westernized girl who didn't pray or fast, who liked to drink, and who had a secret boyfriend. Not exactly the sort to fit in.

I was really only happy with Arash.

My birthday was approaching, and Arash was arranging a party for me. It was a combo of my college acceptance and my birthday—two in one. I told him he had to do separate parties, but he just told me to relax!

That night I told my parents another lie: that I was heading to Elham's for the night. I stashed my party clothes in my duffel bag and threw it down the stairs so I could walk out of the house with some books and an apple. I liked to convey the idea that I was heading out for a nerdy night with a friend.

I arrived early to Arash's, to help him get ready for additional errands.

As always, his place looked spotless and clean, and he had hired catering and ordered good wine and drinks. I was both excited and worried. I had invited all my friends, and Arash had invited some of his, and we were going to have good drinks and no chaperone! I had given my parents Elham's home number, and even though she'd promised that she was having the number diverted to her cell, I was still stressed over the idea of my parents catching me.

It was an important night, in more ways than one. I felt that all the people at this party had helped me understand and cope with the newfound, alien craziness of this strange country, in one way or another. Arash was at the head of the line. From the moment we met, I had discovered a hidden passion and love within me that he drew out, and I managed to experience it with him, at dinners, the Lavasan mini-trip, meeting secretly in Shomal, and the underground parties he had exposed me to. Our souls had joined, and I knew for sure that I was in love.

Soon after I got there, guests started arriving one by one, and each of them made me happy because they all were carrying gifts. I wondered how on earth I was going to sneak these gifts into the house! Bahareh told me she had bought me the *Firoozeh* gemstone (turquoise stone), the original found in Iran's Khorasan Province, and that they had specially designed a pair of matching earrings, bracelet, and pendant for me. It was awesome, and the minute she told me I had to open it!

We ate, drank, sang, talked, and took lots of pictures to remember my first birthday in Iran, thrown by my first boyfriend and including my first friends in Tehran. Arash had a balcony and was grilling some meat at my request, so we moved outside to look at the Tehran sky. You could see every single star ... or maybe I only thought that because I was with Arash.

Neda and Saloomeh from Tatbighi had come too, and were hitting on some of Arash's friends. The norm. After her hip movements, Neda joined me in my third piece of steak and said, "Happy birthday, woman! By the way, I have some news for you."

"What? Please do share!" I exclaimed.

"We're moving back to Los Angeles in a month or so," she said casually.

For some reason, it hurt me when she said that. I liked Iran, but wanted to go back to the US so badly. Why was she returning and I wasn't? Why had her father decided she had to go to college in LA when mine wanted me to stay here?

"That's awesome!" I said. I was upset for myself, but still excited for her, and had to congratulate her as a friend would.

She had a long future ahead of her, and I knew she was in love with UCLA and the whole beach vibe there. It was fitting for her to go home.

And it would have been fitting for me to be doing the same.

"What do you plan on doing when you get there?" I asked.

"First things first—throw away this stupid scarf and jump in the water!" she said, laughing.

The moment she said it, a million things jumped into my head, and I realized something: No matter how good life in Iran got, it would never be good enough. Not without the freedoms I'd had in the US. Iran had given me my family and Arash, and it was my homeland; the homeland I was developing a very complicated relationship with! It was all good, I told myself ... some things I couldn't find in New York, I found here.

But were they enough?

Arash came by to join the conversation and added, "If we would have known, it would have been a goodbye party too!"

"It's never too late to announce the number three!" Neda said, laughing.

"You mean you are pregnant?" said Arash teasingly.

"I think she might be…" I added some spice.

"Shut up, guys!" said Neda jokingly. "I think Saloomeh is also headed back, but I don't know when. Her mom is fed up with Iran," she added.

Saloomeh was busy flirting and getting drunk, so we didn't spoil her fun. I didn't want to hear about her leaving, anyhow, because it would have made me even sadder.

Arash noticed and kissed me lightly on the cheek without saying a word.

We brought out the cake, which Arash had ordered, and was the shape of my lips! While blowing out the candles, I had one wish: to head back home to New York. It might have seemed like a pipe dream, but it was the only dream my heart desired. Of course, with Arash!

We did another toast before everyone started to wrap up and leave. The cousins, friends, and caterers all went home, then, and all that was left was an awesome memory and Arash and I standing in front of each other. I walked toward him and hugged him so tightly, feeling how much I had grown to love him.

I tilted my head up toward his ear, and whispered, "Thank you for the party…"

"I would do anything for you," he replied softly.

We gazed into each other's eyes, and then he took me in his arms and eased me into a kiss. I felt his heat, his tongue, his body against mine … and knew that with him, everything would be all right.

He tickled my ear with his lips. "Del, you are the best thing that's ever happened to me…"

I knew my feelings were just as true, and hearing him say this made it all the more real.

I turned to his ear, gently kissing it, and said, "Right back atcha…"

And we stood there, listening to each other breathe, listening to our souls surrendering to one another. I felt like dew from a secret flower for him, and looking at him brought on an intoxicating dizziness. It was like floating on some magical cloud on a potent drug, allowing me to step into my femininity.

With him, there were no taboo thoughts ... and everything was lost in the timeless moment of being with him.

"Can you sleep over tonight? I just want you to sleep next to me..." he asked, very quietly.

Without thinking of the consequences or what in the world I would tell my parents, I said yes.

"What are you going to tell the emperor?" he asked.

"I don't want to think about that. We'll let Elham be the mastermind," I answered.

I lay nuzzling and cuddling with Arash, whose languid grin appeared permanent, and gave no thought to the outcome of this, either. I think he was fed up with trying to think of *this and that* too.

I woke up and found the sunrise brushing the wall with gold. I wanted to stay next to him, but Cinderella had to rush home! The pumpkin ride was long overdue. I called Elham before leaving and she said my dad was sick with worry and my mom was practically in critical condition.

"Just go home. Your dad is so mad it would take the Persian and Roman Empires to keep him in place! He kept asking me where you were, and I acted like I couldn't hear him and hung up the phone!" she said nervously. "Glad he didn't have our address. I swear he would have come to my door to ask for you, woman!" She was so upset that she had lied. Her parents were chill—nothing compared to the emperor. "Did you at least have a good time?"

"I did, but nothing happened! But it was good ... without worry and cuddling and kissing and cuddling and kissing..." I said, giggling. "Ok, I'll talk to you later. If I live!" I was just as nervous as she was—probably more. I had no idea what was waiting for me at home, but I knew it wouldn't be good.

Chapter 23: Finding a Niche to Freedom

The cab pulled up to the house and as I was walking toward the elevator, I could already feel the negative energy through the doors. I walked into the house and walked straight to my room without looking around. I didn't even want to make eye contact, but from the corner of my eyes I could see both of my parents watching TV on the couch.

After I settled in my room, I put on the Three Stooges and waited. They'd already done the worst by bringing me to this country, so what could they do now? Ground me? Give me more restrictions than I already had? Throw me out of the house? I knew they'd never do that—it would damage their reputation. I knew that I hadn't done anything wrong, and I wasn't going to let them treat me like I had.

After about thirty minutes, my mother came in my room and asked me to come out because they wanted to have a talk with me.

"What is this about?" I asked, looking at the TV screen.

"You know what it is about, Delkash…" she answered.

"Actually I don't, because as far as I know, I am living my life and not bothering anyone else," I said casually, annoyed.

I paused the video and walked into the living room. The emperor was there and waited for me to sit. At that point, I really thought the title fit him well!

The first question out of his mouth was: "Why did you lie about where you were?"

The tone was so intimidating that I felt like he was asking why I'd murdered someone.

I couldn't deny anything, and at the point where I didn't even *want* to. This wasn't just about rebellion anymore. It was about getting out of that hide-and-seek culture. I was tired of lying, tired of pretending to be someone I wasn't. This is who I was, and this was how I operated. Label me Easternized, Westernized, traditional, stubborn, or whatever. I wasn't disrespecting or hurting anyone; on the contrary, I felt I was being tortured with customs and beliefs I was forced into.

"Because *you* forced me to lie. If I had told you I was at a party with my boyfriend, would you have allowed it?"

"What? Boyfriend?" His voice escalated.

"Yes! Boyfriend! I have a boyfriend, and he threw me a birthday party!" I said loudly.

"Lower your voice, Delkash. I don't want Aziz Joon, the neighbors, and the whole word to know we are having a fight and where you were last night," my mother said.

I glared at her, knowing that she knew exactly what I was going through. She could have sheltered me, could have helped, but she'd bowed to social pressures instead.

"Mom, I am not speaking loud. I am frustrated by how all you guys care about in this stupid country is what Mr. X and his lousy gossipy wife Mrs. XYZ view me. Frankly, I could care less, and to add to that, I could care less about all this traditional nonsense of how a girl should be and should not be!

"Oh, and leave all the Islamic beliefs aside, because I don't believe in it at all!" I added.

"Don't shout, Delkash. I can hear you! I won't accept you partying with just any guy, and I definitely won't accept you having a boyfriend!" my father said firmly, as if we were negotiating the treaty between Palestine and Israel.

I didn't want to be disrespectful to them and say it was none of their business. But that was what I was thinking.

"You know, we wouldn't be having these fights if I were still living my beautiful, happy life in Brooklyn. Maybe I wouldn't have wanted a boyfriend and maybe I would have known what I wanted to study. Maybe the pressure to be *someone* here is not what I am accustomed to! I mean, who brings a seventeen-year-old back to Iran? Who does that? I had already formed my identity, and right smack in the middle of my development years, you brought me here! All my friends are moving forward there, and you rewind back to a country stuck in the 1970s!" I said angrily, almost shouting.

He knew I had a point, and he knew he had made a big mistake, but no one—not even my mom—had the courage to tell him. I mean he was an Iranian man! Whatever! He'd taken me to a country where I had no foundation, and expected me to blindly accept it. Well, he had another thing coming.

The worst part was that I had lost my best allies—my parents—the moment we stepped into this country. And as long as we were here—as long as *I* was here—I'd never get that back.

"Del, we are trying to be supportive of you, but you have to accept some rules here. What part of telling the truth do you have a problem with?"

"I don't have a problem telling the truth, but I do have a problem with you pushing your rules and beliefs on me. So if you want the truth, you also have to accept that I have my own beliefs and they are definitely nothing like what you, Mom, these black crows, or the neighbors believe!"

"Del, lower your voice. We won't have that in this house!" my mother said in a warning tone.

"I don't want to *be* here! Living here has brought all this confusion upon me, and you were both the cause of this!" I said, this time shouting at the top of my lungs.

Both my parents were shocked, surprised, and taken aback. They had never seen me like this because I had kept it in the whole time.

"This is your country," said my dad, regaining his voice. "Why don't you want to get in touch with your culture, heritage, and live here for a while and accept the differences?"

"Because I don't *accept* shoving mandatory beliefs down my throat, and I won't *accept* being someone else just to be accepted!"

"Ok, Delkash, this is going too far. You are clearly not opening yourself up. I am not even going to ask you where you spent last night, but you are grounded until further notice. No more Elham, no more Bahareh, and no more of this person you call boyfriend!" he said angrily. "There will be no lies in this house, and all the calls will be screened. Don't think that as soon as I walk out, you can call whoever it is you are calling. You are smart, and have so much ahead of you, and at this age you are dating!" he added, frustrated.

"People get married at my age!" I cried.

"The *right way* ... not by dating!"

"And I assume the *right* way is by some lame intro by someone and him coming to see you and *you* making the decision. Is that '*right*'?" I asked sarcastically.

Now I had stepped on the lion's tail. Big time.

"Go to your room and don't come out until you make the decision to accept and respect rules and traditions in this country," he snapped, looking straight at me and pointing to my room. "We can't go back to the US because I have invested in our lives here, so don't even think that will be a solution, either."

"Don't worry, I don't expect *you* to go back. And remember, if you have another kid, don't torture him or her like you are doing to me! You didn't think of me when coming here; you only thought of yourself and how you missed your beloved country. And for the record, I am not a liar, but I am true to myself and stand up for my own beliefs and way of life. I have done *nothing* wrong!" I said rather loudly. I stood and went toward my room, ready to burst into tears, and ready to be away from my parents.

God, what did a girl have to do to just *be* these days! I curled up with my pillow and blanket and turned on the TV. I wanted to talk to Arash, to have him comfort me and tell me that it would be okay. I had no way to get in touch with him, though, and didn't even know if I had the energy.

I felt so alone.

*

I had made friends here, gone through an internship, put a scarf on to cover my hair at all times, and dealt with leaving my life back home. Now I felt like a depression tornado was coming my way, but I wasn't going to allow it in. I *did* have so much ahead of me, and knew this was a phase I would overcome.

I started writing aggressively at home. Highly emotional stuff: love, sorrow, my deep sense of loss and sadness ... anxiety and fear. The writing was trying to cure the bleeding, give me some sort of solace and understanding. Opening up to the pen and paper, I realized there was one element shining within me—passion. I could still smile.

Yes, I could smile at this situation. No one could rob me of my smile.

I wanted to explore life, and everything it had to offer. I had the energy and passion to fly through it. And that passion wasn't anywhere near dead…

What had died was being blown away—the ashy remains of an inflamed argument. But the love was still alive, as was my passion. And that was the only thing that mattered.

The probing questions, guilt trips … just exemplified how we saw life. Fine; even if I was thrown off the boat, I could still swim.

*

After a couple of days of intense thought, I felt like my wings were in repair-mode. I was still upset at my parents, and let them see my sadness when going for bathroom breaks outside my room or getting some food from the kitchen. I acted like I was in some depression, although I was faking part of it. They had to see and feel what they had brought on me … and I didn't think they got it. I wanted independence and felt I needed to bring on a revolution!

I knew they were concerned for my heath, and they never wanted this to happen. But they also knew my nature, and should have realized that I would have conflict in this country, rather than fitting in. And if they'd realized that, they would have seen that the first people I rebelled against would be them.

My instincts told me my dad had bluffed about the phone line being screened. We didn't have a caller ID, and this was just part of his full house poker strategy. So one night I took out my secret phone and called Arash.

He picked up immediately. "Del, where are you?" he asked impatiently. "It's been *four days* since you called me. Are you okay?"

I felt bad for not calling him these couple of days, but I needed to find myself again after the explosion. I didn't know whether he would answer, or act upset. Regardless, I had to call him. He was my only SOS backup, and my support system!

"Well, *salam* to you too!" I said, giggling.

"*Salam* back," he said, now feeling assured that I was alive, but half-angry and half-happy.

"I needed some time to myself. I had this massive argument with my dad and felt the world was going to crash down on me," I said. Suddenly I felt weak again, but managed to tell him the whole story.

"I need your help, and I have a plan. Can you help me? I really need to get out of this stupid country before I commit suicide," I said.

He knew I wouldn't commit suicide.

"What's up, *azizam*?" he said, trying to calm me.

"I need your help twofold. To buy me a ticket to the US and to let me know how I can do this with all the rules in the airport," I said.

"Del, are you out of your mind?"

"Yes, *I am*! I don't like it here, and no one understands! My parents think it'll pass. The only part I look forward to every day is you!" I said, holding back my tears. "I feel like an alien that everyone looks at when they hear I am from New York. I can't stand pretending and lying over and over and over again…"

"I think you can talk to your dad about this. C'mon, you are being a bit irrational, *no*?"

"Arash, just look at my situation and tell me what is irrational. My father has his ways and they will not change, and my mother tries to be the glue when deep down she knows I am right. There is no way to fight this, and I am tired. I want to go back...."

"What will you do when you get back? You have no money. No place to stay..."

"I will go to Krista's house until I get a job somewhere. There, I have opportunities and know my way around. I can find my way there. Here I feel I am in a maze! You can meet me over there ... in New York. We can be together on the other side without the bullshit I have to deal with here," I added in a pleading voice.

"*Azizam* ... this is something big. Why are you running away?"

"It looks like I am running away, but I'm not. I'm just going home, and will call them in a bit, after when I get settled. I don't hate them but feel I am going insane here..."

"Del, what's going to happen to us?" he asked quietly.

And there was the big question. It was the only part of the plan I didn't like—leaving him behind. "I don't know, but Iran won't help our relationship either. We are a team, and I need your help," I said. We had become part of one another's life. Spending so much time together, sharing so many thoughts and moments, had brought us closer than even we thought. I just prayed that we could find a way to make it work somewhere else.

There was a deep silence, and we both knew we were playing with fire, but I hated Iran. I didn't think I would survive there. Even with Arash to hold me up.

"Del, I care for you and know you are in a tough spot, but let me help you talk with him. Maybe if I introduce myself and he gets to know me, it'll be better...." he said.

"Arash, I hate living in this country! There is nowhere to go from here, especially with all the limitations for females. I don't like the belief system and what it dictates. Why do I always have to watch if my scarf falls off and have a third eye for the *Komiteh*? Anyway, I don't want to get married now, and if you come forward the emperor won't sit and watch us dating! He'll try to make us marry!" I said miserably.

I felt awful doing this, but I needed to breathe. Arash connected with me and surrendered to my request. We talked until the sun rose and I started to pass out.

I wanted to open up my eyes to the streets of New York. To buy a donut and coffee on my way to school. To go back to where the world made sense.

*

Arash bought me a ticket to leave the week after. But like everything else, this country had a catch, even when you were leaving!

In addition to an exit fee, which had to be paid (thank god for Arash), unmarried women must have permission from their father or guardian before leaving the country! I was outraged when I heard that! So unmarried women were slaves, and if an unmarried girl wanted to leave the country, she had to have her father's permission. And if he didn't give it to her … she was stuck.

Even married women needed their husband's permission to hold a passport. Husbands could ban their wives from leaving the country at any time! This mentality meant that women should have owners, were slaves. Arash told me the majority of people not allowed to leave Iran were either women who didn't have the permission of their husbands or tax evaders. Modern slavery.

So my father had to apply in person, then my passport would be stamped to indicate how long I was allowed to be out of the country. No escape without his permission. How the hell was I going to do that?

I did the only logical thing. In a top-secret mission, while my parents were out and I had been left home alone, I snuck to the private safe where I knew they kept all the documents. I opened it up and grabbed my US and Iranian passports.

Yes, the US passport ... my golden ticket out.

Arash knew some guys that could provide fake documentation and stamp my passport for the father's permission, to make it look legit. I told him I would pay him back with whatever it took once I started working in NYC. He wasn't even worried about the money, but more about me. I think he thought I would most likely sink into depression and hang myself if I stayed there!

After putting all my ducks in one row, the night finally arrived. I had previously given my bag to Arash, so when he picked me up there wouldn't be additional noises and we didn't have to waste time.

I spent the whole day outside—my last day with my parents. I would definitely miss them. I loved them so much, but despised the fact that they'd taken me to this place. My mom, the dearest to my heart, and Aziz Joon, Bahareh, Ghazaleh—all my girls, who I couldn't say goodbye to because I didn't want anyone to know... I was going back home and leaving them behind.

I hoped they would understand later, when they found out.

That night, I climbed out of the back window and jumped into the stairway, then tiptoed down very slowly, making my way to Arash's car. The night was dark and I felt scared. Scared of what lay in front of me. I had no security waiting on the other side ... only freedom, and a prayer that my friends would help me. Part of my soul was being left behind, and the other part was sad but very happy at the same time. Why? Why did this have to happen? Why hadn't my parents given me a better choice?

Arash held my hand as we drove toward the airport. "It's going to be all right. You are a survivor and I will come in a couple months to visit you..." he said, kissing my hand.

I would never forget Arash and how he helped me. He was the angel sent from above.

As we pulled up to the airport, I wanted him to leave because I didn't want him to see me burst out crying. I loved my parents, my cousins, and him ... most of all him...

In the dark, he kissed me one last time before I looked away, grabbed my stuff, and jumped out of the car. I walked toward the airport praying for the strength I needed to get through the next hour or so. To get on that plane, and leave Iran behind me.

I checked in my bags and passed passport control. Everything worked out fine. Then I waited until my flight was ready to board, the tears rolled down my cheeks as I gazed out at Tehran's sky for the last time. I knew I'd never be back.

Made in the USA
Middletown, DE
22 July 2015